MASTERS
OF THE
NIGHT

Elizabeth Brockie

Black Lyon Publishing, LLC

MASTERS OF THE NIGHT
Copyright © 2012 by Orlena Beth Brockie

Our books may be ordered through your local bookstore or by
visiting the publisher:

www.BlackLyonPublishing.com

Black Lyon Publishing, LLC
PO Box 567
Baker City, OR 97814

This is a work of fiction. All of the characters, names, events,
organizations and conversations in this novel are either the products
of the author's vivid imagination or are used in a fictitious way for the
purposes of this story.

ISBN-10:   1-934912-49-2
ISBN-13:   978-1-934912-49-2
Library of Congress Control Number: 2012943573

Cover Model: Jason Aaron Baca
Photographer: Portia Shao

Published and printed in
the United States of America.

Black Lyon Paranormal Romance

This book is dedicated with love to
David, Lauren, Dave, and Nicole.
A special thank you to Kathi and Cynthia
for their support and encouragement.

1.

One sweep of the second hand on a clock. That was all Henri De LaCroix needed. In that one tiny, luxurious moment he swept through the halls of the deserted park museum like a silent wind. His eyes pierced the mystic's, and she lost herself. Her violet orbs fell fully into his bottomless blue wells, filling with crystalline power. He easily whipped sticky, mesmerizing threads around her thoughts.

Her lips parted, but no words fell from them. She was captured, caught in his beautiful web like a helpless butterfly while his sapphire orbs broke her, melting her will and her heart onto the threads of the web.

But not enough, he realized. A mystic's defenses were not easily defeated.

The mystic shook herself as though from unwanted sleep. "I'm sorry. Did you say something?"

"Do you prefer Renoir or his friend, Monet?" he asked, his voice coffee-rich and thickly Parisian.

He stood next to her gazing up at the wall of paintings, and risked a sidelong glance. She was impetuously beautiful, this mortal mystic, beautiful in her dazzling green sequined dinner dress and diamond earrings, with blue eyes so startlingly deep they appeared violet. The silken tresses that framed them shone like burnt gold in the soft museum light, and her face glowed with the innocence of a Disney princess.

Deceptive innocence. Liora Anjanette Carter was endowed with rivers of power.

Mystics were that rare breed of mortals with the uncanny ability to sense the unseen, see the unknown. To "know" things. They walked within the twilight world, the chasm between space and time.

And through their second sight, they could see and read auras, those wondrous radials of color that encircled the beings who moved across the earth.

Their blood was sweet, powerful.

Poison.

Poison to the vampyre who lost control. Bleeding out a mystic would cause horrors in the brain—insanity.

Neverthless, hunger gnawed at the shriveled chambers of the French vampyre's heart, and his veins craved to pulse and throb with mystical essence. He was certain he could survive her.

He placed his eyes on the magnificent painting hanging before them, the Renoir portrayal of a man holding a woman close as they danced.

"*The Dance at Bougival.* On loan from the Museum of Fine Arts in Boston," Henri offered informatively, inviting conversation. "The background is airy, reminiscent of his Impressionist days, but the dancers are a return to solidity for Renoir." He turned to her. "A man asked Renoir to paint him dancing with his fiancée. Do you know much about him?"

"The dancer or the artist?" She laughed lightly, as though pleased by the unsolicited attention from the suave, well-toned Frenchman. He had inky black, shoulder-length hair, disarmingly blue eyes and a brilliant white smile.

A voice suddenly boomed through the room, startling her. "Hey Angie babe! Got us dinner! We can go over to the park next door. Lots of table space since most everybody is vacating. Speaking of, we'd better get our butts outa here before museum lock-down."

As she spotted the grease-spattered, fast food bags in the young man's hands, the Disney princess smile waned and her shoulders drooped a little beneath the sequined spaghetti straps.

"Well, enjoy Renoir," she sighed to Henri in parting. Then she turned back briefly, coyly, her smile returning a little. "And *The Dance* is a favorite of mine."

"Good evening, mademoiselle," he returned with a smile and a nod.

Her gaze flickered with uncertainty as he looked at her one last time, but only briefly. And she left.

Secretly moving through the trees, Henri followed them to a picnic table secluded in the cool dusk under an ancient cottonwood. Climbing easily to a high branch cloistered in a corridor of leaves, he let his long black trench coat drape the limb. He watched her through the shadowy skeins.

Her violet eyes were sad.

"You could have at least told me dinner out meant outside, Bobby," she said toward the face buried in the fast food bag.

A pity, Henri thought as he grimaced at the bag seeping spots of brown. She was worth far more.

While the mortal with barbell muscles and a dopey smile finished his fries and hers, she boosted herself up to the top of the picnic table, and crossed her shapely legs beneath her tight little sequined dress.

Henri drank in the sequin draped thighs, the depth of sweetness male dreams were made of.

She stared at the romantic park pond with its sprinkling of water lilies and emerging starlight, and sighed again. One sandaled foot swung back and forth in sad little sweeps while the other nudged at a crack in the cement bench.

Dusk deepened. A nearby walkway lamp came on and the leaves on the tree lost their summer green under its pasty haze. The whole place, in fact, seemed to take on the dead of winter. The pond became flecked with gray as though ashes of the dead had been scattered across the ripples, and even the glass green sequins of the dinner dress now shimmered gray-green as though a layer of grave dust covered the bodice.

While evening slipped away, Bobby continued chomping and asked the mystic if she wanted her limeade. Pushing a plastic cup toward him, she turned her violet orbs from "dinner out" toward a northern sky becoming shimmery with stars.

"The Dipper's beautiful tonight," she murmured.

The Big Dipper was tipped, pouring milky stars into the universe. Henri gazed at the Dipper's points of light for some moments, then moved his gaze to the southern sky.

Above the wavy horizon of park trees, the constellation Scorpio curled into the heavens. Three bright, diagonal stars for the head, a sweep of stars arcing downward from the center star into the body, a curve back up again at the tail—and into the stinger.

Henri wanted the young man to leave so he could slip down beside her. And sting *her*. He would enjoy the stars with her first, of course, telling her how Scorpio was his favorite constellation. And that Sagittarius, the archer, was not. Then tell her why.

"Liora Anjanette. Such a beautiful name," he murmured. His words in the dark were no more than the brush of the night breeze against the sky.

Yet she looked up as if she had heard the whisper high in the branches of the gnarled, old tree.

And she shivered! Though the night was not cold!

"Ah, Eleanor," he whispered, excited, stroking the night bird that lighted on his shoulder. "She is aware something is amiss in the portals of the night. And now she searches the very night itself for the dark disturbance. And of course, the disturbance is—me."

His deep, dead eyes tingling, he continued to watch her, captivated. The mystic was now looking directly into the canopy of foliage that held him secretly in its embrace.

Her violet eyes reflected starlight in every shimmery facet. His cold blue sapphires reflected a scarlet soul, tincture from the world of the damned. Could she see the red glints emanating through the leaves, he wondered, the fire in the depths of his pupils if one looked too close? Or too long?

But no. She did not see him. This one's talent was raw, needing honing ... She was reluctant to trust her instincts.

She shrugged away her tremors of warning and placed her attention on her lover again—or at least Henri supposed the young man with the food bag smile was her lover—and she wasted a soft gaze that was totally lost on Bobby Billboard Boy.

She's languishing in sequins and pearls and you're oblivious to her, Henri thought with disgust.

Henri drank in every curve of the femme fatale body the foolish fellow couldn't see, and enjoyed the perfume wafting upward through the leaves.

But how the night carries irony in its black talons! he thought. *The night is waltzing on her sweet perfume, the wind whispering into her hair, and they both seduce her past the innocence of a heavenly dipper, to a scorpion. To me.*

Look toward me, Angie.

In heavy French he pronounced his name for her in a slow, sensual thought threaded through the branches. "Ähnrē, De La Cwah."

She smoothed back a rope of golden strands that had fallen forward, and as her fingertips brushed the nape of her neck, Henri's eyes could now look nowhere else. His fangs dropped, and he beckoned her toward him again. He was determined she would be his. Forever.

Look toward me, Liora Anjanette.

She looked up toward the highest leaves, toward him.

Fierce delight coursed through him. Her disappointing date with her escort had left her vulnerable. He had been able to deliver the subtle suggestion into her mind as easily as if she were a rag doll.

She began nervously toying with a gold chain at her neck. The strength of his thirst, his hunger, the excitement in the challenge to see if he could survive blood that was poison to the undead, the swell of false breath in anticipating her life in his veins and her afterlife with him, had penetrated her senses.

Henri became mesmerized by the links of gold sheen caressing her jugular.

The chain twined downward, disappearing into a plunging neckline.

What was the necklace hiding? Did the tiny rope of gold hide some charm?

An amulet, perhaps. Or maybe a heart-shaped locket. A locket with a tiny treasured picture of herself and her paramour—

Surely this wad of human spit was not a lover she cherished enough to hold next to her heart!

Angie and her mismatch.com began arguing. Apparently, the beauty dressed to the hilt in a sparkle of green and high-heeled sandals cradling little pink toes, hadn't realized dinner "out" meant a weed-encrusted, poorly lit county park on a pigeon-poop picnic table without even the benefit of a bit of moon to offer solace and salvage a night gone sour.

Irritably, she pushed back the soft golden tress of hair that the breeze kept tussling into her eyes. Then the vivid, violet gaze began to burn with anger and disappointment.

The starlight in them was gone.

Cinderella didn't even get a pumpkin, Henri thought.

The feces-laden discourse continued. She had tickets to a hockey game on Saturday. He wanted to work on his motorcycle.

She said he had promised. He said he had only mentioned it.

Would the argument turn violent? Henri thought hopefully. What was an angry mystic like who became out of control with her own feelings? Would her escort stomp off in a huff? Would she stomp off in a huff? He felt the rush of excitement become almost uncontrollable. Could he possibly hope for so much? That she would end up alone in the park fast becoming deserted as dark settled in? Would it be that easy? Could it be too far-fetched to think that Fortune would smile on him tonight? That the desire of his dead heart, to take the mystic as his own and into the Realm, would come to pass?

Surely the dumbbell would not leave her in a desolate park alone.

Utterly alone.

She would be Henri's, his for the taking.

Unless, of course, that gold chain held a cross.

In which case, he would go to bed hungry in the morning.

Henri glanced down through the branches at the young man who had finished cramming food into his mouth. Something about him disturbed the vampyre's instincts. The large hands were tensing, the eyes staring down hard at the cement table top as though he was dissecting every grainy crevice.

Henri sat up straight. Her young fool was not dumb.

He was deadly.

Eight hundred years on earth had taught Henri how to sense and recognize the spoiled wine in humanity.

He had brought her to this isolated park to kill her.

2.

Slipping noiselessly from his branch, Henri began moving down through the tree swiftly, a mamba through the jungle vines—

He stopped. In a pretense of anger, Barbell Muscle Maniac was stomping away toward the heavier, thicker park foliage.

Where he could hide. And wait.

The mystic was rubbing little wet tears from her cheeks.

She is probably wondering why she ever left California, Henri thought.

"I could run and catch him, I suppose," she murmured to herself. "Beg him to take me back while I agree to be his little grease monkey." She pursed her lower lip and straightened her back. "I think not."

But she slid despondently from the tabletop. The night had lost its flavor.

Her shoe strap caught on the bench corner and broke. "What a lousy week!" she said dejectedly as, taking off her shoes, she began walking barefoot on the soft, cool grass down to the pond.

The park was nearly deserted now. An occasional jogger, a bicycle now and then, a couple of kids on skateboards. A few ducks calling it a day as they flew in low toward the pond. Nothing else.

Maybe she's thinking a stroll along the water will lift her spirits, Henri thought as a touch of sympathy rippled through him. After trailing her for weeks he knew her life was not easy. She was working at a dead end job. She was twenty-four and by herself, and her life had taken a turn for the worse since she left her home state to "make it on her own."

First a flat tire. Not a blowout, just a weary, gradual collapse. Like her life. Her car was sitting at her apartment useless until payday. And her Internet prince had turned into a website frog.

A frog who was waiting to zap her like a fly.

The prescient mystic glanced uneasily at the path woven with deepening shadows. An impending night was filled with foreboding, and she perceived its dark smile.

She just didn't know the danger was to herself.

Would Angie try to dismiss the electricity on her skin, Henri wondered, deny the Jekyl night becoming a hellish Hyde, tell herself it was just her nerves, she was just imagining things—too much TV, too much eleven o-clock news, too many shows about paranormals? Was she wishing she was safe at home—home with a safe, warm bed, late-night TV and a sandwich? Would she deny her gift tonight and pay for it with her life?

She should be running, fleeing.

Still barefoot, she did quicken her steps somewhat as she left the pond. But she was not hurrying excessively. She was remaining poised. She did not want to appear the fool to a passerby, and have to admit she was terrified when there appeared to be nothing, basically, to be terrified of. But her eyes were wide. She knew something, somewhere, was frighteningly out of kilter, out of sync. And frighteningly close. Her mystic synapses were firing.

A sensation began to grip Henri, one he did not expect.

He wanted to save her.

"Something wicked waits in the darkness, Anjanette Carter."

Henri's whisper of warning whipped along the paths and bolted toward her ears like thunder on the wind.

Finally, her sad little form began to run barefoot across the park, her sandal straps dangling from her fingertips.

Gasping, Henri doubled over as a heartbeat spasmed through him, gouging him like a needle.

He fought the unwanted human emotion.

I am a Royal. What should I care that she is about to die? I will kill him too, drink every drop, then make the Disney princess a minion princess.

The unpleasant sensation left.

She slowed her pace as she reached the walk, fumbling pitifully through her handbag.

To see if she had money for a cab?

Pity eroded his veins again. Damn. He was going to save her

life. He could feel it. He was going to have Barbell Bobby's double patty, sesame seed blood for breakfast instead of the luscious sugar cookie he wanted.

"If I were that young man, I think I would have liked hockey," Henri said softly, gliding to her side.

Looking up to find the man from the museum no more than a foot from her, Angie gasped and dropped her handbag.

The contents spilled across the sidewalk and into the grass.

Apologizing for startling her, Henri began helping her pick up lipsticks, keys, wrinkled receipts, a few pennies. Then he moved closer to her.

She instinctively recoiled.

She was now clearly nervous and frightened. He could hear her heart pounding like a hammer on an anvil.

"Do you sneak around the park often, eavesdropping on every couple you see?" she spouted as she jammed things into her bag. She was trying to sound angry, trying to sound—unafraid.

But she was trembling.

"I was walking my bird, Mademoiselle. And I am sorry, but I could not help but overhear the—discourse? I apologize if I appear to have intruded on your privacy." He kept his voice gentle, and hoped the husky French accent he usually used to entrap female victims would intrigue her, draw her toward his voice and away from her trepid heart.

"Did you have your bird in the museum?" she asked, surprised, though her breathing was fast, shallow.

He smiled. "She was leashed to a small tree outside. She is quite tame."

She closed her bag without checking to make sure she had everything. She wanted to end the conversation, get away as quickly as possible. Beads of perspiration formed on her forehead, her face, her neck.

His violent blue eyes followed the tiny beads of salty wet, mesmerized by them as they trailed down her throat and disappeared into her low neckline between her breasts.

If he had been able to breathe, he would have been breathing hard and fast himself.

He handed her a lipstick, careful not to let their fingertips touch—if they touched, he was certain she would feel the vampyre essence and flee like a frightened fawn.

He averted his gaze to his bird, pretended to adjust the leash.

A couple of bicyclists stopped near them to rest for moment and take a drink from their water bottles. When they demonstrated an interest in the bird preening its glistening black wings, Henri invited them to pet her. Angie seemed to relax a little, even brighten.

Henri appraised the intruders. They looked to be in their late teens or so. And were naïve to the difference within him that the mystic could sense so acutely, but not identify.

Their young, strong hearts beat heavily from the invigorating ride, and he could hear the blood pulsing through their veins.

He looked away quickly. Before the mystic could "see" the intense excitement within him created by the scintillating closeness of full, young veins. Or sense the empty heart exploding with want, and clawing at his chest, demanding replenishment. His shriveled veins throbbed, expanding in painful pulses, demanding he exchange life for life and end their misery.

Where the hell was Barbell Boy?

"Does it have a name?" the young girl asked amicably as she reached out her hand to pet the bird.

Her pulsing wrist smelling of sweet perfume passed so close to Henri's lips that he almost swooned at the scent, almost bared his fangs.

The girl had a pleasing smile. Innocent.

Would she be difficult to seduce into his world of darkness? he wondered. As a minion, perhaps?

He shook himself inwardly, reminding himself it was the mystic he wanted. He was resolved that one night soon, when she had warmed to him, he would taste power and pleasure he had only imagined in his dead dreams. An ecstasy of power! And she would join him, relishing the dark power of the Realm. They would celebrate with golden bowls of wine that he would spill lusciously across her breasts while he urged her legs apart and thrust his body against hers, over and over, delighting in her, and she in him.

And yet ... He smiled delightfully at the girl.

"Her name is Eleanor," Henri answered pleasantly. "And mine is Henri. Spelled H-e-n-r-i, but pronounced, awn-REE. It is French."

"Awn-REE. Works for me, Frenchie," the girl teased flirtatiously, laughing, seduced by the moist eyes that briefly brushed hers.

Angie was watching him closely now. "You take your bird for walks often?"

Her cherry-glossed smile, though cautious, was dazzling, and made him ache to be human again. Shimmering, luscious, her lips wreaked havoc with his desires. Not to mention the low neckline barely covering the "other" assets he wanted to have and to hold.

"Oui, Mademoiselle. She enjoys the walks," he answered, averting his eyes to the bird.

"And it doesn't offer to fly away?"

"But of course. That is why I have the leash."

The bicyclists complimented him on the pretty black bird, then pedaled away to resume their ride.

"Did your young man leave you without transportation, Mademoiselle?" Henri asked carefully, in a concerned voice.

Her heartbeat quickened again in spite of his attempts to keep her calm.

"I have a way home."

He admired her honesty. She had avoided telling him a lie. One's own feet were, of course, an acceptable mode of transportation.

"If I may be so bold," he said, "your dinner date was a fool to abandon such a beautiful young woman."

Unaffected by the flattery, she looked straight into his eyes to admonish him, but faltered under his fiery blue gaze. "Have a nice walk with your bird."

She began walking rapidly away.

Refusing to acquiesce, he was instantly beside her again. "You should not walk alone, Mademoiselle. The night is an uncertain traveling companion. And not trustworthy. The night, like the promise of romantic love, can deceive and beguile."

He walked her to a phone booth, and gave her money for the call and the cab. Then he lingered until the taxi drove up.

The bird's leash suddenly broke at the harness, and the bird, feeling the loosened bindings and its new-found freedom, flew from Henri's shoulders.

"Oh!" Angie cried, ducking into the cab as the bird swooped close in its flight toward the low branches of a nearby tree.

"Take her straight home," Henri commanded the driver as he

closed her door.

Then he turned, shaking his fist in the air and crying, "Nasty bird!" as a pair of disobedient wings could be seen flitting down a side path. A string of French curses followed.

"Miscreant! Impudent bird!"

He began chasing after the night bird, not knowing Angie had climbed from the taxi, bewildered, but wanting to help—

Without considering the consequences.

3.

Pushing aside low hanging tree branches and snarls of brush, Angie tried to follow the man pursuing his bird, but she was running haphazardly, and soon found herself in the older, denser part of the park.

Gnarled mangles of ivy that had been allowed to run rampant snapped at her ankles, threatening to coil and trip her as she tried to follow pieces of broken cement that had once been a walkway.

The night became wicked.

But neither the black feathers and fluff, nor the strange Frenchman, was anywhere in sight.

Her steps slowed. She could hear a rustling, behind a bit of scraggy hedge.

The bird?

Something glinted through the wands of leaves, metal …

She leaned in to peer closer.

A pair of powerful arms reached out from the leaves.

She gasped, caught in a grasp she could not break.

Cold steel pressed against her throat, warning her to silence. Whispering, "Good girl, Angie, don't scream. My little friend here is antsy," her assailant held the knife close, oh, so close, to her jugular.

Then the arms hauled her backward, toward a small stone building devoured by ivy vines.

A groundskeeper's shed?

The iron door was an easy push for the weighty arms. Angie was plunged into utter darkness, silent shadows of stone.

In a frenzy of disbelief, she tried to steady her breath, while terror kept threatening to choke it from her. "Bobby! What are you doing?" she cried.

His sweaty hands shoved her roughly to a cement floor. "Shut up!"

A speck of park light filtered in through a tiny, cut-out window, illuminating his eyes. Angie shrank in horror of the vile gleam.

Her eyes darted frantically around the room.

This dark little square was not a gardening shed at all! Frescas and stone pillars were not what one would find in a tool shed.

A low, cement slab like a coffee table rose from the concrete flooring.

Angie's heart pumped hard with fear as she realized the slab was to support a coffin. She was in a mausoleum ... in the cemetery that adjoined the park.

What was he going to do to her?

Grabbing her painfully by her hair, he began hauling her backward across the room to the slab.

She dug her feet into the cement, twisting her body, trying to impede him. Her fingers clawed at his hands, tried to pull her hair from his grip.

He tripped on an unseen piece of debris on the stone flooring, a broken branch.

With a mighty shove, she rolled and jumped to her feet, grabbing the branch.

Hands like steel slammed her back, flat against the coarse, rock wall.

Rough stone scratched at her bare flesh, scraped and tore. She saw her cross falling. The precious symbol her grandmother had given her when she was a child, a memento from her mother, was falling to the ground, its chain broken. *No! It's mine!* Her hand reached out toward the golden sunburst splayed behind the tiny, notched beams becoming buried in the dirt.

The iron door began to close with a great groan, scraping on its creaky hinges.

"No!" she cried, whirling. Clutching the branch, she leaped toward the door, grasping the ring, pulling at the ring, trying to stop the iron door that was locking and sealing her in.

With him.

She fled to the furthest wall, and struggled to control her rapid, terrified breathing.

He was crossing the room …

She shrank from him, clinging to the branch that seemed so useless in the face of the slim steel menace slicing the air, coming for her.

She ducked under his arm and headed for the window. The fight wouldn't be long, she knew. But it was all she had.

Grasping the window ledge, she stood on tiptoe, screaming for help through the tiny opening, trying to see someone, anyone.

Her screams sailed out onto empty air.

The park was closed. Budget cuts. The county workers were gone.

Collapsing despairingly against a stone pillar, she turned to him.

For what seemed an eternity, he just stood there with a grotesque smile behind the slab, watching her. Just watching her. Why didn't he move? Why didn't he get it over with?

He was taking his time, letting the terror linger.

He was cruel.

"You bastard!" she flashed at him, with tears stinging her cheeks.

He moved toward her. The knife lunged.

She ducked, fled to the opposite wall. But in an instant, the knife slashed and blood spurted, poured down her arm as she threw up her hand to protect her face. Then the blade pierced the air and descended again.

She blocked the blade's point with the branch. The knife went flying, clattered across the stone flooring, slid into a crack in the grout, and was swallowed up by the earth.

But her attacker still had his hands, monstrous, murderous hands. He came at her, threw her against the wall, and a new flow of red poured against the jagged mortar. Crying in pain, she tried to beat him back. But his fists found her over and over again and the walls found her body over and over again. Screaming for him to stop, screaming for someone, anyone to help her, she stumbled around the room helplessly.

No one came. The assault became relentless, merciless, and did not stop until she had collapsed to the floor, exhausted, broken, and bleeding, defeated. Still clutching the branch she had futilely flailed at him, she looked up through half-shut eyes.

An evil grin, the shape of sardonic pleasure, demonized the billboard perfect face.

"You dirty, damn, dirty, sorry excuse for a human being," she moaned through a broken breath.

A black blur sailed across her field of vision.

The night bird.

With screeches and screams that seemed to rise from some wild, forgotten place, the bird hurled itself toward her attacker like a piece of black night torn from the heavens.

He tried to beat it off, flailing his hands futilely against the fury of feathers, beak and talons.

He fell, blood gushing from gaping orbital holes that only seconds before had been eye sockets. He groped, but found only dust and cold, concrete floor.

And a pair of eyes.

4.

Through half-closed eyes behind a drape of soft, black eyelashes, Angie looked up in awe at the beautiful vampyre emerging from the shadows. His black hair flowed around him in inky, silken swathes that fell to his shoulders, and his powerful form was liquid as he moved. The folds of the loosely buttoned, black silk shirt rippled softly, as though a tender wind blew against him. He seemed more a dream than reality, more of the night than of man.

His long, black trench coat swirled out away from him as though from a wind.

He seemed to be floating through airy veils of lustrous, pale blue light that emanated from his eyes—enveloping her, they pulled her into their depths and away from her pain.

He lifted her gently as he would lift a fallen sparrow, and placed her carefully on the coffin slab.

"My cross," she begged weakly. "Do you see my cross?"

"I am sorry, chéri. I do not see your little charm. I will look for it—later."

Gingerly, he touched her arms and her sides, and her body, assessing the damage.

"Are you here to take me to the hospital?" she asked, barely aware.

"No, chéri."

"I—don't understand."

The French vampyre gathered her into his arms, cradling her, unable to fight the sorrow wrenching his heart. "I thought you had gone. Why did you not leave, Anjanette?"

He smoothed her golden hair gently away from her neck.

As his gaze fell into hers, Angie tried to appear unafraid of his violently blue eyes. Her grandmother had told her tales of vampyres.

But her grandmother was as crazy as a loon. She'd been locked up for years!

Sticky pale blue strands from the power of his eyes were suddenly all over her, spinning a web. The room dissolved.

"I can save you, Angie ..."

She understood. "I'm dying."

Beyond them, Angie could hear her attacker moaning where he had fallen. A strange gurgling sound was replacing the labored exhalations of breath and moans.

Then nothing.

The bird lighted on a beam above her, its beak bright with ribbons of red.

"You were in the tree, weren't you?" she said, touching the vampyre's shirt with her fingertip. "I felt you."

"I was there."

"Damn you. Was I chosen at random, just tonight's dinner and dessert because I was there?" She paused to draw in a breath, but inhalation was like a rake across her lungs. "Or was I on the menu to become a vampyre princess?"

His lips curled into a small smile. "A princess? Your power would surpass my own, Liora Anjanette. You would be a queen."

Her heart sank. He knew who she was, what she was.

At twelve, her grandmother had explained her heritage, the legacy of mysticism. But with her cataract eyes widening like saucers, she had raised a gnarly finger in warning to beware the night and keep her windows closed.

Everybody said the demented old woman was off her rocker and had no right to scare a child sleepless with her loony bin ranting, so Angie blew it off. Sort of.

"You must be crazy, wanting a mystic."

He only shrugged. "No. I'm bored. I have watched men act like fools for eight hundred years. Nothing changes but the tide and the times. For one night of the kind of power and ecstasy you offer, Anjanette, you were worth the risk."

"You were out of your mind to think you ..." She stopped in mid-sentence as a sick thought hit her. "Or you're a master."

"I am a master, Angie."

"You belong in hell with Bobby," she sobbed through her pain.

"You are not happy, Angie. You have a gift no one of your kind even understands. Come with me. Where you can be appreciated."

"No."

"Use your talent with us. The way it was meant to be used. I can teach you."

She tried to shake away the webby film in her brain. But he was oh, so carefully spinning across her thoughts as she lay dying in his arms. The room felt hot. Yet so—cold. Perspiration beaded up in her palms. Then dried up like dust.

His voice was as rich as cream, mocha as it played across her skin. "You don't have to die, Angie."

"Do you think I would even choose?" she spat woefully.

He sighed and mumbled something about her obsessive spirit. "It would seem you have already chosen."

He kept her in his gaze, a gaze that was now clearly revealing his thirst, and a hunger so deep it drove a new horror into her heart. A hunger for more than her blood.

He wanted his queen.

Her thoughts began to ramble like lost rivers. *Have to—get— out of here.* She pushed at his chest, tried to free herself from his embrace. He eased her back onto the slab. She tried to rise. Sand replaced the stone slab, and she felt as though she was sinking.

Is this what it felt like to die?

The wall. Find the wall. If I can just reach the wall, and the door. She put out her hand, as though to reach for the wall.

There was no wall.

She fought the swells of confusion, the wall that wasn't there. Everywhere, everything was dissolving around her. Then, for a moment, the black gravelly stone was clear. She could see the room, the dirt, the debris, the murderous bird on the rafter ... and her cross. She reached out, tried to reach for it.

The vampyre was softly calling her name. The room, icy with mist, floated, and he was a visage through pale veils as he leaned over her without form or shape ... so handsome and desiring in the soft wind.

He lifted her into his arms again, so close she could have felt his breath—if he had any. Then he touched the nape of her neck.

The brush of wind blew through his raven hair. "Come to me,

Liora Anjanette."

She fought the hypnotic voice.

He was haunting, horrible.

Magnificent. Beautiful.

"I have never fought a demon of darkness …"

"Right. Sorry. You have only one foot in hell."

He took a lock of her hair in his hand and curled it softly into his palm, inhaling its fragrance. "I have felt you in the portals of the night for a long, long time, Angie. Have you not felt me as well?"

The mocha voice was so soft. "I don't know what you mean." The air felt hot.

"Of course, you do, chéri. On those nights when you suddenly would stop and turn and search the darkness. As though someone was there." He paused. "But of course, it was only me."

"No," she protested weakly.

"You sensed me, Angie. Do not deny it."

He described the nights he had followed her, and even walked beside her in crowded streets. He had walked the halls of her apartment building, paced in front of her locked door, and rustled the hawthorn to catch a glimpse of her violet eyes when she would turn, searching for the intruder who was not there.

Indignation rose up in Angie in a fury. With a sudden, mighty push, she rose up toward him with the broken branch. She would stake the monster!

He loosened her fingers from the limb and tossed it away.

"I'm going to try to save you, Angie," he said. "You will live. And I will live through you." He paused. "A pity you did not train your talent. You would have been a warrior, an opponent worthy of battle. You would have killed him, and probably me as well. As it is …"

His dark, black silhouette enveloped her.

Her life was over.

She cried out, tried to push him away.

"Your wings are broken," he whispered. "Do not fight me."

"I won't let you mesmerize me," she sobbed.

He shrugged and sighed—and stroked her hair. "You are going to fight me?"

"With the last breath in my body."

"It doesn't have to be that way."

The essence of his intent permeated the very air like thick oil, taking her breath.

The imminence of death.

"Surrender. Your pain will fly as the dove in morning."

"Another deception," Angie choked bitterly. "If I surrender, surrender means you would be able to call me back as I died, and I would have to yield—give up my mind, my body, my soul to you." She paused for breath, her inhalations weak, shallow. "Mental slavery to you as I relinquish my mind and will, and become a slave to hell as well is not my idea of a fun afterlife."

She looked into the sapphire eyes filled with fire and hunger—and something else, something she could not identify. Lust? Surely it was not love she saw in the fiery, blue depths?

"Take a walk in the sun, De LaCroix."

Try as she might to struggle, Angie finally could no longer strain against the hands holding her pressed to the cold stone. But she was determined he would not get near her soul.

Build the wall, brick by brick, she told herself as she began stacking bricks, one by one, in her thoughts. Brick by brick and block him out.

"Stop, Angie."

Brick by brick ...

"I just have one question. Did you love him?"

The vampyre's ploy worked. She was caught off guard. The wall fell.

"Who?" She tried to force a fuzzy brain to think. Keep him talking. As long as he's talking, he's not sucking you dry.

"The boy. Surely you did not love him."

He sounded too hopeful. Like he wanted to make a vampyre lover tonight.

"He's a piece of junkyard chrome," she coughed, struggling to breathe. "So are you."

"Then why did you do it?"

"Why did I do what?"

"Go out with him?"

"All the junkyard of life has is scrap and crap."

"Ah," he said, understanding. "You were lonely."

He massaged the nape of her neck. To coax wounded vessels to flow.

"Just remember," she warned him, her voice, raspy, weak. "One drop too much and it becomes poison in your veins. Not only will you suffer forever, you will become mad. Forever."

The mystic's comment did not faze Henri. The vampyre pressed his fingertips against her pulse.

The throbs were weak, erratic.

She was badly bruised and broken, her veins torn.

She looked up at him with her beautiful violet eyes glistening. Then the lids closed softly, and the lashes became wet with tears.

Compassion coursed through him again, smashing into his heart like a meteor. He felt her despair as he had felt no other's. She was closing her eyes against the pain, against him, against her dream of love lying dead on the floor, and against her sorry life.

He pricked her carefully to lessen the pain since he'd been unable to mesmerize her.

Twenty minutes later, she lay in his arms unconscious. Barely a murmur of life pulsated through her veins.

Immersing his being with hers, he offered her at least a semblance of life in his world.

She refused to accept the price.

He leaned back and gazed down at her. With the next and careful last drink, as he left the one drop that could not be taken, her heart would stop.

But when he closed his eyes and leaned forward, all Henri saw were her eyes—the beautiful jewel eyes, the beautiful sad jewels. He drew back and looked at the face, still beautiful, but pale now, and cool. She was dying, and she had never really lived.

He felt her heart. Still a beat or two.

The beautiful mystic had been left so sadly stranded in the park.

Sighing, he slashed his wrist.

And broke Realm law.

In denial of the Realm's precepts, Henri De LaCroix let red drops fall against her lips to give her his strength, knowing she would not give her being to him. He should have known it was useless to offer a mystic immortal hell. Even now, she could probably see hell's gate opening in the drops seeping past her lips. Yet—

He could not let her die.

He immersed her in his essence to preserve her life. Her human life ... A terrible conflict erupted within him.

He was a Royal. Sworn to the Realm. He had walked the courts of kings in life, and the courts of vampyre kings after life.

He was not just a vampyre, he was an Old World vampyre. Key word "pyre." The funeral wood on which the dead were burned, in a rage of fire.

He moved his lips toward the waiting punctures. He could not let her live. A Royal's essence could not remain within a mortal. If she lived, she would taste his knowledge, his appetites, his memories.

She would know how to sail, how to ride stallions in the wind, how to choose and enjoy fine wines.

All the things she had never experienced ...

Lifting her into his arms, he carried her from the mausoleum and began to fly with her toward a distant steeple.

"I hope I don't regret this," he muttered to himself as he lighted and laid her gingerly on the rectory porch. For if she lived, she would also taste—his power.

He hammered the buzzer, then stepped back and yelled at the upstairs window. "Stephen! Get your butt out of bed!"

A light came on in an upper story window, filtering to the stairs, then the foyer. Henri backed in the darkness below the porch steps.

The porch light came on and a young priest opened the door, looked out, then seeing no one, stepped out, almost stumbling over the crumpled form that lay in front of the door.

Quickly bending down, the priest turned her face to the side to check for a pulse. His hand jerked back and he gasped in shock at the blood on his fingertips. Then he looked wildly around, looking for the assailant, looking for—the vampyre.

Grabbing the unconscious young woman by her wrists, he dragged her body inside, then banged the door shut and began waking the house with urgent shouts.

Henri moved away, dissolving into the last edges of twilight.

But as he hurried to daysleep, the power the mystic had brought to him began to flow like starlight in his veins. Intense. Magnificent. He was but a vapor in the night. He was the night!

Ecstasy? What was ecstasy when compared to living power? Ecstasy was for the moment. But this, this strange new strength washed through the chambers of his heart in fierce surges ...

If she lived, would Angie feel the same? From him?

5.

Golden light streamed into Angie's eyes. Then nothing. Slumber called her back.

Dreams—a blur of violent blue eyes with flames in the pits, passed through her sleep; blue eyes with feral red flames burning behind the pupils, burning into her own, making her ache to be with him.

He leaned over her and as he pricked her, her veins felt hot and odd, as though the flow was reversing backward into a northern sky. She fell from the sky, through the clouds, into a park pond where the ashes of the dead had been scattered across the stars.

Veils of blue gossamer, a shroud of death, floated down across her body and she drifted on the pond's stars. She was drowning. And he was becoming powerful, commanding the tributaries from the chambers of her heart to flow, and replenish his. He called to her to join him, to share his eternal misery, to live condemned in darkness with him and run through the black rain of night.

Her sorrowful sob broke through the stars—and into the suctorial heart sloshing like a languid sea ...

Angie opened her eyes.

Her body felt like lead.

She willed her arms to move; they refused. She tried to turn. Her body ached with deep pain.

Her veins were in spasms, but she could not cry out, only lay in her prison of pain, a stone.

The golden light was in her eyes again. A golden cross gleaming in the rays of a sunset.

She averted her eyes from the brightness. She needed to focus, needed to think. The strange weakness invaded her very bones.

Someone near her was speaking in low, even tones. What was he saying?

"She will heal, somewhat, if we were not too late."

So that's it. I'm hurt. I'm all busted up inside. I must have been in a car wreck or something. They're giving me the last rites.

"I'm not Catholic," she said. Or at least, she thought she said it.

"But are you a vampyre?" a voice asked close to her.

Her eyes shot open wide. The voice was—

French.

He was back! The vampyre was in the room! Waiting to tempt her again.

She threw back the covers writhing and fighting, slapping at the hands that tried to force her to lie back down, tried to command her against her will.

A twinge in her arm, a quick pinprick. She turned her head to the side to see what had caused the tiny, sharp pain.

A syringe.

Sleep called to her again and she could not refuse its beckoning. She fell back against the pillows.

The next time Angie awoke, she was calm. It was morning, and she was clear-headed. She looked past the cross hovering over her forehead from its leather rope to the somber face behind it—a handsome face, tanned and with a strong jaw line, but tense. And his blue eyes were far too serious beneath a shock of inky black hair.

"It's broad daylight, Father," Angie said, pushing the cross to the side. "If I was a vampyre, wouldn't I be in a dead sleep by now or something, instead of coming out of one?"

"Not necessarily."

"Oh."

The priest left the side of the bed, went to the window directly across from her, and gave the drapes a hard yank.

The room was splintered with light.

Angie threw her hand upward to shield her eyes from the sudden, blinding brightness.

The priest glanced past her and spoke to the opposite wall. "She seems adverse to the light. Could she be a minion?"

She followed his eyes. Another man was in the room standing by a chest of drawers.

He was short, small-boned, with thinning dark hair, a goatee brushed with gray, and beady black eyes that seemed to be perpetually busy, watching every inch of the room.

By the way he leaned his elbow on the edge of the chest to make himself look taller, Angie deduced he was probably self-conscious about his height.

He was well-dressed. A high collar black shirt and black suit, but no tie.

Was he a doctor?

"I doubt she is a vampyre's servile," he said as he stroked his goatee.

The voice startled her, as it had before. It was French.

"I—don't know what that is," she answered in a voice suddenly gone small. There was no more sarcasm. She felt lost and alone and afraid. And she could remember nothing beyond a pair of mesmerizing, sapphire eyes that had stolen her from herself. "Perhaps I am."

"Serviles, minions, live to serve their masters, and to keep them alive. You do not seem to have any symptoms other than a bit of sensitivity to light, which may be temporary."

The Frenchman crossed the room and stood beside her. "He let you live," he said as he studied her with his beady, busy eyes. "Why?"

What did this Frenchman want with her? "I don't know why. He didn't intend to, I don't think. But I can't remember much yet."

"Only a master could have taken as much life from you as this one did and still leave you with a heartbeat. Then he gave you a vampirical transfusion."

"A what?" she asked, dumbfounded.

"He gave you a couple of pints of his best," the priest said. "Or worst, depending on how you look at it. In other words, he changed his mind."

The Frenchman stroked his goatee pensively. "I seriously question whether his decision to let you live was without malevolent motive."

Malevolent motive? Transfusion? The words sent knives through her.

"You were badly beaten," he continued. "Vampyres do not normally cause those kinds of injuries to their victims. Do you remember what happened?"

Angie struggled to remember. "I was in a park, I think."

He stroked his goatee. "The severity of the attack has caused a memory lapse, perhaps?"

"Perhaps." Angie felt her limbs suddenly become icy. She began shivering uncontrollably.

The Frenchman took her shaking hands into his warm ones. "Stephen. Bring another blanket. She is cold."

His hands were slightly calloused, Angie noticed. As though he had worked in—carpentry perhaps.

As the priest smoothed a blanket across her, the Frenchman stroked his goatee. "Do you suppose Sister Margaret could create some of that horrible chicken soup she fancies the whole parish likes?"

"She's tearing around the kitchen as we speak, God help us," he laughed.

The woman who shortly appeared at the door with a bowl of noodles swimming in broth and carrots was not what Angie expected. There was no stern black habit hiding her hair, no "sturdy" black shoes laced up to her ankles, and no saintly, thick black stockings. She was sporting a bright smile, blue jeans—and she was pretty.

"She's a street nun," the priest explained in answer to Angie's look of frank surprise. "And she may have met your—assailant."

The nun handed her a glass of carrot juice. "Closest thing to whole blood nature has to offer." Then she stood guard to make sure Angie finished the whole glass.

She was a nun all right.

"You met him?" Angie asked as she handed her the empty glass.

"He caught me by surprise one night," the sister answered, "but could not seem to move toward me. He stood for a long time in front of me, puzzled, as though he was trying to understand why he was being prevented from coming any closer." She paused. "I think I frightened him. He didn't know what I was."

Angie turned her gaze away from the bowl of soup. Something, she wasn't quite sure what, didn't feel right inside her, inside her thoughts. They were filled with places she had never been, people she had never seen, and murderous monsters, brutal, without mercy—vampyres.

And she was looking at it all through a vampyre's eyes!

Her heartbeat became runaway as she saw victims trying to flee, trying to escape the horrible, beautiful blue eyes, and heard their screams—a cacophony of agony. There were maidens, blood flowing down across the beaded necklines of their medieval dresses. Young men in top hats, their waistcoat collars spattered with red. The red hood of a Victorian cape hid all but the violet eyes of a female vampyre. Carriages carried music and death in the air, and wisps of dark shapes moved through thick fog, moving silently, stealthily, toward the lone traveler, the solitary, unsuspecting rider, the hapless homeless.

Gripped with terror, Angie wanted to cry out to her rescuers that the vampyre had done something horrible to her. But she swallowed her voice back into her throat. The Frenchman with his glittery, iron eyes looked for all the world like he would stake her if he even thought she wasn't human anymore. And even the kindly priest was still wary of her, keeping the cross around his neck grasped tightly in his hand as they spoke. Only the street nun seemed unconcerned.

Angie forced the hot, tasteless soup down her throat, perhaps more to prove to herself, rather than them, that she was untouched by a vampyre's world of darkness, that she had been violated, but not corrupted.

That she was still human.

"You don't happen to have any Merlot?" she asked.

The priest left the room, and returned with a glass of red wine. Angie took the glass with trembling hands. She had asked for Merlot without even knowing if she liked it! She knew nothing of wines. But as she sipped the red-black liquid, she found herself richly enjoying it.

Henri De LaCroix had enjoyed this wine, she thought, startled. A new knowledge flowed through her. A knowledge not her own.

With the last, terrible, delectable swallow, Angie knew what had happened to her. She had been taken into irrevocable union with a master vampyre. And his tainted drops had sealed the deal. *Hide it, girl. Hide it, or they might kill you.*

Keeping her terrified soul in check, Angie forced down the last of the soup as though to remove any and all doubts for them that she was mortal. Then she handed the emptied bowl to the nun, and said, quietly, "I would like to go home now."

All three of the people in the room exchanged looks she couldn't read.

But she had a feeling she wouldn't be going home.

Home. She had left California, driving alone to Seattle despite the overwrought pleas from her overprotective grandmother, but she had felt she was suffocating in the tightly sheltered life. She needed to breathe. And she deeply desired to find love, real love. The problem was finding the right man in the twenty-first century. The pickings were slim. No more meeting the "right young man" at a Sunday Social, snaring the boy next door, or bringing home a date for dinner. For Angie, there were only the noisy pick-up bars, the well-meaning friends arranging introductions, and the internet dating services.

"Why do you suppose he let her live?" the Frenchman queried the air.

"To return for her later?" the priest shrugged.

Angie stared at them aghast, a new horror in her heart. He had said she gave him power. Was it something he would want again? Like a narcotic drug? Would his prison of want demand he return? "Surely he wouldn't!"

The Frenchman turned to her. "There has to be some reason De LaCroix let you live."

"You know him?" she cried in surprise. "You know him?"

"Oh, yes, we know him," the priest said.

"Maybe he was—afraid—to let me die," she answered hesitantly. "I—can't remember—"

The Frenchman's eyes narrowed. "There is little that would cause a vampyre fear." He appraised her slight frame. "And I don't think it's your size."

"I'm a mystic," she finally admitted.

"That would not deter Henri De LaCroix."

"Then I don't know," she said, her shoulders slumping unhappily.

The Frenchman's eyes studied her intently. "At any rate, you can't go home."

He sat on the bed and began to question her, about her life, her childhood, the crazy grandmother she inadvertently mentioned, and her "gift."

"Do you know what you have been given?" the priest asked her.

"A curse. Apparently, it almost cost me my life." She touched the side of her neck where the vampyre had struck, then gazed at the small bottle of holy water and a tiny branding iron in the form of a cross on the night stand. There was no longer any visible evidence she had been bitten, but the knowledge was there as deep and raw as any wound that would not heal.

The priest approached the side of the bed. "Perhaps it's time for introductions," he said. "This dire little Frenchman is known as Andre DuPre, a master slayer. And I am Father Stephen—De LaCroix."

6.

A fireball of fury rose up in Henri, white-hot. He had not given Stephen the mystic so that horse butt, Andre DuPre, could proselytize her!

Angry and disappointed in his cousin, Henri stomped through the rain and mud and churchyard gravestones to the rectory. Sequestered by a crepe myrtle, he peered in past the front window drapes.

Irons of fire erupted in his eyes behind the veils of rain beading from his thick, black eyelashes. Sitting around in the parlor light, congenially drinking brandy and beer, and laughing, and getting to know the mystic, were DuPre's slayers, his "Shadows" as he called them.

Oldest of the troupe at twenty-six, James Lauren sat across from her in a thumb back chair. His crossbow rested beside him, and his lanky legs stretched out comfortably in front of him. He swilled a brandy and took off every stitch of her navy leggings and beige satin tunic with long, easy glances from his beer-bottle-brown eyes.

Henri felt his blood burn.

A vampira in alliance with DuPre stood behind the crossbow slayer, her hand relaxed on his shoulder.

Her azure eyes moved to the window. The Vampyre of Light had sensed the Royal's presence.

Not that Henri cared. He knew Kathryn Beucherie would not betray his presence unless he posed an open threat.

A skinny little Nebraskan with a pouch full of stakes strapped to her waist leaned against Stephen's credenza and sipped a sweet, white wine. She was a black belt; she could leap high and come down tight. Beside her, DuPre's stocky, cocky, street-wise nephew from Northern Ireland cleaned his nails with a stake point.

Brandi Davidson and Mack MacKenzie.

Henri curled his tongue across his lips. If he had not been in atonement, he would have liked to have made the little Midwestern wine-sipper his minion. Then had a taste of Northern Ireland.

The crossbow slayer, he would simply have killed.

An Ethiopian, beautiful with skin like smooth caramel, entered the room from a side door, and Henri instinctively backed away, deeper into the shadows.

Taniesha Telahun was an African night fighter.

Deadly.

And she normally did not travel with the Shadows.

There had to be more to this parlor party than met the eye...

Andre DuPre pulled a hardwood dining chair close to Angie, and began explaining they were going to do a genealogy search on her.

Something to do with a cross her grandmother had given her.

What is that damned DuPre up to with her? Henri thought hotly, his fangs dropping as his emotions roiled and instincts ruled.

Fear and hatred for slayers flared from his lips in a heavy hiss.

Angie was sipping a nice Merlot. Henri smiled, the fangs receded. She was enjoyably experiencing the taste of life he had given her.

He let his eyes travel along the leggings, desiring a thrilling moment or two with her himself.

A fang-laden frown erupted again. DuPre was discussing taking her away. Tonight.

To England.

Why?

The master slayer informed the group they would be traveling by train from London, their destination a small village to the north.

A small village to the north ...

A cross her grandmother had given her ...

Henri flashed away from the window, a silhouette parting the beads of rain as he raced to the park where Angie had been attacked.

Stripping a slender, short branch from a sycamore sapling, he entered the mausoleum.

The body of Angie's assailant was still on the floor. No one had discovered it yet.

They might never discover it.

Stepping over the bloating corpse, Henri began poking around in the dust and debris.

A bit of sheen in the dirt next to a wall. He scooped the chain and cross from its tiny grave on to the stick and held it up to a moonbeam streaming in through the window.

If it was possible for a vampyre to be shocked, Henri was.

Well, this is definitely an OMG, he thought.

He gazed, immobile, for several moments, at the gold sunburst soldered to two, tiny, intersecting silver beams centered with four baguette diamonds.

There was only one cross like this in the world.

Careful not to touch it, he slid the bit of jewelry into his trench coat pocket. And grabbed the red eye to England.

Liora Anjanette Carter was quite possibly far more than just your everyday, radial-reading mystic. A lot more.

•

As soon as he reached the English burrow, DuPre had targeted to hunt down Angie's ancestors, Henri took the cross to a jewelry store to have it repaired and cleaned for her—while he planned a way to get her the hell out of England and away from a past, that if proven to be hers, could shellshock her.

"You have perhaps seen a short Frenchman roaming the streets, Monsieur?" he asked the jeweler casually as he held out the cross, dangling from its stick.

"Ah, the historian," the man returned, as he tossed a questioning glance at the sycamore branch, then at Henri.

"Silver causes an allergic reaction," Henri said in response to his look.

"Unusual piece," the jeweler commented as he fixed the clasp. He shined the sunburst, then dropped the jewelry into a velvet pouch. "No charge for the bag. Oh, and your Frenchman has leased a Tudor home in the country."

Henri took up residence in the barn.

Pacing the hay-strewn floor restlessly, he waited until the rain-rich, low-hanging clouds darkened an oncoming dusk to semi-night, then glided as a raven through the faux darkness to follow

Angie as she left the house. Andre was sending her to the town library.

A brief stop at a small dress shop, then happily on to the library rising into the cistern skies of an English evening—totally oblivious to the horror about to rise on her horizon like a bad sun.

Henri lighted on the tiled roof. The library was impressive for a small township. Stately pines flanked either side of the stone steps, ribbed pillars supported an arched portico.

Inside—the wonderful smell of cedar and books. Books crawled up the walls everywhere. Shape-shifting into the tiniest of mice, he scurried through the door and across the library floor.

Angie stood in jeans and cap-sleeved blouse, gazing upward in awe at the wealth of thought rising around her. And Henri gazed upward in awe at her. Her golden hair curled from the moist English air, her blouse was dew-damped around her breasts. Henri could not take his eyes from her.

She pulled a note from her shoulder bag, briefly studied it, then, wadding it into a ball, tossed it toward a nearby trash can, unaware as she turned away that the crumpled note had hit the can rim and popped to the floor.

Henri padded swiftly across the waxed, hardwood floor, grabbed the wad in his teeth, and whipped behind a book case. Smoothing back the edges with his claws, he studied Andre's scrawls. The prince of penmanship Andre was not. Meticulousness was not one of his most notable attributes. Except when he was cooking. He was a chef to rival the best, Henri had heard.

The note was listing editions of several old newspapers in the library's basement archives.

DuPre was hot on the trail of the bloodline best left in the grave.

Henri hurried out from behind the case to find Angie.

She was standing at the top step of a dimly lit basement stairwell. Wistfully, she glanced behind her at the staircase that spiraled upward into the poets' brightly lit realm.

She turned around, walked to the center of the library, placed her palm over the baluster finial knob, and ascended the spiral staircase.

Apparently, DuPre and her family tree could wait.

Scampering up mahogany stairs so highly polished he would have been able to see his reflection, if he had a reflection, Henri followed the mystic.

Chaucer and *The Canterbury Tales* moved past them on the right. Homer's *Iliad*, Greek mythology, and Europe's art arced around the lustrous wood balustrade to the left. The history of kings shone out from a shelf of their own at the landing, the dark brooding romances of the English moors lay hidden further back.

A column of art and music, then, the poets. Angie's gold locks fell away from her face revealing an open fascination with the magnanimity of it all.

Taking a small, blue, hardbound from a crowded shelf, she let her shop purchases slide from her arms, and scooted into a secluded study nook.

The window gave her an intriguing view through rain buttons of the dark blue clouds and the park below.

Henri shimmied along a ceiling beam to where he also had an intriguing view—down into the book—and down into the front of her blouse.

The philosophy of the poet masters the mystic liked best, it seemed, struck a common chord with her own. They believed that inherent human goodness will, sooner or later, eliminate evil from the world and usher in an eternal reign of transcendent love. Ethereal idealism.

Why did she cling so veraciously to such an ideal when her own life had been one of flat tires and futility? Henri wondered, intensely curious as he leaned his chin on his paw and drank in the cleavage of the human mystic he was beginning to desire beyond reason.

A gnarled and weathered branch from an ancient tree rubbed against the window, its leafy fans smearing the pane with wet. Henri blinked toward the mist spattered glass and down to the park.

Everywhere the world was a canvas of watery green—green grass deepened to dewy splendor, and lush, leafy satiated trees.

Il commence à pleuvoir! I love the rain! Henri thought. *I love to walk in it, talk in it, and I want to kiss Angie in the dark in it. Kiss her in doorways drenched in watery curtains, behind rainy veils under porchway eaves, kiss her into beads of pleasure that will melt her will into my own until she is one with me.*

I'm such a fool, he thought suddenly. *Here I sit in vermin's clothes, stinking, carrying God only knows what filth on my claws, and for what? Just to glimpse her.*

Angie's violet gaze suddenly left the book and centered on the beam, or more specifically, the mouse. "Enjoying the view?"

She had sensed his presence, who knew for how long?

He scurried across the beam, dropped to the floor, became himself, and was sitting across from her at her little reading table before she could exhale.

A universe of emotions passed through her eyes. None of them the desirous stars he had hoped for. She stared at him as though a nightmare had just materialized before her, a horror of discovery. The vampyre who shared her being was indeed real and right in front of her.

"Slaying for DuPre must pay well," Henri said sardonically, eyeing the lavishly wrapped parcels. Then he kicked himself in the butt mentally. That was not what he wanted to say. He had wanted to say—hell, he didn't know what he wanted to say. But not that.

Her cheeks reddened, and her body tightened. "What—are you doing here?" she managed, her hand shaking as she fingered a page of the book.

He leaned toward her, and his watery blue gaze swept through her opaque violet one. "What are you doing with The Breakfast Slayer Club? I left you with my descendent cousin, with Stephen. I didn't let you live so you could become a slayer. I wanted you to—have a real life. Some fun, some adventure." He paused and arched an eyebrow slyly, invitingly. "With me perhaps?"

"I'd rather eat a handful of live wasps!"

He studied her, puzzled. He had expected a measure of aggravation with him perhaps, but not this, this open animosity. He had saved her life, after all. "You sound—a little irritated."

She pursed her lips. "I would kill you right here, right now, if I had the power!"

Holding his arms out to his sides in a mock gesture of surrender, he flashed a sly smile. "Ah, but you do."

Her next words were a bitch-slap. "When I learn to use it, I will."

The glacial coldness in her tone seared him to the core, an odd pain reaching into his heart. An ache that stole his control. The emotion of feeling hurt, wounded, was new to him.

Or perhaps so old he had forgotten.

At any rate, he quickly pushed it aside. He could deal with human frailty later. There were more pressing matters at hand. "Why are you with DuPre and that scurvy band of stake throwers?'" he demanded.

"I'm not your minion," she spat. "I don't have to tell you anything."

"You clean up nice," he said, tossing her a brilliant, white smile. "Spunky, perky, impertinent, and maybe even a little sexy."

She half-rose from the nook to run, but in a flash, he was putting his hand of power over her soft, human one. "Don't, Angie. I'm sorry. Please. Sit back down. I only came to talk. I'm a vain, arrogant bastard. I know that. I guess it happened when I was bitten."

"I think you've probably always been one," she said, but eased back into her seat. Slowly. Watchfully.

Henri could feel the pulse in her wrist racing. She was scared. With no memory, apparently, that he did what he did to save her.

She does not yet remember she was being beaten to death by her mortal lover, and bleeding out, he realized unhappily.

But he knew as her eyes became brackish, that she was sensing acutely the irrevocable union with him.

He also knew she was acutely aware that experiencing her in return was pleasuring him all the way to his groin.

"I am a vampyre, and you are pleasantly gorgeous, but I'm not going to hurt you, Angie," he said softly, his voice coffee-rich as he stroked the back of her hand lightly with his fingertips.

"Then why are you here?" Angie was barely able to ask, wondering at the sensation of pleasant warmth his moving fingers caused as they pressed lightly against her skin.

"You need a guardian, Cinderella. You couldn't throw a stake and hit the broad side of a barn."

"Maybe not today," she retorted with a Cimmerian tone, closing the book of poetry and withdrawing her hand before the fire in her brain drew her into flames of surrender.

"Andre should have left you with Stephen, where you would be safe and protected by that crazy nun of his."

"Why do I need protection?"

"Because the world is not heaven. It is more akin to hell."

For a long moment, her violet gaze cut into his.

"You are thinking you should stake me," he said, as her fingertips eased to her belt, where a drawstring pouch bulged slightly against her hip.

She curled her hand into her lap. "Eventually, Henri, the Shadows will come for you. You must know that."

"But that day is not today, yes, chéri?" he answered, unconcerned, his voice a cool waterfall.

The blouse was dry now. A pity. He had wanted to gaze at the hard little, wet nubs pushing against the rain-kissed blouse.

Ah, well.

Emitting a semblance of a sigh, Henri admitted to himself he was obsessed with this beautiful mystic he had salvaged from death. Possessed by her. The myth of insanity was true. But it was not the insanity of a lost mind. It was the insanity of a mind lost. Lost to desire. A fire burned at his very core, a violet fire striking him every time he envisioned her eyes.

And to make matters worse, his one moment of human weakness had cost him. His heart had throbbed with a great burst when he saved her, an explosion of life, hurling him into a remembrance of being human.

And into atonement.

He had not been able to drink from even a useless drunk since.

Mystics. He should have known to leave well enough alone.

"Hate me if you must, Angie," he said, "But I feel—responsible for you." He paused, and grinned. "Since you seem to be carrying a bit of a vampyre in you, chéri."

"Damn you!"

For want of anything else to do with her hands, she clutched the little book, so tightly her knuckles turned almost white.

His eyes moved to the little volume of poetry.

"I have somewhat of an affinity with poetry myself," he said, comfortably leaning back and clasping his hands behind his neck.

Henri kept his indulgence in human poetry secret from the Realm, away from their glowing, prying eyes. The powerful, perfect, faster than a speeding bullet able to leap tall buildings and able-to-kill-with-a-single-prick Royal was expected to move through the night with his soul masked.

Weaknesses, especially those associated with humans, could earn you a night, or a century, in chains.

"We are as clouds, traveling 'crossed a wanderer's midnight

moon," Henri murmured, creating poetry, as he had centuries ago.

Radiant, we slide and glide, and ride the moonlight!
To pale the very stars we seek,
As moonbeams through our ebon profiles streak
Then the day, and we were but darkness laced in night
Sleep poisons the dreams we would keep ...

A vampyre's poem. But it was all he had. A violinist who could no longer play the haunting melody, only haunt the melody.

"What do you know of your past, Angie?" he asked, leaning forward to place his chin on his hand and study her.

"My mother died when I was very young. What is that to you?" she answered warily.

"Is that all you know?"

"My grandmother didn't tell me much about her. And I don't know who my father was. My grandmother is in a home. She has dementia or something. All I have of my childhood with my mother are some little books of poems, a few legal documents, some other books and I had a cross—" A sadness paled the violet in her eyes. "I guess I lost it."

"The cross. Was it from—your mother?" he asked carefully, keeping his voice gentle. She was tossing him a few crumbs of trust, and he did not want to lose them.

"I think so." She shrugged. "My grandmother gave it to me for my twelfth birthday."

"What is your grandmother's name?" he ventured.

"Jennie Mae Wessin."

Wessin.

So. Mae Weston had changed her last name.

Mae Weston. The daughter of an English duke whose legacy traced directly back to a royal court. The duke was murdered the day Mae's daughter, Allison, gave birth—to a girl.

The last Henri had heard in the vampyre courts, Mae had fled with her daughter and granddaughter to America to save them from the family horror, a violet-eyed vampyre named Jane who had made a secret pact with the Realm to deliver up the royal babe for a purpose that had made even Henri shiver.

"And your mother's name?" Henri probed carefully.

"Allison."

Ah, Liora Anjanette, Henri thought, sighing inwardly. *Your little*

keepsake necklace has marked you, revealed you.
  And Jane is roaming the earth.

7.

Angie's eyes rested, but not demurely, on the library ceiling beam. The violet gaze burned into the wood.

"When I saw that mouse—with odd little eyes, unusually bright." Her gaze whipped to Henri's. "You're a shape-shifter! Andre told me only the most powerful ..."

"Andre's a fool."

He crammed his hand deep into his trench coat pocket. To keep from making a fist and breaking the table.

The velvet pouch met his fingertips, and a bit of burnished gold. He pulled the oval locket from his pocket.

A tiny painted portrait had once occupied one half of the inside. The Lady Jane Weston had been twenty-six, so to speak. Was still twenty-six, so to speak.

He was thirty-two. So to speak.

He pressed the locket's tiny latch with his thumb.

As the locket popped open, Angie glanced at it in surprise. "It's empty."

"I, umm, tore the lady's picture out."

"Pissed you off, did she?"she smirked.

But the snow in her eyes was melting.

"No. She was—a little pissy to begin with."

She was beautiful, Angie's ancestral aunt, the vampira who had taken him from the mortal world and become the owner of his soul. Provocative, twilight violet eyes, skin as smooth as tea with cream, though cool, and raven-black hair that could dew into a mass of unruly, little-girl curls.

Like Angie's blond ones.

Perhaps the resemblance had unconsciously struck him, been

the reason he had been drawn to the mystic.

Adding to nature's gift of sweet deception, Jane had appeared fragile. But unbeknownst to him, unholy strength had laced every sinew in her body when she walked the earth at dusk, and walked with the mortal who lived in the royal courts, distant cousin to the queen.

He had walked willingly with her in the royal gardens with little fear of her winsome smiles.

To his demise.

Henri rose from the desk and flashed away to run from the mystic, run from the fear he might hurt her, run from the disappointment of never being human.

He glanced back only once.

Angie was staring, perplexed and bewildered, into the empty space where he had been only seconds before, and at the locket left open on the pages of the book.

The golden token of his destruction. He smacked the library doors open and stomped outside. He had kept it. All those years. Why?

Beads of rain were forming on the library's ribbed support columns, and puddles were beginning to dot the stone steps.

Umbrellas began to bob.

Henri pulled his trench coat collar up around his neck to ward off the rain, and brushed the water from his eyelashes. He didn't like the rain so much anymore today.

Henri walked two blocks, then the hellish sting of atonement ripped at him. The mystic was unskilled, alone and vulnerable, with no one to protect her if she went dragon slaying with Andre's wild bunch. Or to protect her from the dragon lady, Jane Weston.

He whipped into a shop and bought Angie a cape-style, hooded raincoat, then hurried back to the library. He would give her the cross, help her remember what had happened in the park.

The study nook was empty.

Duty to DuPre had called.

The little book of poetry was still on the desk. And the locket. Henri left the golden oval where it lay. It was time to move on.

His eyes traveled to the basement steps. Being entombed in a windowless cellar with a bunch of dusty, faded newspapers did not appeal to his sense of adventure or spirit any more than it had Angie's, any more than shape-shifting into vermin—he was French, after all—but he wanted to know what Angie would find.

A thin, little elderly woman in a gray skirt and prim white blouse was manning the information booth and looked up pleasantly over the rims of her reading glasses as Henri approached her and asked for access to the historical reference section.

Smoothing back her salt and pepper hair, she inquired conversationally, "Are you all right, sir? You look a little pale."

"I'm fine," Henri said. I've been pale for a few hundred years.

"Are you of local ancestry?" the woman smiled amiably.

No. I am French. And I am the ancestry.

"Most visitors who want to take a peek into the history of the city are usually tracing their family tree. If that's the case, the church might also have birth records you'd be interested in," she said invitingly. "And then of course, there is the churchyard—if you want to search through the headstones."

Not likely.

"I'm a genealogist, a historian of sorts" he said, mimicking Andre's misnomer for his slayers as they tramped across the graveyards of the world.

Henri was amused at the woman's instant interest as she breathed in admiration, "How fascinating!"

"I'm actually trying to trace the existence of an ancestor for a client," he continued.

"You are the second person today!" the librarian exclaimed brightly, directing Henri toward the basement. "Just ask if you can't find what you're looking for. And good hunting, dearie. You know, we may not be among the most well known cities of the world, but we do have a few intriguing skeletons of our own. The House of a Hundred Rooms, for instance—if you're interested. It's said a vampyre once owned the place!"

She still does.

"When you're finished, you might want to end the day in the lovely little French restaurant just past the bridge at Ridgeway Turn," the librarian offered, her dentures in a full smile now.

Henri assumed she had made the suggestion because he was French. He thanked her and descended into the unappealing basement disheveled with old magazines, newspapers and periodicals—and air layered with dust.

The room was permeated with dust, and the smell of musty shelves and old paper—and Angie's perfume.

Taking a deep, delicious whiff of the lingering fragrance, a scent of forest florals, that, magnified by his heightened sense of smell, pleasured him to distraction, Henri followed the florals and found her secluded between two back shelves at a table strewn with stray newspapers.

He glanced over her shoulder at the newspaper she was intensely reading, enjoying her scent. Another paper lay to the side.

She lifted her eyes under their beautiful veils of lashes to his. "Why did you come back?"

"Would you rather I left?"

"Whatever." She shrugged unconcernedly and returned to the paper.

"I brought you a raincoat," he tempted, sitting down beside her. "You should not be running around in a downpour in summer clothes. You could catch a cold."

She looked up at him in surprise. "You bought me a coat?"

"Do you not need one? DuPre should not have brought you halfway around the world without a proper trousseau, Anjanette."

"I ..." Words failed her.

"You're welcome," he said, draping it around her shoulders.

Sunday edition, June 12, 1850, Henri thought with distress as he glanced at the date on the paper. He swallowed hard, forced himself to seem only semi-interested. "Is there a Wessin?"

"Andre has me looking for anyone and everyone named Weston. He talked to my crazy grandmother, and she not only said she changed our names to Wessin, but that she once lived in England, had relatives in the Gold Rush, and so on and so on. I couldn't believe he even listened. But I did find a couple of references to Weston in the archives here."

"So DuPre has you looking for your past in old newspapers. Why? What difference does it make now?" He stifled an impulse to yank her forcibly from the table and run with her, hide her.

"Andre said he would explain more later, but he thinks I may be descended from royalty or something," Angie said.

Or something, Henri thought.

Apparently, Andre had chosen not to tell her yet the significance of her necklace.

"He said he needs to verify that I'm really Allison's kid," Angie continued, "since my grandmother said my parents died in a car collision, then switched gears, to 'Allison died in a train wreck.'" She paused and became thoughtful. "Maybe I was adopted."

Not with those eyes.

Henri watched Angie's soft hand tremble slightly as she turned the pages that sensationalized an exciting era in the history of a young America, and he wanted to touch the satiny hand again, stroke her arms, became sensationalized himself, and take away her uncertainties, take her to bed ...

Or brush the clutter from this tabletop and coax her soft thighs to his right here, right now.

But her mother may have been murdered and now was not the time. He forced his attention to return reluctantly to the excerpts from the past she was buried in. Intriguing ads boldly soliciting adventurer and settler alike to America.

She continued reading, but he found his eyes drifting to the fly on her jeans. So much easier in days of old to have a woman. Just lift a skirt, drop a petticoat or two, or fourteen and "Voila!" Petticoats and pantaloons dropped so easily. Jeans were problematic. Especially if they were tight.

Angie's were tight, hugging her thighs like a second skin.

"As long as you're here, I may as well show you this," Angie said, pointing with a reference card at a photograph taken in late evening, under a caption proclaiming a man could become rich in day. Three prospectors in scruffy pants and boots were leaning happily on their picks and shovels and showing off a six pound nugget of gleaming gold, two Americans, and one supposed Englishman.

A woman wearing a richly adorned riding dress was standing near them, partially concealed in the shadows of a shed, her features unclear.

"The paper says the woman was the financial backing for the venture," Angie said. "Jane Weston, the Lady Jane Weston."

Henri's eyes darkened.

"But that's not the eye-catcher. A hot California sun should have weathered and prematurely aged the youngest gold seeker in spite of his youth," Angie continued, becoming exhilarated. "He should be sun-wrinkled and heat shriveled, but he's clean-shaven, and his short, sandy colored curls are freshly washed while the other two look like the Sasquatch brothers."

"He does seem none the less for wear," Henri added, trying to keep his voice even.

Angie drew in a long breath. "The grueling work of digging out a square of dirt next to hundreds of squares of dirt being shoveled out by sweaty adventurers could tire a man quickly, draining his vitality and youth before he ever found a single golden flake. But this man does not seem fazed at all by the hard work."

The sandy-haired prospector was holding a bowler hat against his midriff and maintaining a gentleman's stance in spite of a wild and woolly culture where men sported such nicknames as Snake-Eye, and towns bore names like Hangtown.

A short article gave the names of the two Americans, and the local Englishman, who had struck it rich in Sacramento, California.

"The young one with the bowler hat must be the Englishman, Nicholas Browning," Angie said.

He was proudly holding the reins of a white horse.

Angie's eyes became intense. "He's wearing a ring, but I can't tell if it's a wedding band. It seems a little too thick. Anyway, look at this—"

Angie opened the second newspaper, dated 1988. Smoothing the paper, she placed a second page with a photo, side by side with the 1850 photo of the striking young man showing off his gold, the handsome young man who had washed his hair for the picture.

"One is a prospector in the 1800s, the other a passenger from a derailed train—in 1988." She paused. "Both photographs of this man were taken at night, and over a century apart." She looked up at Henri. "He hasn't aged a day."

"Well, maybe a day," Henri said weakly.

A knot formed in Angie's throat, and she became silent. She could feel the Bowler hat within Henri's transfused essence. Henri had known him.

She swallowed the knot and pressed her fingertip to the article below the 1988 photo headlined, *One Found Dead On Train.*

"Apparently, he's a hero. He was credited with helping the passengers after the derailment. The obit Andre had me looking for, Allison Weston, my mother apparent, died during this train wreck. She was killed when an ensuing explosion threw a railroad tie spike, right through her heart. She was in a rear coach car, but the blast sent it all the way past the engine where it happened?" She paused, and looking up, cut her eyes sharply to Henri's. And the violet depths welled with tears. "Is that how it happened, Henri?"

"I do not know, chéri. I did not know your mother." That, at least, was the truth.

"And the vampyre?"

"We were associated for a time. But it was long ago. I have not seen him in several decades."

Decades. Acutely, Angie was reminded that the being sitting next to her, exotic, exciting, and an Excalibur of strength, was not human.

She folded the newspapers, stuffed them under the raincoat he had given her and buttoned it up.

"I don't think you're supposed to take—" Henri began.

Vampyres. Okay to suck you dry, but stealing newspapers from a library apparently is ardently frowned on.

"Andre needs to see these," she said. "I'll bring them back."

Sneaking the papers past the librarian was a piece of cake. First, the old lady was sorting through bunches of returned books, then she was looking for her glasses, then she was looking for her date stamp. She was absent-minded, and seemed more concerned with her tea and chocolates than the two visitors leaving the library with an obvious weight gain.

"Well, I'd invite you home for coffee," Henri said as he opened Angie's car door for her and smiled, "but I live in a barn."

"I know," she said, with a half-smile.

He drew his hand down the sleeve of her raincoat. She tensed, her trust fragile, and Henri knew if he took her away by force, even though it was to protect her, she would hate him. The act would override the reason, no matter how he tried to explain it.

He kept his eyes cool, and let her go. But compelled to safeguard her, he trailed her.

Vapors of her fragrance on the rainy breeze followed a road out of town and into the woods.

The rain diminished to a misty fog, draping him as he shape-shifted into a wolf and ran into the trees.

He tracked her rented mini to a wooded area wonderfully messy with wild flowers—pink dog roses, tubular foxglove in pink purple, patches of wood anemone and yellow Tormentil.

As she parked and walked through the flowers along a small foot path, the mystic's flaxen hair became as beautifully misted as the wild garden around her. Her fair skin glistened, and she appeared as exquisitely fragile as a serene, gliding forest spirit.

But Henri knew Angie Carter was on her way to becoming lethal. Underneath that deceiving, delicate demeanor, she was carrying a brimming ladle of his power. Laced with the undiscovered country of her own mysticism.

Was she also on her way to becoming a mystic slayer?

Absorbed in the kaleidoscope of color and fragrance around her, she did not see the wolf who watched her through nebulous whiffs of fog. She turned and gazed at him in fascination as he eased out from between the trees and padded toward her. Bending down, she stroked the silver and cream fur in curiosity. "Well damn, don't I feel like LadyHawke."

He took up stride beside her.

"Tormentil. Such a strange name," she murmured to herself as she paused and plucked a few of the yellow flowers growing on long, shiny, green stalks. "But they are rather pretty, don't you think, Henri?"

She touched the petals. Her jewel-colored eyes moved from the flowers to the path.

A little pile of leaves that had been lying undisturbed swirled upward as though tussled by a breeze, then settled back down again. Then another and another.

Her gaze followed the flurries of leaves. It was as though a tiny whirlwind was traveling along the path.

Or invisible footfalls.

Henri felt an importune shiver, frosty with a sense of familiarity, and he knew—

A ghost disturbed those leaves.

"What do you want?" Angie called out, trembling as the portentous figure became visible.

Slender, in a tailored gray suit and top hat, he acknowledged her by touching the brim of his hat with the head of a silver-tipped cane.

His hair, dark, carried a skein of gray at the temples, and his thirty-something face was not extraordinary. Until one looked in his eyes.

They were a dead gray.

"Go away. Or I'll have you exorcised!" Angie warned shakily. "I know a priest, y' know!"

He popped open an umbrella as if to protect his expensive gray suit from the mist floating through him, twirled his cane, and ambled away into the fog, whistling.

"I've stepped off the edge of the friggin' universe," Angie groaned, and she raced to the safety of her mini, leaving the wolf on the path.

She seems a little distraught, Henri thought, observing her. *It was just a ghost.*

She looked as though she wanted to choke something, anything, with her bare hands.

Henri felt it best not to follow her, considering.

The car's engine revved and shortly became far away. Henri dissolved the wolf shape in a vapor and became himself.

Glancing into the woods where the spirit had dissipated, he puzzled over the ghost's appearance. Andre's troupe of no-goods usually just unearthed vampyres, but it seemed they were unearthing a top hat with a cane in their quest of Angie's lineage.

Interesting.

Ice slushed down Henri's spine, then warmed, a warning his own kind was near—

He swept quietly through the mist-swathed trees, searching, but the woodsy paths did not give up their secrets.

He sniffed the air. The perfumed scent of the mystic was still lingering in the mists, and ... vapors of another presence, one he couldn't identify.

The Realm had dispatched a Lammergeier. A lamb hawk.

To kill him. And carry away the mortal infused with forbidden power.

They did not yet know who and what Angie was.

8.

The rural road panning the hilly English countryside had become a maze in the fog. Washes of creeks, bits of trees, fence posts, floated into Angie's vision then receded back into obscurity.

She was as lost as a rabbit in a snake hole.

And all she had wanted was a glass of wine to calm the jolts of a day that had ended with a ghost instead of good coffee. So she had turned onto this woodsy two-lane to find the French hideaway the librarian had suggested, patterned after the famous Caravelle.

She pulled off the road to get her bearings.

Odd. Something, off to the right moving through the marsh, parting the reeds and tall grass, cutting a rapid path straight toward her, but she couln't tell whether it was animal or human or ...

It disappeared, sliding into the bog as another silhouette became visible in the murky evening.

Henri.

He walked toward her across a low land bridge through feathers of fog. His long trench coat was open, flowing out away from him, and his white cotton shirt was unbuttoned to mid-chest.

He was wickedly handsome.

His casual Italian slacks were cut low and sensuously relaxed around his hips.

A Molotov cocktail exploded within Angie as she gazed at him.

He was well endowed.

Framed into the mist, Henri was a heart-stealer. A cavalier.

Angie climbed from the mini, her heart beating like a rabbit's. He excited her, but her heart was roiling. She was remembering his fiery red drops against her lips. He was the master of stolen souls.

Nervous, watching him, wary of him, she stepped cautiously

onto the bridge.

He slowed his steps, his blue gaze falling full across her, penetrating splinters of ice blue.

She slipped her hand into her belt pack. Warm wood met her touch.

Not much security in that. The stake felt like a toothpick in the face of such power.

Slowly, Angie withdrew the stake, uncertain, wanting to trust, unable to trust—

Where did he go?

He was in front of her, her stake in his hand.

She stared down at her empty fist, aghast, then at him.

"How do you think I have survived for eight hundred years, Anjanette?" he said quietly, his Parisian voice *sotto voce.*

"Obviously very well," she answered.

The stake became cinders in his hand. "Were you not headed home to 'Dinner with DuPre,' Angie?"

"And you're concerned because ...?"

His voice was gentle. "I—do not trust the evening or the night with you. Where were you going, lovely mystic? You seem lost in the fog."

Angie could not isolate the mystical perceptions bombarding her as his eyes drank her in as though tasting mystic wine. This baffling, mesmerizing creature had brought her as close to death as a human could be, yet now seemed to have no malice toward her whatsoever.

"I was trying to find a restaurant called The French Reconnection," she managed.

"Ah, excellent cuisine I've heard," he said, his perfect mouth forming its usual brilliant smile. "You're not too far actually. I could take you there." He held out his hand for her car keys.

She did not even try to protest. She couldn't stake the broad side of a barn. The world was more akin to hell and it was obvious he wasn't going back into the fog.

Settling comfortably into the driver's seat, he ran a hand through his inky hair and tossed a sly glance toward the backseat. The purloined newspapers lay in plain view. "You're quite the little mystic thief. Couldn't you just have told DuPre what you'd found?"

Angie cast a sly glance of her own toward the muscular chest rippling with comfortable power under his barely-buttoned shirt. "I want him to read the articles. My grandmother said my mother, Allison Wessin, died in a car wreck. If she lied and also really changed our names, maybe the reason had to do with Jane Weston."

A trace of rigidity passed through the vampyre's muscles at her words, a taut ripple. But it left very quickly.

Henri pulled easily out onto the road, and a small restaurant soon appeared in the fog wrapped hills. Henri parked, and pulling the raincoat he had bought her close around her shoulders. He led her inside. She trembled under his touch, under his closeness. Walking next to him was like walking next to lightning.

The French Reconnection, a relaxed restaurant and club with white tablecloths and sexy little table lamps, was patterned after its famous larger twin.

Murals of Paris parks and streets rimmed the walls evoking the illusion of Paris street scenes.

"Il est adorable," Angie murmured as they entered.

Henri slipped the hostess a fifty-dollar bill for a secluded table in a far corner—out of earshot and eyeshot of the rest of the patrons.

Angie slid into the chair he held out for her, and concentrated on the menu, avoiding the eyes of moist fire under the cavalier eyelashes.

He lowered her menu with his fingertips. "I promise I will not offer you anything this evening that you do not want, Angie."

She leaned her cheek on her hand and studied him. If he wanted to kill her, he could have done so on the land bridge and just dumped her body in the soupy little marsh. "Scallops sound good."

The waiter grinned broadly and greeted them in French. "Bonsoir, vous êtes prêts à commander?"

"Ah oui. Je voudrais les coquilles St. Jacques," Angie responded, ordering the scallops.

"And for a wine?" Henri asked.

"Bordeaux?" she suggested.

"Nous voudrions une demi-bouteille de Bordeaux pour mademoiselle," Henri's resonant voice requested from the waiter.

Angie watched Henri DeLaCroix with intense interest—the rich voice no one could turn away from, the muscles with sinewy strength unfettered by mortal limitations, the slight trace of warmth under the loosely buttoned cotton shirt.

Warmth ...

How could a vampyre have any traces of warmth?

The wine came. He poured them both a goblet to sip until her food arrived.

As Henri lifted his wine glass to his lips and relished the bouquet, the color and the taste before he drank deeply, Angie caught a change in his eyes, just a flash, a flicker others might not have even noticed. The pleasure in his eyes was rare, from another century.

Then the gaze centered on her, deeply focused. "Angie, that night, offering you damnation with me to save you— Yes, it was probably not the best decision I've ever made, especially considering you are a mystic, but you were dying. Your lover tried to kill you. Do you not remember?"

She was barely able to answer, the shock smacked so hard. "No, I ... My lover?"

Was he telling her the truth?!

"The human mind often blocks what it cannot accept, trauma too deep to relive," he said carefully. "Can you believe me though you cannot yet touch that night?"

The scallops came, but mostly she just pushed them around on her plate, her appetite lost, sloshing around in a nervous sea with her bile.

"I sense good in you, Henri. But I don't remember much of that night," she finally said. "For me, for now, you're a vampyre, and a few good notes don't necessarily salvage a bad melody."

"Perhaps I can at least work on the lyrics?" He pulled the little velvet pouch from his coat pocket. "Open your hand."

She gazed at him uncertainly.

He took her hand in his and turned it palm side out.

She felt her breath catch as he held her hand. He didn't just walk in lightning. Electricity once again traveled along her arm in a bolt of pleasure.

A notched silver cross with a sunburst fell into her palm from the pouch.

"My cross!" Angie cried elatedly.

"You lost it when you were struggling with your attacker," he said, releasing her hand. "I had it repaired."

The sunburst caught the soft light from the table lamp in its rods and shone like translucent gold.

The master vampyre seemed to find it difficult to take his eyes from the golden sheen. Was it a longing, a wish, just to see a sunrise? Angie wondered.

As his eyes moved to his wine glass, she wondered if perhaps like her, he had decided long ago that wishes and dreams were for fools, lovers and old men on park benches. Though she kept trying to believe otherwise.

She slipped the cross back in the pouch.

"You are not going to wear it?" Henri asked curiously.

"Do I need to?" she countered softly.

Lightning streaked across his eyes. Then it was gone. Taking the pouch by the satin strings, he dropped it into her blouse breast pocket. "It would be better if you didn't."

Although he did not touch her, Angie felt the essence of him, brushing her like the quick edge of a sea wind.

She took a quick sip of her wine to steady her nerves. "You said you're eight-hundred years-old?"

"Eight hundred and thirty-two." A tease curled into his smile.

"That's a lot of lovers."

"No, that's a lot of sex. I have only been in love once. And it was a disaster. My lover was not what I expected."

"Apparently mine almost killed me."

"Mine tried."

He poured them a second swirl of wine and raised his glass in a mock toast. "Here's to disastrous love affairs," he said, his laughter rich and solicitous.

She touched her goblet to his, then lifted it to her lips and emptied it.

"Liora Anjanette!" he laughed. "Should I dare give you a third?"

Drinking the rich wine like it was water warmed her far too swiftly and left her light-headed. She ate some of the scallops to put some food on her stomach.

After downing his own second glass of wine, Henri poured her a third then eased his chair around the table close to her. She lowered her eyes, fearful to look into his. Fearful she might see her heart reflected in his blue wells.

"Angie, lift your luxurious lashes and let your violet eyes enter mine," he coaxed whisperingly.

She looked up into his blue storms.

"I should go," she said, her throat dry.

"I know," he said, softly stroking her cheek with the back of his hand.

A flash of pleasure warmed her, desire for foreplay.

"I really should go," she said again, taking his hand from her cheek.

"I know," he said, wrapping the hand in his.

He pressed her palm to his chest.

The hint of warmth as her hand came in contact with the soft cotton shirt, with him, capsized her defenses like a paper boat on a wanton sea.

He rubbed her hand caressingly across his shirt.

"Explore me, Angie," he whispered, pressing her hand harder against his chest. "Touch me. What do you feel from me mystically? Trust your senses."

"You're filled with fire," she said, her own heart smoldering.

"Do you not want the fire's flames, Anjanette?"

He eased her hand in under the open shirt and onto his bare chest.

A fountain of heat rose within her, from him. "Will this path prove fatal, Henri?" she breathed, exploring the strong muscles, lost in him.

Reluctantly he pulled back to put space between them and let her recover from his touch. He became engrossed in his wine, watching the lamp light shine in its depths.

When he looked up, his eyes had lost their fire. The gaze was—hauntingly sad.

"The path could prove fatal, but not from me. We're in danger, Angie."

His words stunned her into sobriety, and she sat up straight. "The great and powerful Oz seems—shaken," she said, but her taunt was weak. His demeanor was that of a knight without a shield.

She opened her mouth, no idea what to say, then said nothing as she heard a familiar voice at the front of the restaurant. Andre's crossbow slayer was asking the hostess if she had seen a young American woman, a blond, come in for dinner.

Angie turned back to Henri.

Henri and his wine glass were gone.

A shadow passed across the wall, darkening one of the Paris murals, then darkened another and another. But only Angie, the mystic, "saw" the vampyre. Silverware chinked, glasses clinked, laughter and small conversations continued unaffected.

"Trust no one," Henri whispered across the room to her as he slipped out a side door.

The Shadow slayer approached the table with a grin, but his brown eyes were somber with concern. "You were running late. The boss feels you need a healthier fear of the dark, my dear."

"H'lo to you, too, James Lauren," she returned. Her words were slightly slurred.

He glanced down at the expended wine bottle.

"Yes, I am becoming magnificently, stinking drunk," she said, dropping her car keys into his palm.

He took the keys, glanced curiously at the bottle again, and then his eyes rested on a small circular indentation in the table-cloth directly beside her. Slight, almost imperceptible.

From a second wine glass.

9.

By the time the mini reached the two-story Tudor home, the landscape was embellished with rainy dark. James hadn't said much, just opened her door for her, and Angie reached over the back seat for the newspapers.

A smattering of Tormentil stalks and petals fell out from between the pages. She slipped them in her pocket, and loading her arms with the newspapers and her packages, scooted out of the car. Still a little tipsy as she entered the house, she clutched the guide rail to the second story balustrade and went directly to her room— a cozy niche with a ceiling sloping to a gabled window, ivory rosette wallpaper and a trundle bed. Pulling the Tormentil from her coat pocket, she tossed them and the newspapers,on the bed, dumped the items from her bags and boxes on the bed as well, then opened the single window to take in huge gulps of air and clear away the lingering wine.

A starling was sitting on the outside sill, staring in.

Henri.

"Are you crazy to come this close to a house full of slayers?" she cried in a whisper.

His response was simply to preen the water from his wing.

A voice silvery, lilting like Japanese wind bells, suddenly filled the bedroom doorway. "Regarde tous ces beaux pullovers! Angie, those are gorgeous sweaters!"

Angie slammed the window shut, smacked the curtains together and turned around quickly, holding them closed behind her. "I have a slight phobia of lightning," she said in response to the vampira's cool but questioning glance. "Blinding white light, fireballs bouncing across the floor, all that."

Kathryn sat down on the edge of the bed and gazed at her quietly. "Are you expecting a storm, Angie?"

Angie quickly held up the two sweaters and asked which Kathryn thought was the better color for her. "I couldn't decide between the two—so I bought them both." She forced a bright smile while her insides churned.

"They're both great," Kathryn said pleasantly.

Then her eyes fell on the third item Angie had not been able to resist purchasing. Kathryn gathered the cloak into her hands, a floor length, deep purple hooded traveling cloak with satin orchid lining. Her blue gaze clouded over as though she had just transported to some undefined place beyond the room, the house, the present. "This is a period piece."

"I found it in the back of the shop in a little corner crammed with costumes."

"This is authentic. I used to have one like it in royal blue."

She placed it carefully back on the bed as though it was part of a treasured trousseau, then looked up at Angie. "Looks like you found some pretty good steals."

"The one thing I couldn't find was a curling iron."

"You can use mine," Kathryn offered.

In a flash she was gone.

And back. "Until you can get one."

She tossed the iron across the room to Angie.

Angie caught it easily with one hand, surprising the Vampyre of Light with her unsuspected quickness.

The movement startled Angie as well. It was as though her hand had been a glove, for an invisible power …

"Andre is training you well in such a short time, teaching your hand to follow your mind's eye like that," Kathryn said.

But she was staring at her as though she wondered whether it might not be as much Andre's training as a staining from the master vampyre who might not have left her unscathed.

Angie quickly made a mental note to be more careful around the vampira.

Let the damned thing fall next time.

Kathryn crossed the room—and opened the window curtains.

"Looks like a new rain is moving in." She turned and dressed her words in a casual tone. "Are you going with us to dinner?"

"I had a bite and some wine on the way in. I think I'll pass."

"See you when we get back then."

As soon as her foot had stepped beyond the threshold of her door, Angie ran back to the window. Had the Vampyre of Light seen Henri?

A rustling on a birch tree branch nearby.

Angie. Do not go out alone. Anywhere.

The words whipped through Angie like a spinning wind.

No! She shoved her hands over her ears, realizing she had heard, within her, the silent words vampyres could spin at each other across the unseen threads of space and time.

Henri's power had opened portals she had not expected.

The threads he tossed traveled and unraveled, along her very spine. Angie turned from the window, stricken.

She slammed her face into a deadpan expression. James was leaning against her doorway, his arms crossed, gazing at her curiously.

"I wouldn't hide too many secrets around here if I were you, Angie," he said. "I won't ask you who you were with tonight, but you need to remember—Andre didn't hire us because we were pencil-pushers. We push stakes."

The quiet young scientist, Angie was learning quickly, was by far the most deadly of the Shadows.

Quiet, deadly and adopted.

Left in his car seat in a grocery cart, all James had as a remembrance from his DNA mother was a ring.

Beautiful piece of pizzazz, Angie thought, glancing at the ring he perpetually wore. The stunning circlet of gold cradled a substantial black sapphire in a bezel setting, and the Greek key of life, symbol of eternity and infinity was engraved, unbroken, around the band.

His smooth brown hair was pulled back behind his ears in a ponytail that reached about mid-shoulder, exposing a plain gold cross swinging from a thick neck chain.

"Did you get the clasp fixed?" Angie asked as she glanced at the chain that had weakened earlier in the week.

"Seems to be okay now."

"Seems to be?"

A slight shrug rippled across his switch hitter shoulders. "I'll have it looked at next time I'm in town."

"Might be a good idea. Considering your profession."

"You could probably use a little extra protection yourself," he said, lifting an eyebrow toward her bare throat.

His eyes fell on the little spray of yellow flowers lying on the bed quilt, and his tone lightened. "Ah, Tormentil. Origin of the name, obscure. Linked somehow, the experts believe, to the fact it appeases the rage in the teeth. The original toothache powder." He glanced out the window at the sky still persistently harboring clouds. "Gonna be a solar eclipse in a few days. Hope we get to see it."

"I wanted to show these newspapers to Andre," Angie said, picking up ye old English news.

The slayer's lips broke into a smile. "Didn't think you were supposed to take reference material out of the library."

"Yeah, yeah, I know. I'm a thief. I'll repent and return them tomorrow."

"Just bring them downstairs after we get back from dinner," James said with a friendly slap to the frame as he pushed away from the door. "He's in his room right now with the door closed. That's a 'do not disturb.'"

As soon as James left, Angie was back at the window looking out into the night, into the trees.

Where are you, Henri?

She was certain he was hanging around, or rather, flitting, around to keep her safe. He had said they were in danger ... She wanted to know why.

She searched within her being to find a path to him.

As though drawn, she looked toward a distant weathered barn, barely visible in the lightless night.

He was behind the graying doors. She could see his eyes, two red meteor points glowing through the rain as the doors opened a slit.

Desperately, Angie, still warmed by the pleasure of him, wanted to run to him, run out into the night into the rain, to explore that protective, tender fire, lay in the hay with him and let him flame against her body wet with rain.

But she also didn't want him dead with a crossbow bolt through his back.

James was a seasoned slayer.

Angie was, in fact, discovering Andre's vampyre seekers were truly warriors in the shadows, even though Andre's assignments often brought them close enough to death to feel the cold breath of the grave on their jugular veins.

They would enter a hang or lair and sweep, as they called it—then move out. No one was to know who they were or where they came from. They were shrouded in secrecy, in shadows.

Except for me, of course, she thought. *I get to spend my time in musty basement graveyards looking through old newspapers. Because I can't throw a stake and hit the broad side of a barn.*

Sighing, Angie began putting away the two sweaters she had purchased, and the cloak.

But as she started to hang the cape next to her only evening gown in the small closet, she stroked the rich velvet and saw Henri's memories within its luxuriant fibers—foggy brick-laid streets, sidewalks lit by gas lights, ballrooms and ball gowns, three-story homes with expansive libraries. Carriages and brandy.

Angie slipped out of her clothes and into her evening gown, clasped a diamond drop pendant around her throat, and put on a pair of modest sized diamond earrings, the only diamonds she owned. Sweeping the cloak around her shoulders, she gazed into her cheval mirror, hummed a little waltz, and twirled in front of the glass. She imagined herself dancing, imagined what it might have been like to have lived in the earlier century, dancing in her jewels with the beautiful burgundy satin dress swirling around her, and the purple velvet cape hanging in the coatroom. Countless little gold curls and tendrils brushed her forehead and the nape of her neck. And olive eye shadow accentuated the violet hue of her eyes, deepening their shine.

Henri suddenly appeared in the mirror behind her.

She gasped. "You have a reflection!"

He grinned. "Most in atonement do have one, I've heard."

"Most in atonement knock," she said, admonishing him as she turned to face him. He was arrogant—she liked it. He was brash, bold—she loved it.

But she was afraid to show it. "You are here uninvited."

"Do I need an invitation?" he grinned. "We are joined, Anjanette."

She became serious, her brow furrowed. "What you need is to leave, Henri. Very quickly. In case you hadn't noticed, I live with slayers. Every room in the place houses one."

"They went to dinner."

His smile spun around her heart. She trembled, wanting him to stay, afraid to let him stay.

His gaze moved to her cloak, and he seemed to become lost in the rich, royal purple sheen of the dark velvet lying softly against her shoulders. In fact, Henri seemed unable to take his eyes from the elegant traveling cloak. He seemed to suddenly flush with color as he stared at it. Angie watched him, watched the wash of excitement, watched him try to resist touching it.

Moonlight slipped in through a window and caught her in a silvery beam. He moved close to her and kneaded the velvety material lightly, briefly with his fingertips, then he brought it up to his face to enjoy the perfume caught in the rich cloth.

"In earlier centuries a young woman would never have traveled or attended a social function unescorted," he said, gentility permeating his tone.

"I doubt I would have had an escort. I would probably have had a shriveled up old aunt chaperoning me, like the English librarian," she laughed lightly, but still on guard.

"You would never have been without an escort, Liora Anjanette. "Que tu es élégant ce soir!" he said softly. "Burgundy becomes you. It deepens those dark Amethyst jewels glittering in your eyes. Que vous êtes belle, Anjanette!"

Angie felt her thoughts becoming cloudy in the presence of the sensual, dangerous creature standing so close to her. The dashing scarf at his throat, the debonair hat, the whimsy in his smile.

He removed his hat and bowed low. "Your coach awaits, m'lady—if you choose to be with me."

The streams in his eyes were becoming tributaries to wash away her thoughts.

"I live with slayers who want to kill you, Henri," she said, shaking away the cloudy streams and sweeping the skirt of burgundy to the side to step past him.

He caught her and swung her toward him. Into him. "But not tonight, yes, chéri?"

She gasped as she felt the muscles seething with power and terrible strength.

But he was sweeping her into visions of his past with him so fast and furiously Angie was left breathless.

The room dissolved. Velvet curtained coaches with romantic lanterns clattered on a cobblestone drive toward a pillared house.

Coachmen were holding carriage doors for party goers, and the scent of roses tinged the air.

A coachman held a carriage door open for her. She climbed out, one dainty slippered foot peeping out discreetly from under the hem of the burgundy dress and rich purple folds of the velvet cape. Henri was pulling her with him into the fantasy of a romantic era when gentlemen courted ladies dressed in satin gowns, and silver candelabras adorned dinner tables laden with food and laughter. An era she had seen only in books, and in her mind's eye from Henri ...

She entered a house filled with gaiety and lively conversation and chandeliers spilling crystal light across an elegant ballroom.

"Dance with me, Angie."

She eased carefully into his arms. He was in atonement, right? And would not hurt her ...

She gasped as strands of weakness flowed through every sinew in her body when his hand moved against her waist—the price of willingly yielding to a master.

"It's all right," he whispered. "You'll get used to it." He swept her onto the dance floor.

Her thoughts burned away like paper in a fireplace.

Then he was turning with her, twirling, whirling, flirting with her, leaving her dizzy, laughing.

As he laughed with her, Henri's enjoyment seemed genuine, as though he was remembering or reliving his own version of *Dance in Bougival*.

The crystals in the chandelier high above her swayed, filling her vision. Shimmering glass careening past her, around her, within her, taking her from herself.

"Are you real?" Angie asked, looking into his eyes, her heart a Roman candle. "Or just part of a dream?"

His eyes cut sharply into her pools of shining violet. "I'm real."

In moments, Angie was becoming part of his being, his strength—his desire, wonderfully lost in him.

"What are you really doing here?" she asked.

"Guarding you," he said softly. "The slayers left you alone. Are you all right, chéri?"

The voice was so tender her knees went weak, and she felt as though she would collapse she was driven so crazy with wanting him.

The orchestral music crested, the violin bow waltzed hauntingly across the strings. Chandeliers and candlelight began to glow like liquid gold.

She swayed with him to the music, his seductive whispers filled the room. He was whispering to her to enjoy him, touch him, excite him.

His seduction was so subtle ... the laces of airy whispers caused sensuous ribbons around her thighs, teasing her, heating her.

"To hell with the past," he said suddenly, halting the dance. Loosening the satin ties at her throat, he pushed the cloak from her shoulders and to the floor.

The chandeliers became circles of recessed lighting, undulating music throbbed sensually with heavy percussion.

She became encapsulated in the rhythm, dancing against him, her hips moving, guided by his hands. She was entwined in a new dream, of heat, of passion.

Gasping for breath, she fought to control her heart—and other places.

The dance ended. The crowd dissolved.

With his arm around her waist, Henri pulled her close and led her to a private table laden with fragrant bouquets of roses, where he spoke of love and her beauty, and they talked softly—and she never touched the food on her plate.

He filled a silver wine goblet for her, then, for a moment gazed into the rich depths.

When he looked up, fire had entered his eyes.

The fire of his desire. Specter cold, yet oh-so-hot.

He stood and pulled the tablecloth away. She reached out her arms to him, sliding them along his, aware of nothing except that she wanted him, wanted him with every pulsing ache within her. Pulling her up from her chair, he leaned her back against the edge of the table, grasped the bodice of her dress to unlock her breasts from their satin prison, and spilled a tender draught of wine onto her lips. Wine splashed enjoyably from the cup's full brim, traveling in luscious rivulets across her bare breasts. Henri caught each with a slow draw of his tongue, groaning in pleasure with each slide, melting her into seeking, wanting, searching for deeper pleasures with him. She unbuttoned his shirt, pushed it from his shoulders and moved her hands across his chest, wanting the cold heat of him again, wanting his body against hers.

His free hand played the satiny folds of her skirt until the hem was at her waist, and there was nothing between them but a tiny swathe of blue lace and nylon. He tossed the emptied cup to the floor. His hand moved to the lace. The goblet's silvery bowl echoed as it rolled, a silvery, light ringing as it spooled away from the table. Ringing …

A phone was ringing.

The music, the roses, the illusion, fell away—broken bits of color.

The kitchen phone was ringing, and Angie didn't have to answer to know it was Andre.

Unwillingly, she flew to the kitchen, picked up the receiver and sighed. The magical evening was over.

After no more than a handful of moments, she hung up.

"Ex-boyfriend?" Henri asked casually, buttoning up his shirt as he came out of the bedroom.

"Don't pretend you didn't hear that. Vampyres have the hearing of a noctuid moth."

"Or a bat?" he smiled.

"You know Andre and the Shadows are on their way back, and as soon as he senses you're here, he'll be coming up those stairs, guns blazing," Angie said anxiously. "Why have you not gone?"

He drew the back of his hand down her cheek and smiled devilishly. "Tell him Nicholas was the one lurking around your bed."

She pushed him to the window. "Go!"

He lifted the latch, but paused as he raised the casing. "Nicholas is dangerous, Angie."

Kissing his cheek quickly, ardently, she whispered, "Then stay close to my dreams."

A small smile played around his mouth—but it was edged with fear for her life. "I'll be close," he said.

He swung his legs over the side of the window ledge and was

gone.

Angie grabbed her lounging pajamas and hurriedly slid out of her dress, to hang it in the closet before the Shadows were opening the front door.

Her thumb slid across a button on the bodice.

A broken button.

Several of the buttons on the bodice of her evening gown were broken, in fact.

And he had been buttoning his shirt …

Not all of his dream with her had been an illusion.

10.

From her room, Angie could hear the Shadows on the porch singing raucously in French. Their voices, not exactly on pitch, were burly and punctuated with laughter, Andre's deep notes and guttural laugh clear above the rest. Deciding the newspaper stories could wait until morning, she went downstairs, asked how dinner was, babbled for a few moments about nothing in particular, then returned to her room and happily fell into bed, relieved. It did not seem they had felt any disturbance within the house. Henri had made good his escape.

At what should have been sunrise, Angie awakened to rain and the smell of freshly brewed coffee. She grabbed a quick shower, splashed on perfume, pulled on a pair of jeans and one of her new sweaters, a soft forest green and clutching the newspapers, hurried down to breakfast.

The dining room in the Tudor style home was more than generous—it was humungous. A huge stone fireplace, oak ceiling beams criss-crossing the ceiling, a pine table and benches that could have seated a horde of Vikings. "Who's cooking breakfast today?" she asked James lightly, avoiding the probing gaze still intent on reading her soul. Could he tell she was beaming a little?

"Andre's our cook for the day," James said, then laughed. "He watches every show on The Food Network. He's in the kitchen as we speak, throwing garlic all over everything to kick it up a notch and 'bamming' everything in sight with his own blend of essence while he explains how the yolk remains in the center of the egg."

"He's not throwing in that homeopathic crap I see him drinking every night and day, is he?" Angie laughed in return, deciding he could put his nosy eyes where the sun don't shine. "To kick us up a notch? The juice you invented for him in your mad scientist lab?"

"His health recipe?" James grinned. "I'm the only one brave enough to swill it with him."

Tantalizing aromas floated from the kitchen—roasting ham and savory eggs. And garlic. The pungent fragrance of Andre's first line of culinary defense delineated the room as Andre pushed through the kitchen door with a bowl of homemade salsa, a large serving platter of warm flour tortillas and fresh cilantro for breakfast burritos. Plates were soon filled with the extravagances of his palate, and coffee filled generous mugs.

To a visitor, it would have appeared seven normal people were about to have a normal breakfast at a normal, if somewhat large, picnic table.

Except the morning conversation was going to be a little terrifying. James had brought his crossbow and bolts to the table, belt packs bulged with stakes underneath lap napkins, a strange little starling with bright eyes watched them from the window sill, and the ghost was, well, about to visit.

Angie could sense the presence of the ghost. He was somewhere in the house. As she plopped the newspapers in the center of table, she asked the group if they had seen the ghost from the woods. "Gray suit, gray felt top hat, silver cane?" she broached cautiously.

Not a look, not a flicker in their eyes betrayed any knowledge of him.

"Sounds like a jolly fellow," James teased. "Anybody I knew in real life?"

"Lame, James." Kathryn's laugh was light, jeweled.

They didn't seem to believe her. Fine, then.

Angie put the subject of the ghost on a back burner and opened the newspapers. "If Allison Weston is my mother, it looks like she died in a train wreck," she said. "And it looks like she was on the ill-fated train with a vampyre."

Andre's eyes flamed like coal oil wicks as he looked at the photos and read the columns.

And a twitch started in his square jawline—not a good sign. That little twitch in his jaw meant business.

"Who am I, Andre?" Angie asked. "Am I related to a duchess or something? The paper calls her, 'The Lady Jane Weston.'"

"All we have at the moment is that a vampyre seems to be intimate with your family," he said. "He and Allison Weston both appeared to be from here in England, but were also in the States at the same time. We might find more about you and these events related to your family, Angie, in Sacramento's past where they may have had more in common than a train. Maybe a passenger's diary or journal is stashed in an attic, someone who observed them before the wreck and witnessed Allison's tragedy. We could place an ad in a local paper offering to pay for information and search for Nicholas."

When her guardians suggested that the Bowler Hat, as he was now officially being dubbed, not only might shed light on her identity, but also be in "atonement." The word caused a brief, but strange sensation within Angie. Like the sting of a stray raindrop on her skin.

"Atonement?"

"We have to be careful we do not go after those who are atoning for their crimes," James explained, then paused. "But this one … lot of pride in that stance," he said as he gazed at the 1850 photo.

The strange stirring again. "How can you know if one is really— in atonement?"

Answers sailed around the table, everything from a measure of warmth that would increase as they neared their return to humanity, to an occasional heartbeat, to shedding a tear or two (though not often), to entering professions where they could offer assistance to humans in need.

Helping those in need, Angie thought.

Protecting them …

A trace of warmth …

Angie's breath became shallow, achy as she fought the yearning rising within her. Her eyes moved to the window to the vampyre of interest sitting on the rainy sill, the master vampyre who had said he was in atonement. She felt a pang of longing ribbon through her. Henri De LaCroix was becoming her heart's desire.

Suddenly, she could have cared less about prospecting vampyres, a mother she didn't really remember or anything else. She was lost in a wish, a misty stroll in the woods with the French vampyre in atonement. His arm was protectively around her waist holding her close, and he was laughing tenderly, teasing her, touching her ... returning to humanity. Then the first deep kiss, his lips moving against hers, coaxing them to part as they melt to the forest floor, their bodies liquid.

Angie pulled the velvet pouch Henri had given her from the pocket of her jeans and shook the little sunburst cross into her palm.

"I didn't have this at the rectory," she said in a small voice, holding it up by the chain. "I think it must have broken. It fell ... before that. But a few days ago, it was—in the pocket of one of my blouses. Perhaps Henri ... Would it be odd for a vampyre to—return a cross?"

She exhaled, hesitant to say more than that.

"If it's Henri De LaCroix, that would be damned odd. Outré," Andre said, eyeing her keenly.

"Maybe Stephen found it on the porch that night and gave it back while you were out of it," James said with a shrug as he poured a second cup of coffee and stretched back in his chair. "And maybe you put it there later? You were kind of mentally wandering for a few days there. And you didn't remember much for awhile."

"I guess that could be." Angie voiced her next suggestion carefully. "Or maybe Nicholas is not the only one—in atonement?"

The response was instant laughter. By the entire troupe.

And the consensus was that if Henri was in atonement, hell must have frozen over.

Angie sighed inwardly. She could not defend the French vampyre. She had no actual proof Henri was in atonement. She didn't even know herself.

She slipped the cross back into the pouch and put it away.

From the corner of her eye, Angie could see James studying her, trying to read through her silence.

The crossbow slayer was too damned sharp, too observant.

"Was my mother murdered, Andre?" she asked, turning to the master slayer.

"Je m'en occuperai plus tard. We'll discuss her further when I return," he said, placing his napkin on his plate and rising from the table.

Then he was out the door and gone, driving in a speedway run toward town.

The starling left the sill.

"Napoleon seemed a little on the flaming side of fiery," Angie remarked as she reached for a last bite of ham.

"You'll get used to him," James said.

"Where did he go?" she asked.

"He's a master slayer. We don't ask him."

A master slayer, apparently, was a man of many secrets. They told her it was once rumored Andre was possibly in the employ of the Illuminati, that infamous secret organization of power moguls hell-bent on maintaining balance in the world economy to keep their money intact. If people knew vampyres were running amok all over the countryside, they would lock their doors and windows, hang out the garlic, and no one would be dining out after dark, late night shopping, or going to clubs, pubs, movies or Vegas. The rumor in the underworld, though, was that Andre DuPre may have been a vampyre himself at one time, and returned to mortality through atonement—or a secret chemical.

Or was he just a rich man with money to burn and needed a cause? Who could know?

At any rate, Andre could wield a stake like a third hand and took good care of his troupe. He said he had been born in the Pyrenees Mountains. They left it at that.

Angie rose from the table, to help clear the leftovers—and steal glances out the window, to search the trees for Henri.

A coldness, like a breath of ice, suddenly swept straight through her. She whirled, gasping—her hair disheveled as though from a wild wind.

Cutting a path across the floor, the iciness traveled across the room then swirled into the ashes of the fireplace smack dab in the middle of the brickwork hearth.

Angie stared into the ashes. A transparent shape took form against the ash-blackened depths of the large fireplace.

The apparition was brief, no more than the wink of an eye, then gone.

Had anyone else caught it?

Angie picked up the newspapers, and busied herself with folding them. *No one saw it, no one else knows ...*

James eased the newspapers from her hand. "Gray felt top hat? Gray suit? Silver-tipped cane? You want to tell us what we think we just saw, Angie?"

Angie looked up. Five pairs of eyes were on her.

"The ghost? I think?" she gulped.

"Duh. Y' think?" James tossed at her while Brandi muttered in disbelief, "A ghost. I don't think I'm in Nebraska anymore, Toto."

"And we're not in an Irish castle either," Mack added, his voice rising nervously in pitch. "So where'd the bloody thing come from? Is this house haunted? Have we run into a real live haunted house?"

"I don't know where he came from," Angie said. "He was in the woods. I guess he just followed me home ..."

"Och! Just followed you home. Like a wee warm pup."

"He seems harmless," Kathryn commented with a shrug. "He just seemed to wander in and out, twirling his cane."

"He just wandered in and out—of me!" Angie retorted indignantly.

"Well, I don't think I'll be for getting much sleep tonight," Mack said, rising. He began to clatter and clang in the kitchen, madly scrubbing at the dishes while he muttered to himself, "We've maybe got a bloody murder on a train, a man who might be a vampyre but appears to have staked her, then saved passengers on the train, and now we've got a ghost. The brickbats on the streets of Northern Ireland didn't chill me like m' bones feel in this instant. A brickbat, I can handle. A railroad spike, I can handle—but a ghost?"

"Look, I think the ghost is probably harmless," James said, then added with a small laugh, "I mean, he wasn't throwing plates and crockery around like Mack is right now, right?"

Angie spent the rest of the day in her room reading up on vampyre atonement on her laptop until she heard the front door open and close. Andre was back.

It was early night.

"I've made arrangements for the train ride back to London and airfare home," he informed them.

Which, translated, meant, "Everybody pack up, grab a nap, and be ready to rise and shine at midnight. We're going to Sacramento." The group became a whirlwind of wiping, swiping and cleaning the house, Lysoling away any traces of their existence.

Angie felt a slow panic unfurling within her.

She had to let Henri know they were leaving. He had said the two of them were in danger. What had he meant? She took a stray glass to the kitchen sink, and the voices bubbling behind her fell away as she gazed out the window past a small meadow to the graying, weathered barn with crumbling doors and rusty hinges—

While the troupe finished cleaning, Angie eased away. Hurrying to her room, she pulled the traveling cloak from the closet. She had purchased the velvet coat on a whim, but now found it had a purpose. Throwing it around her shoulders, she tied the satin laces of the hood under her chin and slipped down the back stairs. The dark cloak concealed her, wrapping her into the night as she ran with determination through the rainy trees and across the small meadow to the barn. Shoving the weather-warped doors open, she called into the dim interior fragrant with hay and cured wood. "Henri?"

He was beside her before she could call his name a second time.

His blue eyes flashed fire from deep within, a quick pentip of light normal humans would have thought was just a sunray hitting the pupil. But Angie knew the hot light rose from the abyss within, not from the world without.

Ropes of desire unmercifully coiled around her heart, desire to have Henri's body of lightning moving against hers.

"Why did you come through the meadow alone?" he admonished her, taking her by the shoulders, his voice anguished. "I told you not to go anywhere alone."

She pushed the hood of the cloak away from her face and let her eyes fall into his blue depths. "I—wanted to see you."

He could acutely hear her breathing, a little fast. "Why did you want to see me, Liora Anjanette?" he asked, an eyebrow arched knowingly.

She answered his question by standing on her tiptoes and placing her soft lips against his.

Angie ... Do you know what you do to me? The barn was quiet, with only the beading of the rain on the roof planks disturbing the silence as Henri took Angie's waist in his hands and caressed her mouth with his, returning the kiss he had been wanting since—

Since forever.

"Welcome to the comforts of my home," he said, his voice husky as he drew away. "Hay dust, wood rot, a leaky roof. Just your usual, conveniently priced rundown barn."

"Warm, sweet hay and you," she smiled.

Her words startled his heart, aroused him to a fever pitch.

He wanted to love her ...

But if he became lost in her, immersed in physical union, he knew the Lammergeier could descend and take him easily.

And thoughts of the horrors that might befall her if he died and the Realm found out who she was ate away at him like crows' beaks.

Angie was a Black Rose, the last female in a royal mortal bloodline.

Black Roses were highly prized, to be impregnated by human male descendents of vampyres of royal birth, to ensure the continuance of the vampyre royal lineage, a lineage of power. After mating, the males subjected themselves to the Realm to become vampyres, and the babes were inducted into the Realm when they turned eighteen.

Angie carried an English crest in her past. And she was a mystic, the missing mystic that had been chosen to begin a lineage reign of royal, powerful, mystical vampyres—who could rule the world.

The Count had two living descendents. Both males ...

"Angie, where is your amulet?" Henri asked urgently.

"You mean my cross? In my pocket."

He tore a small piece of wood plank from a stall wall. "Let me have it."

"I don't understand ..."

"I'll explain later. Right now we need to hide it. You must trust me."

She reached into her cloak and pulled out her grandmother's gift to her. Then, reluctantly, she hung it from the end of the piece of wood.

He stuffed it down the throat of a rabbit he had killed earlier when he was out scrounging for food in the woods, then he pulled up a floor plank, hid the rabbit in the cavity and replaced the board.

"I'm going to take you back to the house," he said, taking her almost roughly by the arm to usher her to the barn door.

"When will I see you again?" she said, bewildered and confused by the unexplained change in him.

He loosened his grip quickly and smiled to reassure her. "Tomorrow if it's cloudy with a chance of rain."

"I won't be here," she said sadly, her shoulders slumping. "I also came to tell you we're leaving. At midnight."

"Leaving? To where?" He stopped abruptly, his eyes becoming dark sapphires.

"Sacramento. To look for passenger accounts of the train wreck—or details from the atoning vampyre from Nicholas if we can find him."

"Atoning?" The darkening in Henri's eyes deepened. How could he tell her that finding Nicholas might lead to Jane discovering her? Nicholas was Jane Weston's paramour.

"Do you know where he is, Henri?" she asked innocently.

"No. But perhaps I can find out." He took her arm again. "Right now, you need to get back to the house before you're missed."

He ushered her quickly out of the barn and through the rain splashed meadow.

But through the night's rain, Angie could sense something, or someone, keeping pace with them in the trees lining the fenced meadow.

Henri's eyes joined hers in searching the span of woods and he hurried her faster and faster until she was breathless by the time they reached the house.

"What's out there?" she whispered in terror, trying to catch her breath as she shook with fear, her eyes wide and terrified for him. He still had to go back to the barn.

"Don't invite anything in, and stay close to DuPre and that jackass slayer who sleeps with his crossbow instead of a woman," Henri insisted firmly as he sent her up the back porch steps.

"But where will you be safe?" she cried, turning, her heart hurting for him.

"In my hovel, the barn," he laughed. "After I search the woods for misfits. This bit of countryside is a known vamp hang. I'll let them know what will happen if they come knocking at your window tonight."

She sensed he wasn't quite telling her the whole truth, but as she opened her mouth to speak, he slipped in his tongue and pleasure warmed through her like hot spice.

When he drew away, she swayed, still lost in him, her eyes still closed.

They were sharing essences in a union that suspended them between space and time, streams flowing across a universe of light and night.

"Angie," he said hoarsely, releasing her from his mental and physical grasp only with difficulty. "I will see you in America."

Pulling the cloak close, she swept up the back stairs, still bathed in his spell, still spicy hot. His fiery blue eyes filled her dreams as she slept, and not until close to midnight did she sleep deeply. She did not awaken, in fact, until an incessant, loud knocking on her bedroom door told her she had overslept.

And she hadn't packed.

She slammed her sweaters, jeans, lingerie and the cloak into her suitcase, rolling the luggage out into the hallway by the handle just as James alerted the house they were ready to roll.

•

Soaring from bedroom window to window with long, boned, featherless wings, giving it the appearance of a pterodactyl, the Lammergeier peered into the rooms of the Tudor house. All of them were as empty as a robbed grave, all stone-cold silent. Not even a footstep in the hallway.

At the back porch door, he sniffed the air. The Royal had been here.

If the slayers had taken off with him, were hiding him, they would die one by one, and not gently.

The door was locked. Curling his gray-blue fingers into a fist, he smacked the middle of the door—it broke from the hinges and crashed to the floor of the mudroom.

Leaping into the middle of the fallen door with raptor quickness, the assassin crouched and his eye slits widened. Red points of pupils darted from wall to wall in the emptiness of a house suddenly hushed.

The house was as quiet as the hour before a storm.

The only evidence any humans had even been in the house were two newspapers laying open end to end on a long pine dining table.

His eyes plunged to the photos, and his thin blue lips drew into a tight line. The Russian vampyre in that photo was well-known, a vampyre trickster.

A chill traveled through his long, hairless arm as he touched the paper, a chill that was not from the dampness in the air or England's rainy coolness but from connecting with something beyond the portals of the present.

The core of constricting cold enveloped his consciousness, pulling him into another place, another time. A time when the Realm had found the power shared by the Lady Jane Weston and Henri De LaCroix disturbing.

The Tudor kitchen blurred.

A woman's hand filled his vision, dipping a quill in ink.

"Tonight, Henri. In the arbor of roses. Bring only your love. And I will wear only my love."

His senses returned to the present. He drew his finger along the newspapers and the essence of another hand, younger with a feather of perfume, filled his nostrils. The woman from the woods. The reason Henri De LaCroix was to be killed.

Slashing the photos with his long fingernails to make them unrecognizable to human eyes, the lamb hawk sniffed the air again and glided toward the barn.

Throwing open the door, he slashed at the hay, scattering the stalks, looking for evidence of where Henri might have gone if he did not leave with the slayers—or where he might be hiding or in daysleep.

Uncovering a dead rabbit, he slung it to the side, looked further through the hay, anywhere the vampyre's essence still lingered. He sniffed again. The Royal's essence went deeper than the smatterings of hay. Was he under the flooring? Droplets of rabbit blood spattered the hay and a board in the flooring. He pushed the hay aside, and began ripping up planks. Reaching in under the boards, he did not find the vampyre. He found another rabbit. For several moments, he stared at it, cocking his head from one side to the other as he studied it, then he threw it behind him, against a pitchfork.

The sound when it landed against the prongs was not a simple thud.

To his keen sense of hearing, something had chinked. Inside the rabbit.

Striding with long thin legs that carried him more like a raptor than bird or man, he crossed to the rabbit, picked it up, shredded it open and reached inside.

The scream that pulsed past his sharp teeth pierced the sunless day and shattered the meadow, scattering the birds from the trees. The Lammergeier shook the rabbit from his hand and clutched his mangled, burned fingers with painful cries.

The barn door opened.

"You just woke the whole countryside with your screeching! What the hell are you doing?"

The Lammergeier pointed at the rabbit.

The woman snarling at him narrowed her gray eyes toward the rabbit's open gut. "Hand me that pitchfork!" she commanded.

Poking into the rabbit's gut with the pitchfork, she caught the links of a small chain on a prong and pulled it out.

"Well, well!" she breathed excitedly, holding it out in front of her. "What is the Royal hiding?" She gazed at the bit of cross as though she had just found the Holy Grail.

And was about to sell it to the Nazis.

11.

Wind turbulence. The 747 rocked in the gusts, and the seat belt sign flashed its warning. Angie buckled her seat belt.

Henri, where are you? she threaded helplessly to nowhere in particular.

Why did he have to go chasing off into the woods like that, going after whoever or whatever had stalked them?

You're probably dead. You purloined my heart, and now you're dead, aren't you, you bastard?

A whip of warmth rushed through her, startling her.

I assure you I am quite alive, Henri threaded toward her from the baggage hold. *I had to leave town in rather a hurry after the barn was overrun with vermin.*

Her breath caught and she gasped. He was directly below her!

She turned quickly from the window to see if the slayers seated around her had noticed she had become ashen. Andre was in the seat beside her, James and Kathryn sat across from her, their first class seats facing hers. The rest were behind them sleeping.

Andre studied her intently, concernedly, his fingers pressed together. "The turbulence is rocking us like a boat on a bad sea. Do you feel you're becoming ill, Angie?"

"I'll be okay," she forced, taking a deep breath. "It is a little rocky. I'm just not used to flying. I've never flown much, especially long distances."

Especially with a vampyre flying along with me in my head.

Andre stroked his goatee and continued his study of Angie 101. "You are not yet trained for clandestine battle, Anjanette."

Yes, I know. I couldn't throw a stake and hit the broad side of a barn.

"We may have difficult days and nights ahead of us as we continue our search of your history."

Henri, help us, Angie threaded. *Is Nicholas in atonement? I believe Nicholas and my mother being in 'ye old local English news' together and in Sacramento on the same train is more than coincidence. I'll wager they knew each other and either she was staked in error, or someone wanted it to look that way. Or he staked her. I'm suspicious of halos that glow a little too brightly.*

Nicholas has no halo. Beware of him Angie, Henri whipped toward her.

Angie averted her gaze from Andre, returning to the mountains of clouds and valleys of sky outside her window. Vapors were floating through her—a darkening …

A visage moved through her mind, moving toward a kill. Moving through the fog in ninteenth-century England with Henri at his side. Nicholas, his fangs dripping with kill …

"There are too many unknowns here, Andre," James was saying. "Including that little English town steeped in too much serenity. There was a strange eeriness hanging over those misty meadows. That house on the hill, for example—that was one scary bed and breakfast."

There are definitely elements unknown here, Angie thought. Include the English woods beyond the Tudor house on a rainy night.

And they did not know what they would encounter as they continued looking into her past.

If Nicholas killed my mother, why would he have killed her? she threaded hopefully into the baggage hold.

I do not know, chéri.

"If we are dealing with an Old World vampyre, we need to proceed with caution," Andre said, his tone solemn. "Old World were not like our city street vamps that can be cleaned out in a single sweep. They were fearless. They were empowered. And they were pure in their evil. An evil that helped them hide. That helped them devour the souls of the innocent. That helped them kill. Ten thousand crosses on your neck would not cause them too much concern. And if it's not touching you, it's useless. They would not be able to take you if you wore one, but they would never back away."

Old World vampyres. According to the books Angie's grand-mother had given her, Old World vampyres were beautiful, hyp-notically beautiful ... and this, this man-thing, Nicholas, was mag-netic. Even from the photograph, he seemed to mesmerize and seduce the world with his soft brown eyes. The books had said a vampyre's eyes could be seductively soft—before they flamed with their evil intent—

"Old World are a rare breed," Andre continued. "There are few left in modern society. In their heyday, they were known as ritual-istic hunters who kept to the night and stalked carefully, hunters of souls. And the dark companions who followed with them could rise up into the night in formless black shadows that terrorized the heart to war for its possession."

Angie swallowed hard. Did Henri have dark companions?

"Why all the PMS over Old World, anyway?" Brandi asked smartly as she popped the top on a can of soda.

"It's the difference between a puff of wind and an F-5, Nebraska child," James said. "One will simply rattle your windows. The other will bring your house down around you."

Andre gave her a disparaging glance. His young night Shadows could be cocky at times, too self-assured. Perhaps they needed a war instead of a sewer battle for a change.

"Nicholas is alone," Kathryn's wind bell voice chimed in softly as though a tiny breeze had tussled the oxygen in the plane's cabin.

Angie glanced at Kathryn. Her aura was softening to pale laven-der. She was taking pity on the creature from the newspaper.

"We have nothing to tell us anything about him, Andre," James argued. "That's a position that could prove uncertain at best, or place any one of us in open peril. What if he's an Old World mas-ter?"

Angie chewed on her lip. Henri was an Old World master.

His memories surfaced, a wildfire sweeping across every gray cell in her brain. Of life and death in the vampyre netherworlds.

And within those memories, a knowledge of what happened to defectors. If Henri was a master and in atonement, the others would kill him. And not gently.

Henri? Why would atoners be killed by their own? Angie sent in a panic, gluing her gaze to the oval window now reflecting a scat-tering of stars.

Henri's answer floated into her heart, smashing it.

As soon as they reach absolution and their power diminishes, the other vampyres will fall on them and devour them, taking every drop of human blood in their veins. Or if they become angry before then, they will throw them in a Sun Well.

Sun Well?

Any punishment with the word "sun" in it couldn't be good.

A deep circular well with smooth stone walls like glass, and a round hole at the top. It is the way they kill their own. It kills all vampyres, even those who walk in the light. In that moment, when the full force of the sun fills the well, the sun kills. The steep, sheer walls are polished to a sheen like black glass, so when the prisoners of the well begin to die and must return to mortality in their final moments and have a reflection, no matter which way they turn, they must watch themselves burn.

"You're staring holes through that window, Angie," James commented quietly.

She turned to find the entire troupe awake and studying her.

She blocked the football sized ball of panic in her esophagus.

When in doubt say something, just not the something you shouldn't say. "Henri knew Nicholas," she said. "I see him as a shadowy figure somewhere within my thoughts."

"The union De LaCroix perpetuated with you is strong—and still lingering," James remarked, his eyes steadily on hers.

Damned wine glass circle.

"As we return to the states, you must all remain aware Henri may be lurking. Watch out for him," Andre warned. "He is a solitary hunter, but none the less dangerous."

Angie felt her heart beat painfully, and she fell silent again. She was with a veritable boxcar of living arsenal who would destroy the vampyre, given the moment.

James' eyes moved to hers, dogging her again, trying to see past the new wave of silence.

She exhaled with relief when the jet finally began its descent toward Los Angeles. The wheels hit the tarmac. In not long, they caught the connecting flight to Sacramento.

The flight was crowded on the smaller plane. The Shadows had to sit apart. Angie bent her knees to let a small man with thinning hair and Ben Franklin glasses squeeze past her. Introducing himself as Virgil Danby from Washington state, he plopped into the seat next to her, and soon began talking nonstop, complaining to her how stressful it had been trying to check a coffin for the baggage hold. A rare coffin, he said. He was an archeologist, he said, and it was a rare find, twelfth century. Very ornate. Then he smiled at her and kept smiling. Then nodded oddly at her over his glasses, as though trying to convey a message.

"The central valley is lovely this time of year," he said as he went on nodding like a bobble head and smiling relentlessly. "Have you ever been on a moonlight tour of the wine country?"

"No, I'm sorry, I haven't," she said, trying to be polite, but he was fraying her nerves. Was this silly little man who was old enough to be her father hitting on her?

"It would be enjoyable with the proper guide," he persisted, handing her a business card.

"Thank you, but no," she said, trying to hand it back. "I'm just here on business."

"I could arrange a night tour under the moon with one of our better guides," he continued to smile. "Perhaps not as romantic a stroll as in the English woods." He slipped the dried petals of a yellow flower into her hand.

Her breath caught. She crushed them quickly, secretly, into her handbag and snapped it shut.

Of course! She should have known when he mentioned a coffin that Henri was with them on the flight!

He spent the rest of the flight reading a travel magazine, she spent the rest of the flight just trying to breathe normally.

The small business flight finally landed.

"A pleasure, miss," the little man said, nodding good day as he pulled his carryon from the overhead compartment and joined the bodies inching a line down the aisle. "I'll look forward to your call."

Angie retrieved her bags from the airport conveyor belt, and the troupe headed for the car rental service. She almost capsized the rolling luggage as she kept looking back, wondering where Henri was.

Her mind and heart were on the Tormentil petals in her bag. Tokens from Henri, tokens of his desire to be with her. She felt hot, stirred with excitement.

Andre leased an SUV for himself and a pickup for Kathryn and

Angie to use. Kathryn calmly drove like a speed demon, and they soon pulled up to the curb in front of a store that had been a dry cleaners in its former life.

By nightfall the long, narrow shop housed two busy-looking desks with computer stations, filing cabinets, and a back room with a hardwood table for quick meals. An oil painting of a friendly, woodsy trail dissolving into a stand of trees embraced one wall.

Angie push-broomed the last of the floor dust out onto the sidewalk, then paused on the walk to look out at the city glistening with the last of the dew of night and street light. Before long, day would be balmy and golden and people would walk by smiling, unsmiling, hurrying, not hurrying, casual, serious—shoppers, office workers, lovers, and mothers—a whole bevy of innocents who knew nothing of the darkness that could haunt the soul and the night.

A wing of breeze shivered past her shoulder, and Henri was beside her, kissing her as he flashed past. She felt she would melt into the cracks in the sidewalk from the wild warmth suddenly on her lips, then gone. A shadowy profile was caught briefly in the yellow glow of a street lamp, then it, too, was gone almost before she could blink.

Trembling, ecstasy delivering throb after soft throb, she turned blankly and went back inside.

The trees in the painting were becoming liquid, moving lines behind a transparent outline.

The ghost materialized in the painting, twirled his cane and sauntered down the trail.

Damned ghost. He was interrupting her luscious, mental afterglow.

She shut the front door and scooted the mat next to the stop.

The ghost melted away into the oils.

"What the hell was that?" Andre directed toward no one in particular as he sat down at the break table and opened a large manila envelope.

Kathryn shrugged quickly. "I do not know him, Andre. I swear. He is no one I knew. He is not here for vindication."

"That he is here at all doesn't exactly leave me with a warm and fuzzy feeling," James grimaced, looking back at the trees and path.

"So long as he does not pilfer," Andre said simply, nonplussed as he began sifting through the contents of the envelope.

"Pilfer?" Angie stared at him in astonishment. "A ghost is running around in the art on the walls, and your only concern is whether he might pilfer?"

Andre looked up and said simply, "Better the painting than sitting here with us at the desk or the dinner table, don't you think?" He turned his attention back to the envelope. "After I saw the newspapers, I decided to do a little more intensive investigation. I found these objects in the library museum in our favorite little English city and managed to talk the librarian into parting with them. For a price, of course."

Andre spilled the contents of the envelope onto the table: an etching about nine by twelve inches, a frayed and well-used prayer book, and a cross about two inches in length hanging from a thick, silver chain about thirty inches long.

The irresistible brown eyes that gazed out at her from the etching, eyes that joined Henri's in her mind, left Angie momentarily without thought.

"Are you in atonement, Nicholas?" she finally murmured.

The etching on the parchment had been done by hand in brown ink, a portrait of Nicholas and another man both sketched from the shoulders up. Was it fifteenth century? They were wearing simple dark tunics with high round necks and a single row of small, white buttons down the front of each.

Chains extended from their necks, but the artist had stopped his work above whatever pendants or medallions were attached.

Angie placed the chain with the large, ancient cross next to the chain in the etching.

Perfect match.

"He was a holy man?" the Shadows breathed in unison.

Andre's tone became pensive. "I've rarely seen a holy man return from the living grave."

Angie rubbed the silver edge of the cross between her finger and her thumb, then slipped the chain over her head to see if she had precognitive powers like Taniesha and Andre, and could read the chain to "see" the past, his past, from the object.

Nothing. She felt sensations, but nothing definitive.

"Make sure you have the goods if you decide to wear that, or you could be a vampyre's milkshake," James said, then with a light stroke to her cheek, he smiled a curvy, friendly smile. "Welcome to the Shadows, California girl."

"The other holy man was murdered, reportedly by robbers he surprised as he entered a church he was visiting," Andre said. "But there was no proof of how he actually died. Nothing was taken from the church."

"So there is a possibility someone else killed him?" Angie questioned as she gazed into the silvery grains of the cross.

"A rather substantial possibility." He paused. "At any rate, it would appear Nicholas may hold a few keys to the mystery called Angie Carter, having known both Jane and Allison Weston."

A maelstrom in the secret places of her heart ravaged Angie. Warnings were pumping through her like gasoline spewing from a broken tank. And a lit match was too damned near. That, she could feel.

She glanced at the prayer book. The cover of the little book was excessively faded, the pages dog-eared.

"He must have been very faithful in his private devotions," Angie said, then paused. "Or guilt-ridden. It's often easier to methodically repeat words than face your own heart."

She took the prayer book into her hands and opened it. Something was striking close to home, to family.

A small portrait fell from between the pages of the book, onto the floor face down.

Angie picked it up and turned it over, then breathed in awe as she gazed at the flawless oval face framed in raven-black, drop curls. "She's ... Jane." As her tone blackened with recognition, her awe furled into a frown. "The same woman who was in the 1850 photo, Jane Weston—but here she's wearing a seventeenth-century French farthingale."

Her eyes flew to Andre. "How can that be?"

Andre's narrowing eyes also considered the picture that was out of place and out of time, and the beads in them glittered sharply.

"How is not as important as why. Perhaps our Gold Rush vampyre can give us the answers."

Angie studied the sensuous, come-hither eyes the same unusual color as her own ... This was definitely her aunt, her ancestral aunt. Caught in pictures hundreds of years apart.

Another friggin' vampyre.

"Answers would be good. Answers as to why I've got a vamp in my history," Angie said.

And is she also—in Henri's history?

Angie sat up straight as she felt the silent words hurling through her like musket balls.

Kathryn ...

Kathryn had shot her a single thought, a mental murmur, through the deepest breadths of her being to see if she would pick up on the threads.

It was too late to bury the startled flicker in her eyes.

Now she knows Henri is still in the psionic fields with me! Angie thought frantically. *She knows I can sense the thoughts that slip past mortality! Any suspicions she had that he is in union with me have just been resolved. And now she has probably also realized I can send them ...*

"Keep this cross close if you choose to wear it," Kathryn said, her gaze without expression as she pulled the chain out from under Angie's collar. "James is right. There are too many unknowns."

As Kathryn's fingertips brushed her skin, Angie felt oddly warm.

Because Kathryn Beucherie was a vampyre.

Angie was beginning to understand and read her mystical perceptions, perceptions that were at the moment manifested through touch. She sat stone-still.

She can feel and hear my blood vessels pulsating so keenly she can almost see them, Angie thought. *Can she control her dark instincts, the instinct to take what she needs, what she wants?*

"Did you know you have an aura?" Angie asked her flatly. She may not have been a precog, but she could read radials quite clearly.

Kathryn looked up in surprise, but only for a moment before a smile broke across her lips. "Ah. Yes, I've heard mystics can see color arcs around those they are with that reveal much to them."

"Yours just turned black."

Kathryn exhaled slightly.

Angie, you are deliciously vibrant, Kathryn threaded. *Your blood would sparkle wonderfully in my veins, and Henri's drops left within you would warm me. But I will not hurt you. I am sworn to*

Andre.

The vampyre moved away and folded her hands together pristinely.

"We—umm, haven't had dinner yet," Angie said, addressing the group and the air with a bright tone of terror. "I'm starving. Pizza and beer all around?"

And maybe some of that stuff James and Andre drink every night to ward off vampyres?

They ordered pizza with everyone putting in bids for their favorites—except Kathryn. While they dipped into fragrant boxes of "hand tossed extra large," she sipped her wine contentedly.

Andre's cell phone buzzed.

"An associate has discovered an ancient earthen jar of water, and a cross, much like the one Angie now chooses to wear, that I want to acquire and which I think we are going to need on this quest," he said as he read the text. Rising from the table, he snatched a last piece of pizza to munch on his way out the door.

He hadn't been gone more than thirty minutes when Angie stopped cold in the middle of her last slice of cheese pizza.

A sound of shirring like wings outside the shop beyond the front door.

A bat? An owl?

The front door's opaque glass darkened briefly behind the blinds. Something was blocking the street light. A jagged, undefined shape.

It zipped away. Then it was back.

"Is something beginning to bubble in my family cauldron?" Angie asked, her voice becoming ashes.

"Something's bubbling," Andre said, coming back in through the door on the alley side. "Unless I'm mistaken, there's a phantom outside this shop."

Phantoms. Formless, wingless things that haunted the night when vampyres are about. The dark companions.

Rigid, the group moved from their chairs like silent arrows. Beyond the door's window blind, something was silhouetted against the street light, something clinging to the branch of a small ornamental tree—a torn black plastic bag?

They looked closer.

It flipped or flew—they weren't certain which—a couple of

times back and forth. More like a blink of movement. Razor sharp.

Angie drew a spike from her knapsack.

"Put it away, Angie," Andre said. "You would be throwing it into empty air."

"Then how do we fight them?" she asked, wide-eyed.

"We don't. You hold on to your will, keep your fear in check, and tell them to move out of your way." He paused. "They won't come in here right now. There is force in numbers. Anyway, they seem to be only—watching us."

The black, formless things cast a chilly shadow over the little storefront door.

"Phantoms," she murmured.

"Someone knows we're here. Someone knows who we are," James said, tensing.

The phantoms left abruptly.

12.

The placid currents of the Sacramento River were spackled with setting sun.

Angie walked near the shallow golden-tinted water sloshing at a bit of pebbly bank and waited anxiously for the cell phone in her front jeans pocket to vibrate. She had left a text message for Virgil Danby, but he had not replied.

Where was Henri? Did he know about the phantoms?

From a nearby walking bridge, Kathryn was watching her protectively, but no one was at the river's edge besides a group of barefoot children panning for gold under a park guide's instruction. Andre had assigned the vampyre of light to accompany the "undisciplined" mystic and check out the first Nicholas they located, a cop who worked at night and lived in the nearby woods.

Diligently, with excited, serious little faces, intent on finding a bit of gold before they had to retrieve shoes and socks and leave, the school children sloshed goldpans to spill the water and sand over the sides and see what was left behind. A whoop erupted near Angie, and the bevy of classmates ran to check the lucky pan. Most of the glitter carried in the currents was mica, of course, but bits of gold still haunted the river and catching a fleck or two was not an empty hope.

A shelf of water had pooled near the edge of the shore. Pausing, Angie picked up several smooth river rocks, spun one toward the center of the pool, and watched the ripples make circles outward toward the river.

Another rock pelted the circle of water.

The two circles of ripples overlapped, then widened, moving toward the center of the river currents together.

She looked up to see who had skipped the second rock.

Henri stood sideways to her on the river bank, his face obscured by the hood of a black wind breaker.

"You came!" she cried. She turned to leap into the arms of the French vampyre whose blood rushed through her veins in a fire she could not quench—

He stopped her.

"She chooses not to approach in the presence of children. But she is ready to strike, Angie."

Angie's eyes darted to Kathryn. She was watching them intensely, her hands braced on the bridge rail, positioned to catapult her over the rail to the river bank.

Henri turned slightly and his eyes revealed to Angie how much he wanted to hold her, touch her.

She felt the wild embers in her heart spiral.

How Danby could have even known where she was, she didn't know, but no matter. Henri was here!

Henri pulled the hood away from his face, and in his countenance Angie could see the deep longing.

But she knew Kathryn was wary, battle-ready. If he took Angie in his arms, she would leap the bridge rail and fly at him with her fangs bared and every kid on the river would forever after have therapy.

She took a small step back, put space between them.

"You returned to the shop last night. You were there," she said.

"I was."

"You sent the phantoms packing."

He smiled. "They didn't like me much."

"Do you know why there were phantoms watching us?"

For a moment, Angie saw the strange sadness trouble his eyes again—and something else, something unspoken that almost surfaced.

"Something's gnawing at you. Big time. What is it?" she probed tenderly.

"There's something you need to know," he said, his tone reluctant. "But just not yet. All right, chéri?"

His words left her cold as bleached bones. *There's something you need to know.*

"Where is the rest of your troupe?" he asked, looking around.

"They're going to meet us at some cabin in the woods to see if the occupant is the Bowler Hat."

"Nicholas doesn't inhabit cabins. He prefers castles," Henri said drily. He glanced at Kathryn again and his tone became fervent. "What do you know of Kathryn?"

Angie shrugged. "Not much. She once ran in rich circles with a notorious vampyre in Europe known as a rogue, a Marquis—until he waited in the alley of a concert hall for a violin player that he wanted to play for him, and only him, and denied the world her music. Kathryn was shattered with remorse. Then she woke up one night to find Andre holding a stake over her heart making her an offer she couldn't refuse—devote her talents to his little troupe of hunters or face damnation. In exchange, she would earn her soul's freedom and regain the life that had pulsated briefly within her when she felt remorse. She's allowed to walk in the light, but not partake of it. If she didn't follow truth, justice and the Andre way, she would—implode."

"Angie, if her freedom is being purchased, she is not in atonement," Henri said.

That's an understatement, Angie thought.

He cast a fleeting look at the bridge. "I need to know she is not a threat to you. I need you to stay here while I approach her. Do not interfere. I will not hurt her."

She looked at him quizzically. "You don't trust her?" Kathryn was becoming her friend. Somewhat.

"I must know."

Henri approached Kathryn cautiously. She had bristled.

"You have a lot of nerve," Kathryn said, turning to him, then added with an acerbic taunt, "But then you are a master. And a Royal. Who goes where he pleases, takes what he pleases, does as he pleases. Even the phantoms must obey you."

"How long has it been, Kathryn?" he said, his voice rolling toward her like soft, heavy fire. "How long since you have tasted?"

The rich, solicitous voice enveloped her with clouds of remembrance and tempted her. Henri moved closer to awaken her thirst with heavier thrusts, remembrances of nights when she and the Marquis ravaged the cities they chose to inhabit.

Kathryn slipped a glimpse toward the mystic's pulse, listening, wanting.

"May I remind you," he said in a lowered voice, "this temptation would in all likelihood kill you. Pain would surge through your veins if you took too much, pain that would leave you screaming longer than the final burn of sunset when the soul enters hell." He paused and shrugged nonchalantly. "Or Andre DuPre would pull your headless body out into the sun. Same difference."

With effort, she was able to tear her eyes away, then exhaled deeply, passing his test, resisting the mystic. She was thirsty but in control.

"What do you want, Henri?" she said, then smiled precociously. "Besides the mystic?"

"You once ran with the Marquis. Now you run with Andre DuPre, with slayers," he scolded her harshly.

"Go, Henri," she said coldly.

"You cannot hide what you are from me, Kathryn," he said. "I'm a Royal of the Realm. You can fight me to protect, but you cannot deny my will."

His eyes became blue webs and he forced her gaze to his, pressing his mind toward the core of her being. He felt a chill shiver her spine as though someone had just thrown a fistful of dirt on her grave.

The grave left open in the south of France when Andre DuPre came calling.

Henri deepened the meld. *Why are you with DuPre?*

Agreeing seemed like a good idea at the time, considering.

How did Andre find you when the Marquis was hiding you so well throughout a whole continent? Henri probed.

Master slayers do not reveal their knowledge of the night. One day he was just there, chasing me down like a dog. With those beady little eyes of his.

Though she spoke offhandedly, Henri could see within her the admiration and respect Kathryn now held for the master slayer. The wiry little man was a seasoned guardian who kept a close watch over his band of warriors. There was no guarantee ever that he might not lose one or more of them to death or worse.

Kathryn he was especially watchful of. She could perish. Her mortal life was being restored in exchange for her allegiance, not through atonement.

Releasing her, Henri drew away satisfied she would not harm, or betray the mystic. She was no longer with the Realm.

Kathryn's brow furrowed and her eyes misted with hurt that he had used his power as a Royal to call her into obedience to him.

"You could have just asked me," she said.

"If you were in atonement, I would not have been able to do that," he reminded her.

"Go!" she hissed, wounded.

Henri left, becoming no more than a blur of breeze on the river paths as he rejoined Angie. "I will not be far from the road you will be taking tonight, Angie. To be sure you are safe." He took her in his arms in spite of Kathryn's warning stance.

The shock of her warmth, the fragrance of her as he buried his face in her hair to whisper to her, for a moment left Henri without words. The subtle power in a mortal woman's body was pleasurable, but Angie left his pleasure heightened, different.

Because he loved her.

He held her until the first star of evening appeared in the sky.

"There are things we need to discuss," he finally said in a lowered voice into her ear. "If this night survives into the next."

He flashed away, becoming part of the darkness in the trees.

13.

"He stood in this very river," Angie said, as she joined Kathryn on the bridge. "Nicholas the gold hunter, getting his boots soaked like everybody else while he swilled a tin pan to catch a slice of the good life."

She shifted her gaze to the shore in mystic vision. *The white horse is taking a cool drink from the river's edge while his master, in his funny hat, is watching the moon rise over the trees. He's wearing a red checkered bandana, but he doesn't like it. He takes it from around his neck, swills water into it to wash his face, then tosses it away. He hates it because it's the color of blood, but he bought it for the same reason.*

A woman stood some distance behind him, in the shadows.

My rather undead ancestral aunt, I'm supposing, if I'm a Weston.

Angie and Kathryn left the bridge. Dusk was being chased from the horizon by the oncoming night, and they would soon be driving into deep woods.

"Are you all right?" Angie asked as they walked to the truck.

"Being probed by a master is ..."

"Sheer hell, from what I could see."

"We are vampyres. Everyone has those who are in rule over them, those we must answer to, and feed."

"So what part do you play in Andre's brat pack?" Angie asked quickly, deciding that was as much information along that line as she cared for at the moment.

"We are not a brat pack. We are Andre's Shadows," Kathryn corrected her curtly. "We are shadow warriors, night fighters, seekers of the damned." She paused and exhaled slowly to calm her irritation with the mystic.

Angie kept her mind steady as Kathryn's eyes moved deeply into hers.

"For as long as Andre needs me, I am his to command. He sometimes tackles very heavy forces of darkness."

The azure eyes moved away. They climbed into the pickup Andre had rented.

Kathryn began calmly driving—like a bat out of hell.

"You always drive like this?" Angie said, tightening her seat belt.

"Yes. We all do."

Meaning, of course, Henri.

Kathryn drove silently for a few moments, then murmured, "Stockholm Syndrome."

"What?" Angie asked, puzzled.

"What are you doing cozying up to the vampyre who captured you and almost took your life?" Kathryn asked, turning to her harshly. "He's dangerous."

"I am not suffering from a paradoxical phenomena of empathy with my captor," Angie answered, feeling a little curt herself. "He was trying to save my life." Briefly, she told her what really happened.

Minus the total immersion thing.

Best left unsaid.

"I don't remember much, but I believe him. I would have died without his help." She pulled a note from her pocket. "The Nicholas that Tani said is a cop on night shift lives off to the right at the next turn."

The police officer's cabin at the end of a gravel drive was flanked with pine trees and warm porch light.

The pickup slammed to a stop, and they cautiously walked up the porch steps.

Henri was standing between them, his arms loosely around their waists before Angie's hand was around the doorknocker. "So. Shall we all greet Nicholas?" he smiled.

"What are you doing here?" Angie cried. "Andre is right behind us!"

"No, I don't think so. He's going to be detained. It would seem a log fell off a truck." He paused and grinned. "Maybe more."

The cabin door opened, Henri smirked, and Angie slapped her hand over her mouth. That they had neglected to enter a rather significant field in their computer name search was obvious.

"Make it quick, ladies and gent," the black officer said, fastening the last button on his uniform shirt. "I'm on my way to work. Are you selling something or just need directions? Most people who end up out here are as lost as city pigeons on a mud hen pond."

"You're right. We're lost," Henri said quickly. "Can you point the way back to town?"

"I'll do better than that," he said with a grin. "Follow me in."

"Well, unless your vamp can change skin tone, I think you can rule this one out." Henri shrugged as the police officer pulled his car out of the garage, and he walked Angie and Kathryn back to the pickup.

"In all the excitement when we actually found a Nicholas of interest, I guess I didn't see that pertinent little fact," Angie admitted. She also did not see the shadowy form that followed the policeman's car from high in the trees.

But she felt it—the sludgy thickness in the air, the presence of the unseen. The evil.

"Something is about to descend," Henri said. "Pedal to the metal, Kathryn. Get her out of here."

He flashed into the woods.

The pickup barreled down the gravel-pitted road to keep the red glow of the cop's tail lights in sight.

"Do I need a stake, or my will power?" Angie asked, inhaling deeply.

"It's a vampyre."

The cop's car suddenly turned crosswise in the road. Kathryn slammed on the brakes, stopping short of a few feet of him.

Angie felt Henri hurry to join them. The essence of his strength flowed like a river of molten steel through the trees. And through her.

The policeman jumped out, waving his gun upward, toward a treetop. "All right, you dirty piece of hog gut! I've got you now!"

His eyes seemed filled with terror, but he also seemed determined to confront whatever was shaking the high tree branches. "You chicken-stealin' varmint!"

The vampyre swooped, and was in front of the officer before he could get off a round.

Fear wracking his eyes, the cop bravely held his ground and was able to shoot twice. The vampyre swept out his hand, the gun flew from the man's hand to his.

"He's a master," Henri warned Angie as he swept to her door and she rolled down her window. "Stay in the truck."

He began walking with firm, determined steps toward the vampyre.

"Move away from that human," he commanded.

Angie eased out of the truck, to see if the vampyre was the Englishman they were seeking. He wasn't. His hair streamed in long, black coils around his arms.

He was menacingly handsome.

Handsome, but scruffy! Like he had been living in the wild for many days or weeks.

The vampyre's eyes glowed neon red and mean in the light of the policeman's car head lamps.

Then they fell on Angie. And scorched.

She shrank in horror. The eyes were shining like red glass, red mirrors, and she could see herself in the mirrors, imprisoned so deeply in the bowels of the earth not even Henri could find her.

She couldn't breathe, her chest was so compressed by the force of the vision.

The creature took a step as if to flash toward her.

"Bad boy," Henri's deep voice resounded through the dark.

Henri was suddenly crashing toward him, a flash of dark light, a master of masters, silent stealth in a haze of crystalline power.

The vampyre with coils did not seem particularly startled by the master's power or the rapier flying at him. His arm swept upward and caught it easily—but not the silver and mahogany dagger that was hidden in its wake—from Angie, as Henri's voice burst through her thoughts and her hand responded to his command. In the next instant, the vampyre was on the ground unmoving, the dagger in his heart.

Astonished but still on the alert, Angie pulled a stake from her pouch in case there were any other "varmints" lurking around.

Pleased with her power, Henri swept a gaze of lusty fire toward her, spearing it across the road and straight into her heart.

Angie dropped her hand, her stake dangled loosely at her side. The gaze burning toward her across the night was filled with such tender fire.

Her heart responded in a flow of flames.

Henri slipped an X-rated kiss into her thoughts, a taste of the depth of the fire he could press onto her lips and into her being, a pulsing warmth that would sear her legs apart for him.

Angie's breath drew in hard and sharp.

"I have to get you out of here," he said, walking toward her.

Kathryn whirled to protect, and Angie could see Henri looking uncertainly toward Andre's vampyre as though trying to decipher the extent of the Vampyre of Light's power.

The next moment he was a blur moving back into the woods.

Henri did not flee from Kathryn very far. Angie felt him halting in his retreat.

Kathryn bristled toward the shadowy woods. "Leave her be, Henri," she warned with no more than a slight parting of her lips.

He stepped out from behind an elm. She went into the stance of attack.

"If you come for her, Henri, I will not stand down," she said, baring a wing tip in warning. "In this you have no command."

The feathery edge shone as though struck by sunlight.

Henri backed off. "Then you are the mythical Vampyre of Light, Kathryn?" he asked.

Before she could answer, he fled to the trees. Headlights were throwing a glow across a bend in the road.

As Andre's SUV pulled to a stop, Kathryn roughly pulled Angie aside toward the brush, out of earshot. "It would seem your master is taking you under his wing. Why?"

"I don't know. And he's not my master," Angie returned defensively.

"He commanded you to send that blade," Kathryn said forcefully. "His voice flowed through you like honey. I felt it. He's in communion with you. I suspected as much when you were able to catch my threads."

Trembling, Angie looked away.

"At the moment, it appears he is either in love with you—or he wants another taste of that loco weed in your veins," Kathryn said sharply.

"I didn't think you, any of you, could feel love," Angie said.

"We feel. We feel the agony of wanting and never having."

Andre and James were climbing out of the truck, weapons

drawn.

"I will keep this between us," Kathryn said quickly, "for now. You are in my charge. But walk carefully. I don't plan on being killed by the Realm because of you and Henri."

"I'm not sure why he was going to take me away, I swear," Angie said in a small voice. "He said we were in …"

Andre and James were hurrying toward the cop. Kathryn ended the conversation and hurried to meet them.

"Danger," Angie finished to herself.

She stood in the road alone, staring into the woods, longing for Henri De LaCroix.

•

Sensing the beautiful mystic yearning for him, Henri gazed back through the trees toward her, his own longings hard and sharp.

Her heart had beat so rapidly when she felt his passion in flight like a burning arrow toward her, beat like it was struck with a match.

Henri receded into the darker reaches of the woods a little, but his eyes kept returning to her. She was exquisite in her little jeans and peasant blouse as she stood in the road wanting him.

"Throwing thoughts of fire is why he was notorious," Kathryn said, one eye on the woods as she returned to Angie's side. "He's a self-serving cur."

Angie clinched her fists. "Bastard. Bastard."

"I know," Kathryn said sympathetically.

I'm a bastard for saving her life? And one little thought kiss? Henri thought, amazed. Then he frowned, upset. Very humanly upset.

"No, no, not Henri," Angie explained swifly to Kathryn. "I wasn't calling Henri a bastard, Kathryn. I meant—" She pointed at the dead vampyre. "Him. I think he wanted to hurt me."

Kathryn gazed at the vampyre gone to hell in a hurry. "That's possible. He was viewing you like he wanted you for his midnight martini."

"He was viewing me with more than that," Angie said .

Henri studied Angie thoughtfully. Was her mystic sight in play?

"I will need to stay close to her," he murmured to his bird as it lighted on his shoulder. "There may be more to this river rat than the night has revealed."

Angie walked back to the pickup with Kathryn silently for a few moments, then asked shyly, "How did you know about the—kiss thing?"

"Your heart started beating like lightning had hit. That and Henri's reputation." She halted and turned to her. "Actually, Angie, Henri probably would not have been able to slip one in on you like that unless you were receptive."

Angie's lips parted as if to protest, then closed. She was more than receptive to him.

She stepped closer to the dead vamp that had not yet turned to dust. "I guess they don't just—go away?"

"Not a master. They can come back to life," Andre said. He bent down and with a single, agile whip of his sword blade, separated the vampyre's head from his neck.

As he watched from the distance, Henri felt a sick hollow wad, like worms on the dead, form in his stomach.

Odd. The crossbow slayer didn't look that well either, as the stench of chicken blood filled the air.

"He will dissipate at sunrise," Andre said.

Dissipate. What did dissipation feel like? Henri wondered in idle terror.

"How long has he been hanging around your house?"

"About four days. He was killing my chickens and the rats in the barn," the policeman said. "Where I come from, there are people, and there are animals, and then there are varmints. A chicken stealing weasel is a varmint. He was a varmint. And you hunt varmints down—and kill them. But I could never catch him."

"A gun wouldn't kill him anyway."

"My auntie used to sit on the porch and tell me stories ..." he began, then looked as though the night had not been real. "I think I'm just going to call in sick, get a pint of ice cream, and watch Jerry Springer—something sane."

In pity, Kathryn offered to take the night from his memory, but the officer backed away from her, muttering something about being "out here in the woods too long, think I'll move into town," and with the glazed eyes of a sleepwalker, he got in his car and went home.

Four days, Henri thought pensively. The slayers had arrived back in the states four days ago.

"I hope we have better luck with the Nicholas who answered the ad for the journal," Angie said.

When Angie was safely away from the woods, and Andre had taken her to the house he had rented for his troupe's stay in Sacramento, Henri flew into the city to the roof of an old museum, to sit on a gargoyle and think. The master vampyre had not been after the policeman. He had been after Angie.

A vampyre, strong, sinewy with dark wings, lighted next to him and gazed out into a star studded black velvet sky. "Give her up, Henri."

"What are you talking about?"

"Odd thing the other night. Jane was vacationing in that god-awful house of hers when a Lammergeier was spotted in the woods rummaging through an old barn. And what do you think he found?"

Henri murmured a profanity, his thoughts roiling.

"The Realm hasn't just offered a reward for the mystic, Henri. Position, power, fresh blood supply for life, whatever the finder wants is what they'll pay. How many of them can you kill? Tonight was just the beginning. How are you going to protect her? And stay alive to do it? Jane will be relentless. The Lammergeier will be relentless. The whole damned Realm will be relentless."

"And you, Nicholas?" Henri asked.

"The way I see it, you've only got three options. Fight us all from the darkness. Or grab the mystic and run."

"You said three options."

"Vampyres can't procreate."

Spreading his dark wings, he shadowed the stars as he flew skyward and disappeared into the night.

14.

"How in hell does a vampyre catch a cold?" Angie asked, shoving a box of tissues across the truck seat to Kathryn as they drove toward a tree-lined drive and a hedged walkway lined with garden lights. A mansion rose behind the lights, majestic, its upper balconies reaching out over a massive manicured estate.

"It isn't a cold. It's a reaction," Kathryn insisted as she pulled a tissue from the box—and sneezed.

A strip of fog, out of sync with the clear night, rolled across the hood of the pickup then down the window weather stripping—and in through the back window of the truck's extended cab.

"If you were going to try human food for the first time, maybe you should have chosen something milder like chicken soup?" Henri's voice spooled over the back seat.

"How did you ...?" Angie blurted, jerking around, then shook her head and sighed resignedly, "Oh, never mind."

"So. You are on your way to the Browning mansion, I see. Built when cattle was king and railroads and Nicholas ruled." He stretched out comfortably across the seat.

Kathryn snatched another tissue. "I don't suppose there's any getting rid of you?"

"Not likely." He smiled deeply at Angie, then added, "I doubt my old friend Nicholai is in atonement. If he saved a mortal and didn't at least take a taste, there had to be a reason, and not necessarily a good one."

Before long, a pillared mansion cloaked in night and the sweet smell of honeysuckle rose out of a stand of laurel pines.

"Somehow this is not what I was expecting," Angie commented as they parked. She stepped back to admire the porch archways trellised with the flowery vines.

"We do not all reside in dank dungeons and cobwebby crypts," Henri quipped, pulling her close.

Do not leave my side, he threaded, squeezing her hand into his own. He did not relish letting her enter this golden cave. But he knew she would go spelunking with or without him. She wanted the chronicles of her past.

There was no response to the bell. They rang again, then knocked.

Angie tried to peer through the sidelights next to the door. "I don't think anyone is home."

The porch light came on. The door opened.

Shock, horror, fear and amazement, a load of raw emotion, passed through Angie as she gazed at the being standing before her.

The only thing missing was the hat.

He apologized for his tardiness in answering the bell, his eyes cut to Henri's briefly, then with a disarmingly charming smile that curled the corners of his perfect, full mouth, he invited them in.

"You called and said you might possibly have a journal that would be of interest?" Angie asked, but didn't move. To accept an invitation to enter a vampyre's lair was to accept an invitation to death.

Henri stepped unhesitatingly into the foyer, pulling her with him, less enthusiastically. Kathryn went back to the truck, sick as a dog.

A chandelier shimmered from the vaulted foyer ceiling onto glossy obsidian floor tiles.

"Nice place," Henri said with a slightly mocking tone.

"Better than a barn," Nicholas responded with a smirk.

Not much like a vampyre's chambers, Angie thought. And not quite the dark and dirty cellars and sewers Andre usually cleaned up.

Wonderingly, as they followed him down the hall to the library, she brushed her hand against the rich warm oak paneling of the walls. Was this the house of a prince, or a prince of darkness?

If Andre or Taniesha had touched the wood, would their retro-cognitive powers have revealed anything of his past, or him?

This was not your usual, bite-you-in-the-alley vampyre. The library was well lit by table lamps, and a friendly fire crackled in the fireplace. Rich furnishings and expensive books surrounded the walls.

An exquisitely carved Spanish saddle was displayed in the middle of the room along with a lariat and bolero. A pair of golden candlesticks and a pewter goblet adorned with jewels glittered from a shelf behind the glass of an antique étagère.

A battered bowler hat and a gold pocket watch were beside them.

But the piece de resistance was on his finger. An emerald. Set in a thick, fifteenth-century gold band intricately engraved with Latin symbols.

A vampyre's ring.

Nicholas tossed a few pine chips in the fire to create an aromatic fragrance in the room.

"So who is the lovely vampira who broke rank?" he directed toward Henri.

"The Valkyrie."

His eyes expressed surprise. "The Vampyre of Light. I thought she was a myth."

Suddenly, in a movement more like a blink, Nicholas was in front of Angie, fully focused on her, studying the chain dipping into her blouse semi-concealed.

"What are you? You do not seem to be entirely of mortal blood," he said, flipping a sly, mocking glance at Henri. Then his gaze moved deeply into hers and he raised his hand to move her to release whatever cross the chain held so he could search her being.

Henri's hand came up like lightning.

"She belongs to me."

He shrugged, and let his hand drop.

"And your name?" he asked her, smiling deeply.

Angie started to give him her nickname, but somehow, "Angie" suddenly seemed plain Jane in the face of exotic creatures with names like Beucherie, Nicholai and De LaCroix. "Liora Anjanette," she said.

"Vous êtes français!" Nicholas said, pleasure lighting up his eyes. "Enchante, Mademoiselle Carter. Est-ce que vous parlez français?"

"Et vous, vous êtes anglais?"

His pleasure was apparent as his laughter became rich, enjoyable. "I would like to think there were stately English castles somewhere in my ancestry," he said. "But they are actually Russian. Being English is a current convenience, you might say. What of yours?"

"That's what I'm trying to find out."

A strange look passed briefly through his pupils. Tossed quickly at Henri.

Then it was gone, replaced with a simple shine from the fireplace flames.

Nodding in the direction of the window as his keen hearing picked up Kathryn sneezing and sniffling in the truck, he arched an eyebrow, and smiled. "Corn flour?" he asked Angie.

"Corn tortilla chips and chipotle sauce."

"She should have tried something a little easier on her system. Chicken soup is less likely to send quasi-mortality into shock."

"I don't think she'll be trying human food again for a very long while," Angie said.

He invited them to sit down. Angie sat on the edge, the very edge, of a brown leather couch. He stood next to his desk, comfortably gazing down at her. "Why have you sought me out? Just for a journal?"

"We also came to see if you were truly wanting to return to the world of mortal men, but it would seem we also need your help."

"A Vampyre of Light with a cold, a semi-mortal mystic, and a renegade Royal need my help," he scoffed with a dry laugh.

In spite of his air of confidence, the Russian vampyre was being cautious, Angie noted. He was ready to flee or fight, intrigued but defensive. His jaw was taut, every muscle in his body tight.

She tried to read his aura.

But there was none.

"Discovering you was an accident," Angie said.

"They were looking for Allison Weston. It seems you knew her?" Henri smirked at him.

A small frown replaced Nicholas' smile. "She inadvertently turned onto a rather trashy street in the older part of town one night, lost, and knocked on the wrong door for directions. I used a little friendly persuasion to keep the occupants from killing her. She became infatuated with me, stalking me for weeks, and followed me on board a train thinking I was leaving town when I was actually trying to outrun a slayer. When the train derailed, a hunter of the damned staked her in the ensuing confusion. I do not know why. I was trying to save a woman with child and was unable to help her."

"You told Angie on the phone you had a journal that belonged to a passenger on the train?" Henri interjected quickly, his own jaw becoming taut, his eyes scissoring the other vampyre.

"It belonged to the woman I was helping. Kara Milstead. She said she had bought it at some little boutique in Old Town. She gave it to me several years ago when she was dying. We—had kept in touch. But I've never had time to read it."

He opened a splendid wood storage trunk beside a wine rack, and pulled out a time-worn, leatherbound journal.

"Thank you," Angie said, as he handed her the journal. She tried not to let him touch her hand as she took the little book, but his fingertips brushed her palm. Deliberately, she knew. He wanted to test the mystic waters.

A cold burst of heat tunneled up her wrist. And a manifestation of mystical warning that this vampyre had little fear, even though he could be burned by the protective presence of the cross on her neck.

They will never back away ...

He had touched her, defying the burn.

He touched her for no more than a moment, an eternity, then withdrew his hand.

"Would you care for a glass of wine?" he asked.

He curled his fingers into his palm.

Touching her had hurt him.

I need something stronger than wine, she thought. *I need Jim Beam.*

He pulled a red wine from an oak cabinet, uncorked the bottle, and poured them all a glass.

As she took her glass, his mouth curled into a deeper smile, and the brown pools in the eyes of the Russian penitent oddly seemed even more beautiful than when Angie had first looked into them in the etching ...

Henri stepped between them, swirled his wine glass in front of her eyes, and she shook away the burning in her brain.

"C'est parfait. This is magnificent," she breathed as she swirled her own garnet red liquid glimmering in the candlelight. "A bouquet like fresh rain after a thunderstorm. This is vintage." The wine had been aged until the bouquet was delicate and beautiful.

"Where are you from, Liora Anjanette?" Nicholas asked, with an odd twisty smile tossed toward Henri.

"Podunk, California," she said with a shrug. "But I've been to England recently."

A flicker passed through his eyes at the mention of England, but he simply grinned and laughed. "I have never been to Podunk."

"I found the English countryside mysteriously beautiful at night," she said with forced calm. "And the forests almost made me believe in fairies, dwarves and wood nymphs." She pulled her eyes from his, and they fell on his ring. "The sea was a shimmering dark emerald. Wonderful, wild waves that threw salty sea spray on my face when I walked the rocks. Waves that exploded with splashes of moonlight."

"You're a poet, Anjanette!" he teased pleasantly as he took a deep draught of wine. "And I am enthralled with your passion for life."

Life. When their victims throbbed with it, embraced it with passion, it would increase their hunger and they would crave.

His eyes began searching hers again, and she sensed his frustration at not being able to reach into the portals of mysticism.

The abstracted look deepened …

He was going to use the darker strength within him to open those portals!

His eyes became coffee colored and shone with splintery light as he began to penetrate her sight with optic thrusts, thrusts that were all too familiar. She had traveled this path before …

Henri's thoughts passed close to her, to give her the strength to resist the master standing across from her swilling wine and wealth. And she could sense a power rising within Henri, magnificent but terrifying in its strength.

He was ready to kill to protect her.

I might as well give up on the wine, Angie sighed inwardly, resignedly, setting it down. Mystic heat burned through the very marrow in her bones from the bombardment of power all around her—and now she was sensing another vamp within the house.

A pair of black, five-inch heels sidled into the library.

The black-eyed vamp with inky, swingy short hair and long bangs greeted Nicholas with a strong Russian accent. "Are we having a party?" she asked Nicholas, her pale eyes lighting up as she gazed at Henri with intense curiosity, then at Angie, the sole mortal in the room.

Hungrily, it seemed to Angie. And she was the party.

"No," Nicholas said firmly. "These are business acquaintances."

Flippant, flirty, flamboyant, she presented herself as "Natalia, just an 'old friend,'" and squeezed his hand into hers, then ran her hand along the back of his shoulder. But Angie knew when she shrank a little before the displeasure in his eyes that she was in awe of him. Was he her master?

Bending her knee, she brushed a bit of dust from the toe of her shoe, told them with a tight smile that she was glad to have met them, then she wished him a pleasant evening, tugged at her tiny dress and left.

"Natalia's really not quite that bad," Nicholas said with a warm laugh as she left, "when you get to know her. She was just curious. She's very loyal."

I'll bet, Angie thought.

The "business acquaintances" finished their wine quickly, just in case any more "old" friends were hanging around the mansion.

But as Nicholas moved to the library entrance, to escort them to the front door, Angie realized she was going to have to walk uncomfortably close to him. If they touched ...

They touched.

As she tried to maneuver around him, he casually stepped back and brushed briefly but fully against her.

Hell was so raw within him she wanted to scream. Her mystic senses came alive and turned scathing. An ordinary person would have felt no more than a slight curious trace of something odd, something different about him, a difference that would have been unconsciously dismissed as quickly as it had come, like a blink of an eye. But Angie was fast becoming skilled in her remarkable talent, enhanced by the vampirical force that shook her inwardly from head to toe like an 8.9 earthquake when it surged.

And it was surging. In case she needed to defend herself.

"Sorry," the vampyre said as he glanced softly back at her.

Biting back the sharp sensation of those Nicholas had killed, perceptions of terror that threatened to strangle her, Angie forced herself to walk calmly down the hall.

If he had felt her reaction to him, he did not show it. He held the front door open for them and said goodnight.

"That was godawful," she exclaimed in an exhalation of disgust as she fell into the back seat.

"Don't want to catch your—reaction," she said in response to Kathryn's questioning glance because she chose the back seat. With Henri.

"He's not just a master. He's a vanguard," Henri said softly as he pulled her into his arms to stop her trembling. "You might as well know what he can do. Are you all right?"

"Just a little—unsettled," she said shakily. Henri's embrace was warm, protective. She pressed closer to him, letting her body language and her eyes tell him that him if Kathryn wasn't in the truck, they could pull into the woods and enjoy that back seat.

"From what I could hear, it didn't sound to me like things were going too badly. What happened to you?" Kathryn asked, glancing at Angie in the rear view mirror, eager for the details of their visit.

"Hell," Angie answered. "Hell is what happened."

As they sped away from the mansion that was too well lit, too well kept, too—pure, Henri pulled her gaze into his blue pools under their black waterfalls of lashes. "You are with me, now, m' lady," he said softly, his eyes moist as he massaged her hand, sending streams of sweetness around her wrist.

"I didn't know you knew French so well," Kathryn tossed toward Angie, while tossing Henri a frown in the rear view mirror. "An inner talent you inherited, I suppose?"

"Henri thinks I should learn foreign languages and have fun," Angie responded with a light smile, flirtatiously glancing at him. Then her tone sobered. "Andre's certainly going to have his hands full with old Nicholas Dudley DoRight, isn't he?" she said. "He seems rather comfortable in his world of darkness."

"Andre's going to have his hands full with Han Solo and Leia," Kathryn clipped from the front as she eased the pickup into maximum speed.

"Who?"

"You and Henri."

She sneezed again.

"Should a' had the soup," Angie said.

15.

Angie began searching the pages of the journal that supposedly had belonged Kara Milstead, a school teacher.

"Here it is," Angie said, effused by an entry marked, "June 12, 1984."

"Today promised to be balmy and glorious. Little did I know it would end in horror ... To begin with, I almost missed the train. But finally I was there on my way to visit Aunt Sarah. We were chugging along when I began to feel a little dizzy. The man across the aisle, Mr. Browning, gave me some cold water and asked if I was all right, seeing I was so pregnant. He's kind of strange, but nice. He's really pissed with the young woman sitting next to him, though. They've argued since boarding. A man several seats behind them seems to be watching them intently. He is, I believe, named Mr. Cranville. The Weston woman speaks with an English accent ..."

"The next entries are of the train wreck," Angie said. "Filled in at a later date."

"The train fell at about midnight. I don't recall exactly what happened. It all happened so fast. The car tipped. I felt it leave the tracks. I screamed, I think. My last thought was for my baby. When I came to, Mr. Cranville was leaning over an unconscious Miss Weston. There was something in his hand—a railroad spike? I passed out again, weak with pain. I seemed to be lying in the aisle. The next time I opened my eyes, Mr. Browning was holding Miss Weston in his arms, and I fainted as I saw the spike. And the blood. She was bleeding a river. Her blouse was soaked. I will never forget her stark gaze. When I awoke again he was carrying me from the train, from the coach that was now on fire. I have never felt such strength as he carried me to safety. I was no more than a feather in his grasp. His eyes were so strange ... or perhaps I was simply overcome by pain and weakness. I had not been able to think clearly through the whole ordeal. He laid me on the ground on his coat, then searched for a doctor. More than likely, he saved my life. I did not know I was also bleeding. I have decided to name my baby Nicholas in his honor. I wish he knew ..."

The entries trailed off after that. In the last entry the teacher had written that she was becoming too busy with the baby to keep up.

Angie closed the journal from the back cover side.

That's odd, she thought, staring at the cover. A bit of sales sticker with a partial bar code was still stuck to the back as though it had been difficult to peel off, a trait of products from cheaper stores. The letters *Wa ... rt* were still somewhat visible, and a date had not been completely scratched out.

This journal was purchased from Wal-Mart, no more than a week or so ago.

What the hell was going on?

Angie's heart was suddenly a lava flow of misgivings. She reopened the journal and lightly traced the handwritten, inked script with her fingertips. A chill traveled from the paper through her hand and up through her arm.

The vampyre wearing the robes of atonement had lied to them. Flat out lied. A vampira had written these journal passages.

With a quill.

By nightfall the next day, the Shadows were packing up their office. James was packing the last box, the fax machine, and Angie was sweeping the back room. The narrow shop was empty, the counter bare.

They were headed for Seattle.

Angie wanted to search the box of papers and books she had stuffed in the coat closet of her apartment, the box her grandmother had given her. Andre had continued to pay her rent for her, for the time when she would be able to face returning, and get her belongings.

One of those belongings was a locked diary.

Her mother's diary.

She had never opened it because she couldn't find the key.

But she wanted it opened now, even if she had to rip it apart.

She had wanted to tell Henri what she had felt mystically from the journal.

But those strange glances he had kept exchanging with Nicholas ...

As though warning him to be careful of what he said.

What was that all about?

To hell with them all. She would find her past on her own.

Damned vampyres.

She swept harder, sending the bits of dirt flying in all directions, her thoughts of uncertainty about the vampyre she loved clouding her eyes with unshed tears.

Almost tripping James as he walked past her broom to go to the van and get more packing tape, Angie did not see the black wrinkle on the sidewalk that seeped in through the open door. A puddle of pure evil.

The black slippery thing flowed unseen onto the side of the fax machine box, then slithered in between the unsealed flaps.

Angie stopped her broom abruptly, her eyes darting around the room.

"What's wrong, Anj?" James asked, returning with the tape.

"I—I'm not sure," she said.

He pressed the sides of the box lid together, taped them shut, and took the box out to the van. Then he came back to lock up.

"The feeling's gone now," Angie said with relief. "For a moment I thought something wicked was lurking again."

"Andre is wise wanting us to move swiftly on this one," James said. "He didn't care much for the degenerates who were hanging around here spying on us."

Angie went into the supply room to put the broom away, but as she turned, James was in the doorway close.

"How do you feel, Angie, about returning?" he asked, concerned. Fate seemed to be moving her in uncertain directions.

"I'm a little nervous," she admitted.

He lowered his voice. "Look, I know you've probably wondered why we didn't go whooping and hollering and chasing after Henri, and waving our stakes in the air like idiots looking for him ..."

"No ... I—"

"Angie, Henri De LaCroix is one of the most powerful master

vampyres in existence. He would simply elude us, or in open battle, kill some of us. Secondly, we're stealth fighters, not combat soldiers. You need to know Andre is hoping to use you in Seattle, to sense Henri in the mists he left in your heart and see where he hides. We can take him out when he is weakened by daysleep."

At the moment, in this hour, on this night, there was not even a smidgeon of mercy in the crossbow slayer's eyes.

Angie felt her heart tighten. Would they find Henri—through her, and destroy him?! Not even Kathryn could be her ally. There was no proof he was in atonement or that he had saved her life. She still could not remember much of that ill-fated night.

"Of course, there is the possibility that the telepathic link may have been broken by now," James added.

Angie averted her gaze. What Henri had done could not be broken.

"That's it. We're finished," Mack called out. "Let's head for Seattle, folks!"

Andre pulled his SUV in behind the pickup.

The SUV pulled away from the curb, and Angie climbed into the pickup beside James. She had slept late that morning from fighting a cold—she had caught Kathryn's "reaction"—and was going to have to return to the house they'd rented to finish packing.

As she reached in her handbag for a cough drop, Angie stole a glance toward the van's driver.

James Lauren's hands were strong as steel as they gripped the steering wheel with ease, and she knew they held his crossbow just as easily. Could Henri be quick enough to sidestep his deadly bolt?

"What happens now?" she asked.

"If the Bowler Hat is sincerely trying to find his way back and fleeing the world of the damned, if he is in atonement, Kathryn will be his spiritual guide and warrior while she leads him back into the world of mortals. And hopefully, he will help you learn more about your mother. On the other hand, if Kathryn decrees the Bowler Hat deadly, Andre will use the entire Shadow troupe to bring him down and possibly also use other envoys to assist. He is Old World, and could command a legion of phantoms and followers, including mortals."

He pulled up to the house. She packed. And they were soon pulling her suitcases down the hall. As they rolled her luggage past the room James had occupied, she slowed her steps a little and glanced inside as a strange sensation swept over her. A sensation of emptiness.

A cross and chain had been left on the dresser top.

"My cross!" she cried.

"That's weird. Why would it be in my room?" James said. "It wasn't there earlier."

It wasn't anywhere earlier. It was in a rabbit!

Her heart trembled.

She picked up the chain and sensed strongly within the room's stillness that the future was boding evil. And something very evil had touched this chain.

A mystical forewarning. Angie was at long last grasping the significance of her "gift."

Angie slipped the cross inside her handbag, but as they left the now silent house, a chill akin to the one she had felt in the English woods gripped her. She glanced back toward the second story toward her window.

Partially concealed behind the plain green curtains hanging in the window, the ghost was looking down at her.

He backed away into the recesses of the room.

But she heard clearly the words whispered in his vanishing wisps …

"Dreams have the power to poison, if we sleep."

•

Henri sailed past the capitol building under a full moon and headed for the house where Andre had sequestered Angie and his troupe. Maybe he could send a thread to Angie, and the precocious mystic thief could "pilfer" some cow blood for him from Kathryn's stash, the way she had stolen newspapers right out from under a librarian's nose. After a night of hunting or more accurately, scrounging for food along the river, he had rousted very little of anything tasty.

It was still dark, still a couple of hours before dawn. He glanced toward the mystic's window. Angie would still be sleeping, safe for the moment at least with her slayers, her breathing soft and even. He would have liked to have popped in and sat on her bed and taken her into his arms to wake her with a kiss, but he didn't want to rouse a house full of slayers, so he opted to pop a few pebbles at her window.

Odd. He could not hear her breathing.

Or anyone else's.

Shape-shifting into a starling, he flew to her window sill and peered in.

The room was empty. The bed had not been slept in.

Soaring from bedroom window to window, panic rising higher within him with each wing flap, Henri peered into the rooms. Not a shoe by a bed, not a thread of clothes in the closets.

Not a footstep in the hallway.

Bracing for what he might find in the emptiness of a house suddenly hushed, he opened the locked window latch with a single thought and flew inside.

There was no blood, not even a spatter on the walls of any room. No dead slayers on the floors. No one lying about, bled out. He felt a rush of relief.

The pantry porch and the kitchen were also spotless.

From the kitchen side window he could see the garage and the driveway.

All the cars were gone.

The slayers had left. With the mystic.

Perplexed by the suddenness of the departure, Henri wondered if the storefront "headquarters" would be as abandoned. Gliding above the city streets still sparkling with a bit of yellow lamp light and a scattering of car lights, he made his way to the Shadow's headquarters.

The store was as empty as the house. And clean as a whistle.

He shadowed and became himself. Leaning against the narrow front counter, he drummed his silent fingertips on the counter top. Where could they have gone?

The only thing they had left behind was a painting on the wall. Odd. The trees in the forest scene seemed to waver, the leaves quiver ...

The ghost appeared on the path and stared out at him from the painting with his dead gray eyes.

"You seem to be alone, Henri De LaCroix."

"Where did they go?" Henri demanded, his eyes piercing the painting. "You must know."

"You seemed to have lost your way when you lost your will. Just a bird singing on a window sill." The gray ghost glinted at him from beneath his top hat.

"She could be in danger," Henri insisted in a plea. He did not know how to beg or he would have.

"The lamb hawk is looking for a kill and looking for a lamb—to steal her will. As is the one who writes with quill." He twirled his cane. "The one you seek, seeks her past, where past was stolen and the future cast."

He turned and became far away on the path.

A whisper floated from the painting and through the room, from wall to wall.

And though Henri's being.

For your life, Royal of the Realm, the slayers also have a playbill.

16.

"Until Andre finds a house, I guess we're roomies," Angie said, pulling her suitcase on its rollers into Kathryn's apartment.

Curled into a swivel desk chair with her arms wrapped around her knees, Kathryn was riveted to her laptop screen, its glow the only light in the room.

Angie tossed a summer cap onto a hook next to the door. "Like my hat? James bought it for me as a souvenir after lunch. This German place we found next to the freeway was great. A dude with an accordion played songs and the whole place all sang and sloshed beer. I had pink cabbage with apples, and roast beef with this dill pickle thing in the middle of it, called Roumaladen and dark beer. Do you always sit in the dark?"

"Rouladen," Kathryn said absently, her eyes intent on her monitor. "It's called Rouladen."

"Yeah. That," Angie said, and glanced out the window as a flash of lightning lit up the room. "Looks like rain tonight."

Kathryn took a tranquil sip of wine from the golden goblet next to her. "I'm going to be with James for a while. Will you be all right?"

James Lauren, the mystery slayer who wears a ring with a mysterious essence, Angie thought. *The little gift tucked into his baby car seat by the mother who ran away into the night—the ring he eternally wears and cherishes. The ring that causes a chill within me every time I look at it.*

"I'll be fine," Angie said. "I want to write a letter to my grandmother."

"I won't be gone long, but if you have a visitor—scream. Based on your perceptions and mine, our atoner is not to be trusted."

"He's a lying son of a—," Angie said vehemently. "Do you think he would be here, in Seattle?"

Her answer was to simply shrug. "Possibly."

A clap of grating thunder filled the night, then the storm hit, an orchestra of nature complete with a xylophone of lightning and cymbal crashes of wind against the windows.

"You can close the drapes if you like." Kathryn smiled up at her. "I remember you have a problem with thunderstorms. Blinding white lightning, fire balls bouncing across the room, Henri on the window sill, all that."

Sheepishly, Angie closed the drapes.

"You've got mail," sang out from the computer speakers into the darkened apartment. Angie read the transmission over Kathryn's shoulder.

"Natalia Ruminski—Russian. Now resides in seedy old neighborhood in seedy old Victorian mansion, north side of city. It appears they followed you to Seattle. Does not live alone. Watch your back and tell Angie to watch her neck. She's known to have an insatiable hunger."

"Looks like they're here," Kathryn said. "You're attracting quite a crowd of hangers-on."

Angie gazed at the message. "Typical girl next door," she said. "Who sent the information?"

"An informant," Kathryn responded simply.

Angie changed into lounging pajamas, and returned to the room carrying a candle with a small flame that kept threatening to go out.

Kathryn glanced at the candle. "You can turn on the lights."

"S'okay." Angie went to the refrigerator and pulled out a tall plastic cup with a tinfoil seal from a group of identical cups.

"What's this?" she asked, sniffing it, curious.

"Cow."

"Oh." She put it back—quickly.

"And the little cups that look like pudding cups are plasma. I don't think you'd like them. Unless of course, you're not of mortal blood." She twirled in the chair, turning to her. "Are you? How much did Henri give you?"

"Apparently not enough. Or I'd be drinking cow."

Angie started to open the meat drawer. "Nope. Don't think I

want to know." She took a bottle of water from the tray in the door. "I hope this is water," she said as she twisted the cap.

"It's water. Would you mind hanging up your cloak and straightening your things while I'm gone?" Kathryn asked, not exactly overjoyed about the prospect of sharing her personal space with the excitable child. But at least she was clean.

The vampyre moved like lightning from the chair, and it was still swiveling, empty, as Angie turned to answer her. "Yeah, umm. I'll have my stuff put away in two jumps of a jackass," she muttered to the closing door.

Angie plopped into Kathryn's chair and stared at the blank computer monitor, lost in thoughts of the master vampyre who had saved her life and thrilled her with his passion for her. But the strange pain written in Henri's eyes every time he looked at her left her heart in shreds. What was he holding back? What was it he couldn't bring himself to tell her?

Suddenly she regretted not telling him she was going to Seattle. She had been miffed at him for his secrecy, keeping secret the reason for those looks exchanged with Nicholas, and for not sharing his heart's pain with her that she could see so clearly. She thought they had something special, and it had hurt that he shut her out. He had been at that mansion to protect her, of that she was certain. But ...

Angie tried to trust her perceptions. When training her, Andre had told her that feeling the sunrays on his arms doesn't tell a blind man if the sun is setting or rising.

Perceptions are from felt from the dew on the grass, hearing the birds flying in low as they would at the end of day, or rising high, or hearing the cock crow. Instinctively within the core of the mystic, perceptions beyond the natural are also "seen" and "felt," becoming a vital force.

Angie wanted—needed to "see" what she was feeling from Henri.

She sent a text message to Danby, lit a fragrance candle for aromatherapy, and searched her heart. The darkened room was quiet, with only the light from the candle flame for company and the pale, blue glow cast by the laptop screen into the shadows.

Thoughts of Henri consumed her, the mystery of him, the secrets behind his eyes, the blatant but wonderful way he openly desired her. The warmth—

Nicholas had been cool, his muscles cool, as he backed against her ...

"If he's in atonement, I'll eat my hat," she said aloud. She sighed and rose from the chair. Taking the traveling cloak from the back of the couch, she touched the soft velvet to her cheek remembering Henri's dance with her, and she swayed into her bedroom in a waltz.

"What is that?" she blurted in a startled whisper as her gaze swept her pillow.

A rose lay across the cream-colored pillow case, a black rose so named for its color, a rose so deeply red it took on the hues of night.

She draped the cape across the bed and picked it up, rubbing the soft petals between her fingers as she returned to the kitchen to look for a vase.

Was the fragrant flower from Henri?

The candle flame next to the computer wavered. And went out. Angie's hands froze, crushing the flower.

Peeking around an open cabinet door, in the blue pallor cast across the room from the computer monitor, she could see—

A fog shadow. Then a silhouette. "What the hell are you here doing ... doing here?" she spat, tingles of fear gripping her. Henri had said Nicholas was dangerous. And here he was, brazen and half naked, and in her kitchen.

With wings.

He was shirtless, baring a pair of dark gray wings that moved slightly in the shadows as his silken eyes stared as though obsessed at a small bottle on the kitchenette counter, a holy water bottle, sixteenth-century. The thick, cobalt blue glass bottle, ornately decorated with etched silver capping, was attached to a solid silver chain.

A chain usually attached to her belt.

"Should I spill that all over you? Are you a good witch or a bad witch? Would you melt?" she said.

He walked toward her. "Don't be afraid of me, Angie. You walk our world. I have no evil intent toward you."

Was he lying? She could not tell. His aura was gray, his smile superfluous. Desperately, she wished her perceptions were clearer, instead of brown streaks on a blurry mirror.

She whipped the rose behind her. "I don't recall inviting you in."

"You placed the ad," he said with a shrug and a sly smile. "Inviting me to respond."

"How did you know I was in Seattle?"

"You should be more careful of the friends you keep," he smiled.

"Who?"

He moved toward her. She backed into the bedroom.

Stupid move. His Fruit of the Loom low rise briefs were clearly revealing the reason for his visit.

Somewhere inside her a tiny voice cried pitifully, *Scream, idiot!*

Her scream stuck in her throat.

He smoothed a hand across the velvet cape and the bed. Then across her throat. She fought his spell, the wicked webs in his eyes. "You need to put some pants on. I would have thought you were the silk suit type."

He laughed from somewhere in his throat, and his Reason pushed hard against his low risers. "I am. It's on your kitchen floor." The wings widened to enfold her, the muscles in his chest rippled. "I could place whispers in your heart, Anjanette, because you walk so close to us."

His words magnetized her, drove her toward him, toward the strange, wicked wine in his eyes. "I don't—want to walk—close to you."

His voice heavy with command, he deepened his seduction. "Fly with me, Angie. I could lift you with me above the city and wrap you in thrusts of love while the breezes high above the mortal streets flow around us and under us, cooling our bodies, but not our desire, our fire."

Desire, the wine of forgetfulness ... Angie thought, her brain beginning to spin.

"I would not, could not hurt you, Angie," he said. "I'm in atonement, after all, and it would be for only a moment. Just a touch. A touch of romance. You would feel sweetness like wine and candlelight with each hot thrust from me. A night to remember in a black silken sky. My wings would cradle you as I held you under me. I'm strong. It would be exquisite with me."

He waited. For her to yield her body to his beckoning, her will to his bidding.

Yeah, right. Dream on, Ruskie.

"A night to remember," he whispered.

And then, Angie thought, *he would finish his designs against me.*

Under the dark fires of his touches, she would float enfolded in pleasure as he caressed her throat before he took her breath away—forever. Then waves of weakness and a cry that would seem to come from a chasm, a cry that would be her own, a sob carried out to the sea on a wave from the sky and a windless, wordless whisper of pain—reality gone awry.

A strange feeling would begin to creep along her veins, and she would need blood. It would spread slowly through her body and invade the very chambers of her empty heart.

And he would fill the chambers.

She would be lifted away from the pallid sky in his arms as he carried her with him, to lay her on his pillows and float with her in dark ecstasy while he spoke softly to her ... before he killed her.

Or whatever it was he was planning for her.

Pursing her lips in anger to fight his hypnotic presence, Angie jerked the limp rose, crushed and bedraggled now, out from behind her back. *Damn you, Nicholas,* she thought to herself. *You put this rose on my pillow because you expected a one-night stand in the sky. Have sex with me on some damned cloud, I suppose.*

"You giving me roses, Angie?" Nicholas asked with an amused smile.

"You didn't give me this?" she said slowly, weakly.

His eyes penetrated hers. "If I wanted to give you flowers, Angie, I'd have them sent—and I wouldn't send just one."

He took the crushed black rose from her hand, gazed at it oddly, and his eyes darkened. Into strange, brown-black fire. "Where did you get this?"

"It was—on my pillow."

His face became rueful.

Then a smile crossed his face that she could only describe as warlock wicked. "You should show this to Henri," he smirked.

He skirted to the kitchen, grabbed up his clothes and was gone. Dissipating in a new shadow of fog.

Dumbfounded by the transformation of man and wing into mist, Angie could only stare in wonderment at the empty space where he had been seconds before. What had frightened him away?

The door to the apartment burst open.

The Shadows swept in, stakes drawn, their eyes searching for the intruder.

She dropped the rose behind her, kicked it under the bed.

"Who was it?" Andre asked urgently.

"Nicholas. But I don't think he'll be back," she answered.

It was 2:20 in the morning. The sun would not be up for several more hours. When the Shadows left, she climbed wearily under the bed covers, mentally exhausted from trying to keep her will intact with a master of the night.

A question surfaced from deep within her, floating into her fading thoughts. Something she had forgotten, but that her dreams brought forth.

What had Nicholas meant when he said Henri was a renegade Royal?

She made a mental note as she drifted into sleep that the next time Henri made one of his dramatic entrances, she was going to ask him what the hell he was exactly.

If he made a dramatic entrance. He didn't know where she was.

She cursed her pride and fell asleep.

Angie woke only once, briefly. An eerie feeling roused her, but she was too deeply entrenched between wakefulness and sleep to probe the sensation. Then it was gone.

She slept softly.

The slumber was short lived. She became filled with restless dreams, brought forth by a presence, a presence she could feel violently even through her sleep, standing over her bed, leaning over her as she slept, studying her.

When morning hit, bright and blinding, she crawled out of bed and went into the kitchen to get an aspirin for a merciless headache.

Andre was pouring himself a cup of coffee. He gazed at her intensely. "We have been with you most of the night. He shadowed and fled at our presence, so we do not know what or who he was. Do you? Was it Nicholas again?"

"This apartment is becoming a freakin' bus stop," she muttered irritably as she poured herself of cup of coffee. "It was Nicholas. It had to be."

Stakes, daggers and a crossbow, weapons of supernatural war, rested on the kitchen table. And the slayers' eyes betrayed their hearts' concern for her.

"What do you think Nicholas wanted?" James asked, his tongue rolling over the vampyre's name as though it left a bad taste in his mouth.

"I couldn't read him," Angie shrugged. "His aura is indistinguishable. Nicholas is murky."

"He's brazen," James said. "He comes waltzing in here like he owns the joint? He's obviously unpredictable. And that makes him dangerous."

That makes him deadly, Angie thought.

"He said he's in atonement," Angie informed them.

"Do you believe that?"

She shrugged and rose from the table. "I'd like to go see Stephen this evening," she said, then added the careful lie she'd been planning. "I'm still trying to put together the pieces of what happened to me. I want to know if he actually found my cross on the porch."

In truth, she wanted to find out more about Henri's past from his descendent cousin. That Royal thing, for instance. And hopefully Stephen would have some idea of how to find him since Danby hadn't called back.

"I would suggest you take one of us with you," Andre said.

It was not a suggestion.

17.

Henri had deciphered the ghost's riddle, but Amtrak's departure schedule and the sun had delayed him in reaching Seattle. Reminding himself not to get too close to the apartments where Andre had sequestered the mystic with his crew, or the Vampyre of Light would catch his scent, Henri sat on his haunches on a rooftop a few blocks away to watch over her.

The evening star rose bright and beautiful. Lights came on in the apartment windows. Henri caught sight of her putting on her jacket as she told her cronies she would take Brandi with her to St. Michael's rectory, but that she wanted to make a confession in private to Stephen.

What is she up to? Henri thought. *She's Methodist.*

Henri left the rooftop to follow the mystic slayer and her corn-town companion.

The street directly in front of the rectory was crowded with cars belonging to condos across the street from the church. Angie had to park a couple of blocks away.

Henri was suddenly filled with trepidation at the gently swaying branches of the elms along the walk. As the two young warriors of the dark made a fast clip toward the rectory, the air became brushed with a chinking, metallic sound. The sound of a choker chinking on a dog's neck.

The soles of their tennis shoes met cement and stone with anxious, uncertain steps.

The sound again, closer, behind them on the sidewalk.

"Hurry!" Angie said, her voice in her throat. She picked up her pace.

Henri could see the drops of perspiration on her forehead.

The mystic was afraid of dogs.

Andre's little Nebraskan Shadow began glancing around watchfully.

Shreddy little pillows of clouds that seemed to move across the sky too quickly covered the stars. Then, it was as though things were in the outlines of the carefully pruned trees in front of the church; creatures with scraggly arms, open mouths, and empty eyes. Even the strings of clouds took on the appearance of wispy, floating phantasms with jointed legs like crabs and open, gaping jaws.

A master of night games was at play.

Nicholas, Henri thought darkly.

Nicholas was a master of the games the undead play at night with mortal hearts—before they kill them.

Henri could tell by her eyes and her hard breathing the younger slayer knew they were in trouble. He flew to the church roof, in case the "Gold Rush" vampyre decided to play too rough. He could have the Nebraskan. But if his fangs went for the mystic, Henri knew he would attack.

His lips parted and he made the semblance of a sigh. Angie had pricked his heart deeply. And he couldn't take it back. He was tormented, tortured, terribly in love. And would defend her to the death. Even against the vanguard who had been his friend.

The chinking again. Joined by a harmony of chinking. And the unmistakable sound of untrimmed claws clipping against the cement sidewalk.

Angie and Brandi slowed their steps and turned.

The phantoms were in the visages of men, but with mongrel faces and paws where feet should have been. Claws, long and sharp, curled against the cement, and their tails swished with a snapping motion.

Brandi stepped quickly to block their attempts to reach the mystic, but one of them drew a hidden length of chain from behind him and slung the heavy metal end toward her. As the links swung through the air, she spun and leaped over them, but landed with her back against the support wall of the church steps.

A pair of hands reached over the top of the wall, grabbed her shoulders and yanked them back hard, butting her head against the stone.

She dropped, out cold.

Henri descended from his perch like lightning. An unknown force had made an appearance.

"Brandi!" Angie cried, spotting the unconscious form on the church steps behind her.

But she could not reach her. The phantoms circled around, blocking her, moving with deliberation, growling. They had no interest in the unconscious Shadow. Their eyes were on the mystic.

Angie took off her jacket and wrapped it around her arm. The phantoms attacked, shredding the jacket from her arms and leaving her hand torn and bleeding. But her power responded. Unafraid, she ripped them as they flew at her all at once.

The marks on her hand dissolved.

Henri watched as he landed, fascinated, pleased with her power, knowing she could handle them while he searched behind the wall for the Lammergeier and whoever owned those hands.

Not a blade of grass was broken.

Nicholas' voice suddenly echoed through the bevy of ravenous barks. He was in the bell tower parapet. "Angie! Angie, listen to me!"

The command was sharp. "They're not real. They're phantoms. I can't fight them, honey. You have to. Think. Why would they use this apparition? It had to be something in your past. Tell them to stand off. Tell them, Angie, or they will tear you to pieces!"

She heard the last words well. "They're not going to tear anyone to pieces," she said. Then she shouted, "Back off!" and with tenacity, whipped her arms through the air as though to clear away a web of spiders.

They retreated a few feet down the stairs.

Nicholas spread his wings, leaped from the parapet ledge and lighted next to her on the steps. "I can't command them, Angie. They're not mine. You have to," he said urgently. "What would cause them to take on this form? Hurry, search your past. They will attack again."

The wings folded into obscurity behind a royal blue cape.

"I don't have to. I already know," Angie said. "I knew when I heard them on the sidewalk. I was eight years old. My brother was five. I was walking him home. We were suddenly faced with a rabid dog. It attacked my little brother."

The sudden surge of guilt in her voice gave them license to attack again. Nicholas flew at them, but they rose into a horror that threw him as easily against the church wall as a plastic bottle tossed from a car.

Snarling, they turned back to their victim and gnashed at her with increasing fury. Her arms and legs and body became lost beneath bristling fur, claws and fangs and ripping teeth. Then an arm shot through the mass, upward. Angie was on her feet, and they were retreating.

Henri debated whether to leap into the skirmish and risk revealing himself, an open target that could jeopardize her if the Lammergeier saw him. Nicholas' only intent at the moment seemed to be to torment her. The abduction would not be in play until Jane herself set the stage.

He flew to a stone sill below a stained glass window that overlooked the steps where cloistered he had a clear view of the grounds. His eyes searched the parameter, constant like a wolf's, on the alert for the Realm's hawk.

A phantom flipped, flew, sat down beside him.

"Get the hell away from me," he commanded.

It became a black smear on the colored glass, then slimed its way to the steeple.

God, he hated phantoms! They were nasty little black things whose presence reminded vampyres they would one day die, and not gently. And they tore and lashed at the hearts and minds of the mortals they conquered without mercy.

These were especially tenacious. They belonged to Nicholas.

What is he up to? Henri wondered. *Letting his own phantoms throw him around and lying to her like that?*

Conquering her terror and her guilt, Angie began battling the phantoms like a hellion.

The horrid things began to fade back into black strips.

Their illusion lost, the phantoms rose like black razor blades and towered over her, their eyes burning like craters of lava, but they did not advance.

"If you have holy water, use it. Now!" Nicholas said urgently, again by her side.

With hands and fingers still aching from gripping and shredding, she grappled with the bottle from her pouch. "I—can't get it uncapped."

The phantoms floated forward again, toward her. He yanked a bottle out from under his cape.

The drops sprayed into the air in a fountain across the inky sheets.

A black rainbow sparkled in the halo of drops.

The screams that followed were like the wail of a lost wind, the loss of heaven. The church door blew open. Nicholas backed quickly away into the dark recesses of the church porch, shielding himself with his cloak as sanctuary light spilled across the steps. The sidewalk was splashed briefly with light. Then nothing. The door closed. The phantoms were gone. The clouds moved on. The night returned to calm.

Angie's eyes shone with amazement.

She thinks he destroyed them, Henri thought, frowning. *He threw open the church door, Angie. God doesn't need theatrics. Only the devil, the devil called Nicholas.*

Quite a chance for Nicholas to take, opening that door considering how much holy light suddenly flooded the place and could have caught him in its rays. And killed him.

But Nicholas was afraid of nothing.

The mystic began sinking weakly against the steps, unused to mental battle of such magnitude.

She was going into shock, Henri realized unhappily. He had misjudged her mental strength, overrated her ability.

The Realm and the assassin be hanged, he flew to her.

The porch light came on at the nearby rectory and Stephen appeared in the doorway.

Nicholas leaped from the steps and ran away into the adjoining church yard and through the tombstones.

Henri's cape swept across the mystic and over her as he pulled her lovingly into his arms. "I am sorry, chéri. I was detained by my own foolishness. It will not happen again."

"Henri," she whispered, rising up and planting a long, full kiss on his lips that cold cocked him. Then she sank back. "How did I do?"

"Like powerful, warm wine," he smiled. "I think I'm drunk on you." He paused. "Oh. You also did all right with the phantoms."

"Stop! I say, stop. You!" Stephen shouted and ran toward them.

Squinting into the darkness, he was trying to identify the dark form bending over a woman.

"I need to get you to the protection of the slayers, Angie. A horror who wants to hurt us is too near," Henri said. "So I will not ask you to relinquish your protection. But it will burn when I carry you to your friends because I must use dark power to run. Do not be alarmed for me when you feel my pain. Just hang on."

Angie threw her arms around his neck.

Henri scooped her from the steps. And cried out as wrenching pain traveled from the cross at her throat into his arms in a burst that made him want to drop her and flee.

But he fled with her. Something was running through the leaves by the side of the church. Toward them.

Glancing back, the only form Henri could see was Stephen, turning toward the sound of moaning coming from the church steps. Brandi was coming to. The priest peered briefly down the street after them, then tended the injured slayer. Henri was too far away to follow.

Lifting Angie into the air with him, Henri swept past an owl, and into the night.

"I don't think we're on the ground anymore, Toto," Angie murmured in astonishment as she watched the church steeple sweep by. She leaned back a little and looked behind his shoulders. "You—don't have wings."

"Don't need them."

He sailed on with her toward the Shadows' apartments.

"Cold?" he asked tenderly.

"No," she said, smiling, drawing her face close to his and clasping her arms tighter around his neck. "You're warm."

"Scared?"

"Not when I'm with you."

He didn't tell her he himself was just a tad this side of terrified. They could be shot out of the sky.

As if in response to his thoughts, the air sizzled next to him.

A crossbow bolt.

He flew higher, faster, but careful lest Angie lose her breath from the speed of the chase. She burrowed her head into his chest to breathe, but began drifting in and out of consciousness.

The bolt had been angled, so he knew the attacker wanted Angie alive. The crossbow was to wound him, to bring them down into the dark web beginning to form far beneath them. A web of wings.

He flew into a cloud to gain momentary obscurity. Hovering, drifting, he held the mystic helplessly, not knowing what to do. He pulled her close, loving her, agonizing in a thousand sorrows for what might happen to her. She was in a world not of her making. A single tear trailed his cheek. "I am so sorry, Angie," he whispered.

Through the misty cloud, he could see the moon shining high in the sky, looking on.

Cold. Heartless.

He looked past it to the heavens. And a silent cry rose from the depths of his being, from the depths of his love for the mystic.

Help us!

He felt Angie's heartbeat against his chest, beating so...

He felt her pouch against his thigh.

"Angie, do you have any holy water?" he asked quickly.

"Didn't have to use it," she said. "Are they still shooting at us?"

"Only one. One shooter. We need the water, Angie. Who blessed it?"

"Stephen."

"He has spent his life making amends for me. They will scatter like crows when it hits them."

She pulled out the vial. Henri flew out of the cloud. "Do you see what is below us?"

She looked down. A patch of city lights was blocked out by an amoeba of black.

"Shower the water over them like a rainfall," Henri directed.

The water fell like rain drops down, down in a cascade onto the undead amoeba.

The amoeba split into smoking wings and masses of screaming bones.

The night held no more bolts. Henri flew hard and fast.

By the time he reached the slayers' apartments, Henri was in gut-wrenching agony, the excruciating pain in his arms becoming unbearable. Balancing Angie in his grasp, he slammed his free hand against the house buzzer.

A light came on in the apartment building foyer. He stepped back—and caught a familiar scent in the air.

Nicholas slithered up the side of the apartment building like a spider to sit on the roof and take in the scene unfolding in the night. He looked very pleased with himself.

But whoever had grabbed Brandi from behind and pursued them with a crossbow had no scent.

18.

Taniesha gasped as she saw Angie in Henri's arms, weak and tattered.

"What did you do to her?" she cried out in anger, drawing a stake from its sheath as she shouted toward the stairs, "Andre! James!"

"Call the doctor, Andre!" James yelled as he rushed down the stairs. His crossbow rose into the air to confront the Royal.

"She doesn't need a physician," Henri said, his eyes fixed on the weapons beginning to mass against him as he lowered Angie to her feet. Stroking her hair away from her face, he smiled into her eyes and said, "Throw some holy water on her. She'll be fine."

"Where is Brandi?" they demanded.

"With Stephen. Her head had a slight run-in with a wall."

"Henri didn't do anything to her," Angie said quickly as the Ethiopian slayer glared at him, tightening her grip on the stake.

Henri's eyes splintered toward the crossbow slayer. The bow string was taut, the bolt on deck ready to fly.

"She was playing dodge ball with a phantom," Angie said swiftly.

So. She did not know there had been another player on the court, Henri realized.

"Get her inside," he said firmly to Andre.

Andre understood.

Angie swooned a little, and Andre yanked her from Henri's side and took her into the apartments.

Threading a melty thought her way of being in bed with her naked, and to put a candle in the window if she wanted more than a thought of his deep thrusts in her tonight, he flashed away from the weapons too eager to end him and became a blur on the walk.

But as he left, Henri could hear Nicholas conveniently appearing at the steps he had vacated, soft talking the Ethiopian night fighter.

"I tried to help her, Tani."

Tani.

Henri became angry. The vanguard was wheedling their affection, getting on a friendly nickname basis with them right off the bat to throw them off his true scent. The coyote coming to the dog pen to pretend to be one of them, even chasing the ball until he could strike and grab them by the throat with his jaws.

The Realm vanguard was about to walk right into their midst, parading as an atoning vampyre.

Henri slipped behind a hedge to listen to his sidewalk sales pitch.

"Your mystic was attacked by phantoms in apparitions from her past," the vampyre said, his tone almost sorrowful. "I tried to take the memory of their attack from her, but she is mentally strong and resisted my efforts. I fought them, but I could not offer her much help. They are not mine to command. She had to fight alone. I'm sorry."

"Whose are they?"

He looked away as though looking into the phantoms of his own past. "They were Janey's—and Henri's."

Henri thought of some choice names for him as he listened to this master of lies.

The Shadows embraced Jane's evil vanguard into their midst, almost with affection.

Were they insane?

Nicholas, the master spinner of tall tales, led them easily. How many vampyres had he promised he would share their blood with when he finally took them? Henri wondered.

Shape-shifting into a raven, Henri flew to the high branches of a sycamore next to the apartments, to alight and contemplate his miserable existence.

His attempts at atonement had profited him nothing.

Now a master slayer would be after his head because of the vanguard's lies.

And then there was James Lauren ...

And that damned crossbow.

And a Realm assassin.

And that damned crossbow.

He heard a sound below him, voices in low tones inside the apartment building behind the foyer's glass doors.

Nicholas stood on the stair landing—with Angie on a step slightly above him. He had license to enter, but no one else could invade the building without an invitation.

His cape was draped around him, and he smiled at her like Captain America.

Damn you, Nicholas, Henri thought hotly.

Explaining his relationship with the Lady Jane Weston, he was interjecting just enough truth into his stories to make them flavorful, believable.

Henri flew to a higher branch and shadowed so the mystic could not sense him.

Not that she would have noticed him anyway in her apparent pre-occupation at the moment with the Russian Adonis and hero as of late.

Jealousy began to eat a hole in him.

"I was her prize," Nicholas explained. "The one she had stolen from God Himself. I fled from her in 1620. When I met Natalia, she—she and the others helped me disappear into the mortal populace, and they kept me hidden from her. She has used phantoms to search for me at night, and she employs mortals in daylight. She even used a mortal niece descendant to try to track me, but the girl decided she wanted me for herself. She was killed in a train wreck. But of course you know that."

Angie's eyes seemed to flood with sorrow for him. "The passenger train."

"And now she has found me."

"What can we do to make this right, Nicholas?" Angie asked, knife points of guilt and regret seeming to fill her voice.

His eyes narrowed toward some distant, indefinable place. "Who better to find a vampyre than a pack of slayers? She is still clever as a fox."

"Why are you running from her, Nicholas? Isn't that a little unusual—a vampyre fleeing from a vampyre?"

"Not when it's The Lady Jane," he said.

"You need a safe haven, Nicholas. Stephen's church."

"You want me to desecrate a holy place, Angie?" He reacted with a mocking laugh.

"The only thing you'll find inside is the glow of a sanctuary lamp and a few candles."

"And holy water that will burn like acid."

"I doubt holy water would do anything to you now, Nicholas. From the looks of it, you've got drops all over you."

He looked at his cloak. It was covered with tiny circles of water-stains. "The spray must have been blown by the wind. I guess I didn't notice the stray mist in the heat of battle."

No, I guess you didn't, Henri thought sarcastically from his branch as he watched the master of deception, deceiving the mystic. His mystic. He began to burn with anger. Violently.

"How is it Henri brought me to Andre after the battle with the phantoms?" Angie asked, her tone changing.

"I had no choice but to flee the presence of the priest, but Stephen is Henri's descendant, and he holds no power over him. I do not know why Henri brought you back. He seems to have—designs—toward you, known only to himself. Designs that require keeping you alive, perhaps?"

Nicholas's eyes rested on her breasts. "I could immerse my being easily with yours, Angie, because you are so like my own kind. I can give you pleasure you could never have, would never feel with a mortal."

Then his eyes spotted the cross of hammered silver peering out from between the buttons on her lace collar. His cross. "Why do you wear—that?" he asked, startled, his eyes narrowing

She tilted her head a little to the side to gaze at him sideways from under her lashes. "Because you are such a liar, Nicholas."

Henri chortled so hard with laughter, he almost fell off the branch.

Nicholas's arrogant, dry laugh filled the night. "I guess this means no sky sex tonight?"

"Or anything else," she said. "When you're ready to tell me the truth about my aunt, if she is my aunt, let me know."

She went up the stairs and into her apartment.

Henri left the tree and summoned the vanguard.

Reluctantly, Nicholas alighted before him in the shadows at the back of the building.

No vampyre could deny a Royal's call. They could resist many demands of those who held reign over them after they were imprisoned between life and death, but in this they had no choice. Their will was sacrificed to the Royals the moment they chose not to die.

"What do you want, Henri?" he asked irritably.

"You having a little trouble getting a mystic to believe your lies, Nicholai?" Henri mocked. "You tried to seduce her by leading her to believe DuPre's envoy is part of a vampira's scheme to reclaim a lover."

"She is quite a beauty, isn't she? She could make any atoner junk his vows."

"Your dog and pony show tonight was quite impressive."

Nicholas laughed. Raspy, wicked.

Henri stepped toward him. "What are you planning for her, you worthless piece of fifteenth-century trash?"

"If she has the English crest in her past, one hell of a hoedown. But of course you already know that. Walk away, Henri. This doesn't concern you."

"The mystic does concern me. She's mine."

"Lucky you were there tonight to catch your little falling star."

"Touch her with malice again and you die," Henri threatened.

"You must have exquisite plans for her," Nicholas smiled, unfazed. "Seal her away, keep her barely alive so day after day you can come to her—keep her hidden from the Realm's dogs, drink her mystic power, bed with her and take the Realm throne perhaps?"

"What makes you think the mystic is the descendent niece? Besides a cross that could have come from anywhere."

"We found the crazy grandmother and had a little tea and blood with her to confirm our suspicions. Loving mother that she was, Allison tried to protect her with that very special cross that could have come from anywhere." He paused. "I hear the Realm has offered quite a finder's fee for this Black Rose. I have not yet decided whether to present her to Jane and let her take the vows—or hand her over to the Realm myself, take the money and run. What do you have to offer?"

"Your life," Henri answered flatly.

"Ah," Nicholas said, arching an eyebrow. "That is, if you can survive the nights ahead. And the price on your head. The Realm gave you a run for your money tonight. You may yet need me, Henri.

As in the days of old, yes? When you were in trouble over some woman? How often did we have to dump your carcass in a hearse and whip the horses til' they dropped to get you out of town before some scorned lovely showed up at sunup to stake your philandering heart?"

"This is different, Nicholas. I love her."

The vampyre's eyes widened in surprise. "Damn! I believe you do."

19.

As soon as the Shadows closed her door thinking she was asleep, Angie threw back the covers and slipped out of the apartment building to hail a cab. She needed to see her mother's words on her own, alone. But as the cabbie dropped her off, her high heels touched the steps leading up to her apartment hesitantly. She knew her laptop would still be on her desk, the photo of Bobby still on her Facebook profile, his false flattery still filling her wall.

Maybe she should just throw the laptop out in the garbage, she thought. It was part of her former life, not the life she lived now.

This apartment was a collection of everyday dishes, mall shop clothes, a single bedroom and a few knick knacks. Now she lived in apartments on the go with a collection of whittled stakes and belt packs, and her knick knacks were bottles of holy water.

She pulled the apartment key from her shoulder bag, took a deep breath and opened the front door.

She stepped into the living room agape. The whole place had been trashed.

Walking from room to room as though in a surreal world, she absently picked up pieces of broken ceramic, ripped clothes, cracked dishes. Pictures had been pulled from the walls, the glass cracked, the photos scarred. The furniture was shredded, the couch pillows ripped open. Cabinets were emptied, the drawers and doors hanging open. The floor was littered with broken plates and dishes like an earthquake had struck. Papers and bills were slashed as though by a sharp knife.

It was as though someone had been looking for something, in a hurry to find it and angry at not finding it.

Angie crunched through the ruins of her former life, and

yanked open the hall closet door. Laying her car keys on a shoe box, she pushed aside her winter coats to expose the back corner where she had stashed her box.

"Looking for this, my dear?" a man's sickly sweet, familiar voice asked in curdling tones behind her.

She whirled, to find Danby standing in the hallway.

Holding her mother's diary.

Angie felt fear rise into her throat. And Henri's words, "Trust no one."

"I would like to have that back," she said, holding out her hand and trying to take it.

Quickly yanking it out of her reach, he held it high in the air, and smiled.

But just as quickly he turned, startled, as the rooms became pitch black. The clouds had choked the moon.

Angie leaped past him, grabbing the diary as she jumped, and ran from the apartment.

"My car keys!" she cried suddenly, looking back as she reached the pickup and realized she had left them in the closet.

He was barreling down the apartment steps, coming after her with a demonic pace in his shoddy shoes.

Kicking off her high heels, she ran down the sidewalk, harder and harder until she could whip around a corner and slip into a night drenched alley and catch her breath.

The vapid space was littered with the debris of civilization— bleary-eyed men and glittery-eyed women standing among the blowing trash and broken bottles of whiskey and wine, flashing narcotic smiles.

Two stark youths bracketed a destitute doorway, covering up their fear of the night and their cement prison with drugs and knives. They were motionless, their faces defensive, distrusting, as they watched the long dark cape pass them by.

They laughed. The running, barefoot woman in a trench coat was eccentric, someone they might find rummaging a trash bin or running out on a drunken wife beater.

"Hey, bag lady!"

She halted, but as she turned, their mouths dropped open in wonderment at her youth, her beauty—her eyes.

She turned away from them.

Your souls can never touch mine, she thought. *You grovel with untrained fists for a bit of dirt from your victim's pocket, then you cower like rats, in the corners of the night!*

Take the night, you fools! It is yours! Embrace her!

Death embraces the night, but not gently ...

In the next instant, she was lost to them, nothing more than a moment that had passed in time as she slipped into an alcove through a broken gate and behind an unguarded door.

Angie collapsed against the door.

These thoughts, these feelings, this affinity with the night, were not hers. They were Henri's!

She hurried on to escape the horrid little man she could hear asking the youths if they had seen her.

They lied, said they hadn't seen her, then they hunted her themselves. "Hey, gorgeous, come on. Let's have a summer party," they called out, searching the alley's alcoves. "No wonder you were running from the old geazer. He's a shriveled up, butt ugly."

She rose before them and threw them both against the side of an oil-smeared wall.

They ran from her in terror.

Crossing yet another alleyway, Angie turned onto a shadowy street. The clouds spit mist now, and the black pavement glistened. A column of gray smoke curled from above a club where a sign blinked in neon orange. Music, hard and metallic, pelted the mist.

"Liora!" she heard Danby call through the music, through the crowd. "There's nowhere to go!"

She looked back, saw him weaving through the partiers making their way to the club.

On the skyline, an aging hotel roof poked at the low-hanging clouds. Below the roof, soot-covered windows reflected only isolated, soiled shades and murky obscurity.

She ran toward it to hopefully hide until he gave up the chase.

Another door. On the alley side. Her hand, through the quickness and skill of Henri's knowledge, coaxed the lock into surrender and her soft soles touched the wooden stairs with feather-light steps as his power moved though her.

Then onto the roof, she took a deep breath and jumped across a chasm to the hotel.

More stairs. This time descending. To just below the top floor.

With a deftness that surprised her, she moved like a spider through the corridors and along a floor covered with decaying carpet.

Then, at the first single room engulfed in darkness, she stopped.

Her hand twisted the doorknob urgently, and the door obeyed her hand's command.

With a single, effortless movement, she was inside. The door was secured and she was at the window, a narrow soot-blackened, rain-stained window—

Indistinct, almost invisible, she edged along the drapes, a part of the hour. Her coat, silhouetted against the thin drapery, doused the tiny, timid bits of streetlight behind her.

She opened the drapes a slit, searched for Danby, did not see him. She stepped back and melted into the shadows of the dingy, dirty room, dropping to the floor.

Henri! She cried in anguish, dirt-smeared tears trailing her cheeks.

As she looked around at the tattered room, her stomach quivered. She peered outside again through a slit in the drapes to look alongside the streets.

"Where are you, Henri? Help me!" she whispered desperately.

Footsteps. In the hall.

Don't let it be Danby. Don't let it be Danby.

She wilted into the wall, the darkness— hiding, hardly daring to breathe, terrified. Danby's cataract eyes had been so filmy, so wide and wild. So determined.

So determined.

Her heart thundered in her ears.

The steps moved on, diminished somewhere down the corridor.

She rose carefully from the floor, slid her body along the plaster wall, then cautiously opened the door and peered out. Seeing and hearing no one, she eased out into the hallway. Clinging to the dirty wallpaper and gummy stairs, she finally escaped the foul smelling building.

She began running across an expanse of parking lot, to go back to the club and call for help, call Andre for help.

Footsteps again.

Hope against hope, she longed for it to be Henri.

But a vampyre would have no footsteps.

Her heart lost its beat as Danby stepped in front of her.

"You left these," he said, jiggling her keys in the air.

As a stray bit of streetlight hit his face, Angie could see the evil lines in his jaw, the heaviness in the rolls of eyelids that hid all but the glitter in his eyes at finding her.

Danby grinned at her, a vile spreading of his mouth across his face. "You need to come with me, my dear."

"I don't understand," she said, stepping back as he took a step closer.

Then she saw the steel glinting in his hand.

She had seen a menacing glint like that before.

She stepped backward again, bracing herself to fight a knife for the second time in her life.

"The Realm has offered quite a reward for you, my dear," the little, balding piece of feces chirped.

"You—" She had been duped. And this was not fighting darkness and the undead. This was an unpredictable soulless human.

"Come quietly?" he smiled, then shook his head and sighed as she drew her dagger from her pouch. "I suppose not. I will have to injure you. Unfortunate."

He leaped toward her, but her mystical power surged and carried the force of foresight. She leaped to the side, knocking his knife from his grasp as he stumbled past her and catching his arm in a slice with her own blade.

He looked surprised. He had not expected mystical strength, or that it would be piggy-backing a master vampyre's power.

But he recovered quickly from the realization and came back with a blow to her side that took her breath.

And sent the diary spinning across the asphalt, under a car.

The dagger went spinning under the bumper behind it.

Grabbing her arm, he slammed her belly down onto the hood of a Ford Expedition to pull her arms behind her and tie her hands.

She felt the antique holy water bottle in her pouch break under the impact.

He grasped the chain at her neck roughly, yanked and broke it, then threw the cross and chain into a storm drain. "My business associates would not appreciate it if I let you keep that, my dear."

"Jackass."

Pushing back hard, she knocked him off balance between two parking posts. He caught himself and lurched forward. She broke off the side view mirror of the Expedition and cracked it into his stomach. He fell back and smashed into the windshield of the car next to them, but as he fell he grabbed her arm again and took her with him.

In the ensuing struggle, the two cars quickly became breaking glass and denting metal. She tried to run, but he threw her to the pavement into the glass and asphalt chunks.

Angie rolled away from her attacker, but her head hit the base of a cement pylon. Moaning, she shook her head against the stars and blackness filling her consciousness, braced herself on the stone post, pulled herself up.

Without a sound, a pair of magnificent gray wings descended in front of her, outstretched, and Nicholas stood between her and her assailant.

As the man backed away in paralytic fear, Angie knew the vampyre had bared his fangs.

The wings folded. Nicholas moved toward him.

In one magnificent sweep, Henri also dropped from the sky like a black wind, and took Angie into his embrace.

"Where did you come from?" she gasped.

"Around," he smiled.

"You sensed I was in trouble," she whispered, kissing him. Loving him.

Danby spotted his knife and made a dive for it.

Henri released her and in the next instant the assailant's knife was his grasp.

Nicholas stepped to the sid, as though this was a familiar stage—he would wait while Henri took the kill.

Henri threw the weapon to the ground, then his hand was around Virgil Danby's throat in a deadly grip, lifting him from the pavement. For a moment that seemed like infinity, it appeared to Angie that Henri was going to kill him.

Or have him for dinner.

Henri released his grasp. The man dropped heavily to the ground. Sputtering and coughing, Danby grabbed his throat with his hands and looked up at the vampyre's rage with terrified eyes.

But the hunting knife was near him.

"Henri!" Angie cried to warn him, clinging to the post again to keep her wavering balance.

Nicholas had already whirled, sensing the threat. He knocked the assailant backward. The man stumbled over a broken bumper jutting out from the rear of the Expedition and fell face-down to the asphalt. He moaned, tried to move.

Henri turned him over.

His knife protruded from his gut.

He looked up at Henri with a glazed emptiness that told him he knew his life was over. "Let me join you," he begged weakly.

Bending next to him, Henri gripped him by the collar with one hand and yanked him partially from the ground. "Who sent you?" he demanded.

"From the English village. I would be richly rewarded by the Realm, they said. They gave me the flowers, told me what to do ..."

"Who was it?" Henri demanded, his gaze deepening to black fire.

"No—names," the man choked through a bubble of blood in his mouth.

"What did they look like? Was one from the English woods? Did you see the Lammergeier?"

"Lammergeier? You are in deep doodoo, aren't you?" the man gurgled.

Reaching out, he gripped Henri's arm and squeezed his sleeve into his bloody hand, his eyes wide. Emitting sounds in his throat like a rat caught in a trap, he tried to raise up.

Then nothing. The hand on the sleeve went limp. He fell back.

Henri pulled the knife from his gut, then stood up and tossed it to the side.

For a moment, as he gazed down at the wound still oozing red, Henri became transfixed, like a man parched with thirst who's just seen the river of life in an oasis in the desert.

"Henri," Angie said gently, touching his arm, drawing his attention away and wishing she didn't feel quite so dizzy. She picked up her cap and brushed the dirt and debris from the brim. She had rarely received gifts in her life, and any little token was precious to her.

"He said he was your friend," she said, also picking up the card smudged with dirt and pieces of flower petals she carried perpetually in her pockets. "He gave me these." She showed Henri what she had thought were tokens of love from him.

"I would have sent rose petals," he said tenderly, then looked down at the dead man. "I do not know him."

"He was on the plane to Sacramento," Angie said.

"Waiting for his opportunity," Henri said darkly. "Now he waits for judgment."

Angie stood over the dead man, crushing the bits of dried flowers and card in her fist into grains, then letting them fall through her fingers like sand onto his chest, detesting him.

"Take her and go," Nicholas said quickly. "I'll tell Jane I had to kill her in battle and toss the body in the ocean so the Realm wouldn't find out. I'll take Jane and go hide out at Stony for awhile until they forget about us."

"Why would you help us?" Henri demanded.

"Hell if I know," he said. "For old times, I guess."

Nicholas turned and was gone over the wall, his dark shadowy wings emerging.

"Lammergeier? In the English woods?" Angie asked, leaning on the parking lot wall, still trying to clear away the strange fogginess the fall had caused. "Had to kill me? Toss the body in the ocean?"

A blur, an instant, and Henri was holding her. "Angie, are you all right?"

"I'm fine."

I'm dizzy as hell.

Vaguely, she became aware it was also harder to breathe.

"Easy," Henri said, steadying her.

But as she regained her foothold, Henri did not release her. He held her, clasped against him. "Love with you would be sheer hell for any man," he murmured. "You're stubborn. You're defiant. You don't listen." He entwined a mass of soft, silky, golden hair into his hand and breathed its fragrance. "Your mystical scent is sweet as honey."

She looked up into his gaze. It had become a gaze of fire.

The embrace tightened.

"It's difficult not to want you, Angie."

His face drew close to her cheek, his inky soft hair brushed against her throat …

She could barely breathe.

"Yes, I know. I am exciting," he whispered.

"Don't flatter yourself. I really—can't ... breathe," she gasped. She moaned. The knives of pain in her side as he crushed her against him were excruciating, taking her breath.

He drew away. His hand moved to her ribs and pressed carefully, gently. "You're hurt."

"I think I have—a broken rib and a concussion," she said.

He felt her waist. "No breaks. But deep bruising." He felt her forehead. "And a knot the size of Alaska. I need to get you to a safe place where you can recover."

Lifting her into his arms, he placed her gingerly in the front passenger seat of the nearest car still in one piece. "I can mesmerize you into forgetting what happened here, if you want," he said as he hot-wired the ignition.

"You have already mesmerized me," she said softly as her head fell against his shoulder. "You have mesmerized my heart. I am lost in you, Henri DeLaCroix." Her eyes drifted up into his. "What do I do, Henri? It seems I am a wanted woman."

"We will find a way," he whispered. He began speeding toward the outskirts of the city. "Do you want to stand and fight or get the hell outa' Dodge, Liora Anjanette?"

She was unable to answer. Her world had grayed to black.

20.

A secluded mountain home of brick and timber was masked in the night by pines, foliage and mist.

"Are we—safe?" Angie asked, her eyes resting on Henri as she regained consciousness while he was parking the jacked car in a stand of pine trees.

"For the moment. We are deep in old growth forest," he said.

Bracing Angie against his shoulder, Henri helped her out of the car and led her along a curving, hedge-lined walkway. But he soon realized the stairs would be too much for her.

When he started to pick her up and carry her, she muttered something—he scarcely knew what—and attempted to demonstrate she could walk unassisted.

She swooned and fell against him.

Henri lifted the stubborn, bedraggled creature he loved into his arms. Shivering, she moaned then slung her arms around his neck and closed her eyes. She was groggy from pain, and he doubted she even knew where she was.

He ascended the porch stairs with her and appraised closely, once again, the flawless soft face with its fragile beauty framed in silken clusters of tousled and mussed ringlets the color of the sun, and he remembered blond beauties he had carried up staircases of his past. For his own pleasure.

You do so tempt me, Liora Anjanette, he thought. Will I break the vow I've made so recently to try again to make you my own and take you into immortal suffering with me? He struggled to remind himself that his obsession to be her protector was her only salvation.

"Sure you're taking me to a safe place?" she asked, reading him mystically. "Your aura seems a little on the dark side."

"I wasn't contemplating anything more than a pinprick, Angie," he lied—a little. "For your deceptions and running with slayers—and running around with that nasty little stake in your bag that could pierce my heart. You wound me, Liora Anjanette. To the quick. I gave you so much."

"You would have robbed me of sleep the way the moon robs the world of color. The red rose is left with pale petals in the shadows caused by those silvery rays," she murmured drowsily.

"Still the poet," he said softly. "I thought you liked the moon."

He pushed open the door to the cabin, but hesitated before taking her across his threshold. The only other human he had willingly allowed through his door was the lab assistant from a local blood bank. Christa Remington knew what he was and helped sustain his existence. And she never entered any rooms without his permission. The plain-faced tech had been helping atoning vampyres for almost twenty years, helping them hide, helping them stay alive.

She was, at the moment, the only one he trusted.

He stepped across the threshold with Angie and struggled with the black knowledge that however much he might love her, he was allowing a mystic slayer into his domain close enough to kill him.

Placing her in a chair, he made up the sofa for her, then gently roused her.

He didn't tell her where the pillows and brocade blanket he placed on the couch were from. She would know soon enough that they were his.

While she sat in the chair and gritted her teeth, he cleaned the laceration on her arm, applied iodine, then picked out a needle to stitch the cut. "I picked up a bit of medical training in the Civil War," he said in response to her surprised expression.

"Don't I need anesthetic or something?" she said, staring at the needle that seemed to suddenly loom into her eyes.

"Oh," he said, and gave her a slug of whiskey. "Supposedly, you won't feel a thing now, soldier."

That wasn't quite true, but it did help.

When he was finished, Henri appraised Angie's tattered appearance. Her clothes were torn and smudged.

Bringing a clean shirt from his bedroom, he asked her if she wanted help removing her clothes.

"No," she said firmly as she took the shirt. "I'm fine, but I'd like to wash." She paused. "So. Can I fly? I seem to know how to do everything else you do."

"Don't try to fly," he said. He showed her where the bathroom was, then walked her there just to make sure she didn't accidentally stumble into his bedroom by mistake.

And discover the long box of twelfth-century soil under his bed.

When he returned to the living room to put away the first aid kit, Nicholas was sitting on his couch. "The Shadows are searching for you, Henri," he said. "And not for an atta boy."

"How do you know that?" Henri asked.

"I went back to the parking lot. I—wanted to get something left behind. They were scouring the aftermath like a paranormal CSI team. Taniesha found drops of water spattered in the dents on a car, and tiny bits of blue glass. The mystic's holy water. They decided she had to fight you, and that the dead man slumped between the cars—they called him 'this poor fellow'—must have tried to come to her rescue."

"Danby?"

"That would be the one. But DuPre looked at his face, and told his troupe he didn't look much like a good Samaritan. He looked more like the phantoms had just escorted him into hell. He used his precog on the wall, read the brick dust and knew a vampyre had gone over the wall. And that the mystic had not. He gave the lot a once over. One parking space in the middle of the battleground was clean, no glass or bits of metal. A car had been sitting there, before and during the battle, then gone. Black tire marks led away from the spot, so he knew someone had spun the wheels in their hurry to leave. He bent down and brushed his hands across the perimeter of the vehicle's vacated spot, and knew she had left with a vampyre, and that he drove." He paused. "And that it was you."

"Did he think she was taken by force?"

"His beady eyes shot toward the deeper parts of the city. He started frowning and said he could no longer sense the mystic. He could feel nothing from her."

"That must have been when she passed out."

"He said the city had swallowed her, and he could not sense whether she still lived. Then he ordered his slayers to search the hangs, and that neither you nor I were to be given berth. We are to relinquish the mystic or die. I am, they decided, a soft-spoken terror who at best seems to want to access heaven—by way of hell. And you're a few rungs below that."

Nicholas laughed then, a guttural, deep, dry laugh. "Andre couldn't find his vampyre of light or the crossbow slayer, and started grumbling that in five years the Shadows had not been without unity, fortified in their purpose. But of course he didn't know they had spotted me, and were chasing me around on the far side of the parking lot while he was on his knees sniffing asphalt." He paused. "Damned fun, that sable-haired little French wench that used to be the Marquis' whore. I'd like to draw a few droplets from her rosy lips and join with her myself!"

Nicholas helped himself to a glass of wine, then grinned and laughed again as he downed the red liquid in one draught. "They haven't had an unruly little mystic in their midst who's being sought by the Realm, and a Royal at their back door courting her."

He heard the bath water draining, and left.

Angie came out, her skin sparkling pink, refreshed.

The large white shirt with billowing, gathered sleeves and open collar swallowed her slight form. The cuffs fell over her hands. Henri smiled in amusement. "Aren't you a little short for a storm trooper?"

"Very funny," she said. She pushed the cuffs up, and the drowsiness in her eyes told him she was spent. "Eighteenth century?" she murmured, inspecting the soft cotton sleeves. "Did you kill anyone in this thing?"

"No." He pulled up the shirt and began bandaging her waist, though she trembled at every lingering touch. He eased the bandage to her back and brought it around, standing close to her, his face almost touching hers. Then he tied off the ends, clipped them with scissors, and helped her onto the sofa.

The tiny, stunned cry she emitted as she lay back and her head touched his pillows and her mystical senses became fiery, tore at his soul. "I have a friend. I'll call her and ask her to retrieve the cross and bring it to you. It will—help," he said. Against the protest in her sobs, he pulled the brocade coverlet up and around her shoulders, a coverlet he knew was flooding her with his essence and imprisoning her. And it was not tender. It was to keep her caged. And out of his inner rooms. "You have to understand, Angie, you are in the dwelling of one of the Realm's elite. If you want to be with me, you need to know what I am. This room, this place, is steeped in what I am. These things are mine—and not only are you an intruder, you are a slayer. The room itself is at DEFCON 1."

When she finally slipped into sleep from sheer exhaustion, he went to the refrigerator for a bottle of wine to calm the traces of hunger still flowing inside him.

"Don't touch her, Natalia," he warned as he closed the refrigerator door. He did not have to turn around to know the impudent Russian vampira was standing by the sofa.

"Henri, Henri, what are you up to?" she said teasingly, with a lightly wicked smile as she looked down at the innocent lying in sleep under his favorite blanket. "You've placed her against your pillows and in your—" She stroked the smooth orange and red brocade with her black tipped fingernails. "Blankie."

She smoothed her hand across Angie's arm to touch the soft sleeve of his shirt, and her eyes glittered with pleasure when the mystic moaned uncomfortably. "And you even have her in your shirt. Isn't this the one you wore when you went sailing on that three-masted schooner, *The Sea Ghost* or something?" She turned and looked at him with intense curiosity. "You're keeping her will deliberately weakened."

Angie turned, restlessly.

"Ah, she knows I'm here," Natalia said delightfully. "You've got a sensitive one. A mystic. She unlocks doors with a single touch, and senses my presence even when she's out cold."

The vampira began watching her breathe, and began to sway, hypnotized by the steady rise and fall of her chest. Henri took a step forward, watching Natalia closely.

She placed her first and second fingertips against the artery pulsing rhythmically at the side of Angie's throat, and her eyes became moist. "She's warm, Henri …"

Like a quick breath he was there, grasping her wrist tightly as he yanked her hand away. "I said not to touch her."

She sighed resignedly and feigned a pout. "We could have had a party, Henri, you and I—" She glanced wistfully at Angie's throat. "And her." She moved away at the command in his eyes, but smiled coyly at him. "If you decide you don't want her, De LaCroix, let me know."

As soon as she was gone, Henri called Christa to bring him the cross. Self-control was not one of Natalia's best qualities. Actually, she had no qualities.

When he answered the doorbell anxiously, Christa's gaze darted curiously at the disheveled woman sleeping on his couch. "What's that?"

"She's hurt," he said. "She had a run-in with a human trying to kidnap her, and got the worst end of it."

She dangled the cross in front of him. "And this was in a storm drain next to crunched car head lights because—?"

Henri looked away from the silver quickly.

"Because the chain broke."

"And she needs it because—?"

"Because it would seem—the whole damned Realm is after us."

Christa's look was more than concern. She was terrified for him.

"Would you like me to bring her some breakfast in the morning?" She picked up the rag tag shreds of clothes on the floor. "And do a little shopping for her?"

She pressed the broken chain into Angie's palm. The cross dangled free in the air from between her fingers.

"Please. If you wouldn't mind."

After Christa had gone, Henri sat in the chair across from the couch and studied his guest. His desire for her was so deep it almost drowned him. Her skin would have such warmth, passion, heat. And if she desired him that passionately in return ...

Their love would be a dangerous liaison at best—twin powers that could collide like exploding stars.

As she slept quietly, he lost himself in her beauty until twilight. Then he moved close to her, and pressed his fingertips to the inside of her forearm just above her wrist—above the hand holding the cross chain. Working the muscles patiently, deeply, his fingers coaxed the muscles to relax, so her fingers would release the chain, and let the cross fall.

Her hand opened outward, the chain slid out of her palm, and the cross dropped to the carpet.

21.

Angie awoke with a gasp. And even as she opened her eyes, she was still staring into the nightmare that had just gripped her.

Her breathing was hard and rapid, perspiration covered her forehead, and the moisture on her cheeks was either perspiration—or tears. Her dream had been a horror from which she thought she would not awaken.

She glanced down the hallway.

The door to his bedroom was closed. Sun was streaming into the hallway.

Her hand moved instinctively to the side of her neck.

It was smooth, untouched.

Which was more than she could say for her sleep.

She had dreamed she died.

But not as a mortal human.

She had died as a vampyre.

Surrounded by his soft pillows, pillows that carried the scent of his cologne and vapors from his being, she had lain jailed by his brocade coverlet in a cell without a lock or key. It had become a weight heavier than iron, holding her down, pinning her into a grave from which she could not rise. Quietly terrified, she had felt, seen and heard nothing as the power of the essence in the pillows and the blanket, his essence, enveloped her, weakening her to allow him easy entrance into her dreams through his unity with her.

For several moments he had fought the need to strike, then as he won, she had felt an emptiness crash through his being, the overwhelming knowledge she was becoming a mystic slayer—carrying the power of a master vampyre.

Using a force as terrifying in its gentleness as it was in its strength, he had surrounded her with a dream of a black void, an abyss claiming her as the sun in her dream climbed into the dawn. He pressed her into an understanding of what the dawn and the day meant to a vampyre. She slept the empty dark sleep of the un-dead, without dreams or thought. This was not immortality. This was the inability to die. She could not see the sun, could not hear the birds. Only the whirring of bats' wings.

Phantoms and horrid things touched her, overwhelming her with their evil. The phantoms slashed her into horrific pain with their formless wings. But she could not bleed. She could only heal. Over and over and over.

The void again. She felt hot, her soul emptied of all hope. Then out of the void a wrenching in her chest, and indescribable terror as the stake struck deep and a spasm in her heart told her she would die now. She screamed as she felt her heart burst. Her breathing went wild.

Through the dream, or in the dream, she wasn't sure which, he spoke to her, refusing to let her break the threads of sleep. "I don't want to die that way, Angie. I don't want to be—destroyed. I won't let Andre destroy me that way. I need you to know how I feel, what I fear when I daysleep."

Then she was running through strange, tunnel-like corridors, searching for him through the cities and streets of his past.

The corridors were empty. He had gone. Daylight called her into wakefulness.

Mercifully, he had at least exchanged the brocade quilt for an-other blanket. The brocade had been folded and was draped across a corner of the couch. Her pouch and belt were on the coffee table next to her. Angie was able to reach them and strap the belt around her waist.

Someone was knocking at the door. She tried to rise, but her side was still painful.

She heard a key in the lock. The door opened and a woman in her mid-forties with pale brown hair and just a dusting of face powder announced herself as "Christa, Henri's friend the lab tech." The room filled with the welcome fragrant smell of fresh coffee as she dropped a bunch of shopping bags by the couch and carried a large styrofoam box and cups to the kitchen counter. "I brought you a breakfast burrito, coffee and orange juice. Hope that's okay.

And I think the clothes will fit. I threw in some shower gel and makeup."

"Thank you—I guess," Angie said in surprise.

"Not my doing. It was your rescuer's request. He also called me a little while ago and said your cross fell under the couch or something. I'll get it for you. How are you feeling?"

Oh, I'm fine. A master vampyre helped me dream I died. That's all.

"I'm okay."

Christa began taking breakfast out of the container, and Angie forced herself to try to get up.

The pain in her side sent her back against the pillows.

Odd. The inside of her arm above her wrist also ached. Yet she couldn't remember hurting it during the fight in the parking lot. She rubbed her wrist and asked Christa for ice. The lab tech brought some ice cubes in a plastic baggie, then retrieved the cross.

"Do you—give him transfusions?" Angie asked as she took the cross and inspected the broken chain.

"What?" Christa blurted, sloshing coffee in her surprise as her hand almost lost the lid she was removing.

"You're not giving him enough. Why?"

Christa sighed resignedly. "How can you tell that?"

"Trust me." She sipped the orange juice and began working the chain to fix the links.

"There's a shortage at the blood bank. He won't take more. Isn't he a sweetheart?"

Angie repaired the cross chain and laid the necklace on the coffee table. "How long have you known him?"

"Long enough to know he's started continually looking back behind him. Would you like the rest of your juice put in the fridge?"

"Yes, please. You trust him then?"

"He's a vampyre, miss." She put the orange juice in the refrigerator.

Angie glanced around the large open cabin with pine ceiling beams, comfortable furniture (if you weren't lying under his blankets), sparse lighting and hardwood floors. He had taken her into his chambers. His domain. "Where he has absolute power," she murmured as she closed her eyes, drowsy again.

Christa stayed with her as she slept, and watched over her for the rest of the day. But when the sun fell behind the city, Christa was gone.

Angie looked down the hallway, bracing herself. He was stirring, and he was powerful.

He opened the door and walked out dressed in a simple blue shirt and black pants. "How are you feeling?" he asked.

"Like I took a walk through hellfire and damnation with you."

He did not even try to deny what he had done. Taking a goblet from a corner armoire, he poured himself a glass of wine and dropped onto a barstool at the kitchen counter. Twirling toward her, he glanced at her belt pack. "You're quite a slayer to get your ribs all busted up so easily."

He took a long draught of the wine. "All this is my fault, Angie," he said remorsely. "Do I deserve mercy, do you think? Mercy for the unwanted, the unloved, the cast-offs, the not-very-atoning atoners?"

He set the goblet on the counter and walked toward her.

His eyes were penetrating, sensual, moist.

"I should go," she said. With difficulty, she rose from the couch.

The heat in the water blue eyes was searing, the ache of desire for her within his body deep and raw.

And it matched her own.

He stroked her hair, pressing the tresses away from her face. Then he pressed his cheek to hers and pulled her close.

He became lost in her, in the rise and fall of her breasts against him, in her breathing.

His hand slid down her arm and onto the belt holding her pouch, her stakes. He unsnapped the buckle. The belt and pouch slid to the floor. Then his hand encircled hers in a caressing grasp. "Not tonight, Angie," he murmured, his voice heavy with yearning. "Tonight there are no slayers, no enemies, no fear. Tomorrow. Tomorrow we can face our destiny."

He moved his mouth over hers, searching, needing, but careful. *I don't want you to fear me,* Angie, he whispered into her thoughts, not wanting to mesmerize her, wanting her to remember his touch, remember him.

Within the powerful embrace, Angie sensed the wildness of him, the fierceness, the depths of the dark night within him. And she felt his heart, struggling to beat again, to embrace life.

Surrendering to that heart on fire, she brushed her lips across his cheek, felt his cold fire and trembled. "Dare I trust you, Henri? Can I believe you? Can I believe in you?"

"Can I believe you will not slay me?" he countered.

"Touché," she said softly.

His eyes dipped deeply into hers. "Tell me, Angie, when you're dreaming, who are you kissing? Tell me. Who is it you see and feel, as you draw your beautiful lashes down over your eyes in sleep and your lips search for dreams of love and desire?"

"I think I need to explore that question," she said, moving her mouth over his.

The unexpected response aroused him to fever pitch, and love and lust became a torrent of passionate entwining. Embracing her as close as he could and still remain gentle, Henri guided her lips, her tongue, her surrender.

When he drew away, she was breathless.

And aching fiercely.

He unbuttoned his shirt and pulled her to him to enjoy her warmth.

"The slayers will be looking for me," she said, physical enjoyment pelting her as the strong, bare chest muscles rubbed her breasts through the shirt clinging loosely to her.

"I know," he said heavily, his hands moving to her hips, pulling her closer, deepening the tantalizing sensations. "I know. Everybody's looking for you."

She closed her eyes and moaned, the strength of his desire consuming her. She could become his minion so easily.

She put her hand against his chest, uncertain.

He was pulling her hand away, drawing her to him again.

"We could be protectors of mortals together. If that's what you want, Angie," he said, his voice raspy as he pressed his thighs harder into hers.

His hands moved in under the shirt he had given her, to the silken skin he wanted.

"Your eyes are wild and hot," she breathed, trembling.

"And your own are not?"

"I've heard when you make love, you also have to take a—transfusion?" she asked.

"I've made love to many women, Angie, and never taken anything—" His lips curled at the corners.

The shirt slid from her shoulders.

She arched her breasts to accept the hands encircling them.

"Henri ..." She lost her thoughts. His hands knew where to touch, where to please. Pleasure spilled through her in luscious streams.

Drenched with swells of physical fire, she could no longer keep the sweet pangs exploding through her in check. Her logic was rushing away in swift currents of forgetfulness under the force of the raw presence within her. Desire reigned. Desire for muscle and fire.

His muscle and fire.

The shirt began to slide, as though smoothed away from her body by invisible hands.

"You're using your power," she protested in a soft moan.

"Do you not like it?" he whispered.

Her panties joined the shirt, sliding down her hips, her thighs, her legs, leaving her body bare and his to touch.

His hand slid downward in a fell stroke that sent her body spiraling into soft, physical fire.

She gasped a tiny gasp of sudden, seeping pleasure. He touched bare flesh, his fingertips skimming milky, silky softness.

"Ah. You're wanting me," he said in a tender, taunting smile

His fingertips began moving easily, pleasurably, pressing hot currents of excitement into her.

"I will not hurt you, Angie," he whispered. "Let my touch please you. Do you not like this? And this? And this?"

"Henri," she moaned. She placed her hand over his, to make him stop—

Her hand was guiding his, urging him on. She became responsive to him, to the melting softness he was creating, pangs of molten sweetness.

Pure pleasure, unwrapped.

Lifting her against him, he eased her to the couch to let her yield to the physical yearnings she could no longer repress.

Trembling, excited, she guided his hands pleasurably along her body.

Lost in him, she barely knew when his clothes joined hers on the floor, only that she felt a muscular chest freed from buttons and cloth, then hard, needing flesh suddenly pressing, moving, rubbing against her, preparing for her as his strong legs urged hers apart.

"Enjoy this night with me, Angie," he said. "Night is always long for my kind, yet not long enough."

"Let the clock chime. We won't hear it," she murmured, kissing him.

"I do not want to take your memory of this, Angie," he said. "When I penetrate you with my body and my being, I want you to remember the penetration of fire, the pleasure with me. But when the sun rises and I sleep, the morning will bring an emptiness within you, and you will yearn painfully but not be able to come to me. The day will be long, unbearable. Are you strong enough?"

"I will never be strong enough," she said as he lowered his body against hers. "I don't want to be strong enough. I want to be forever devastated by desire for you. Why do you want me? You must have devastated hundreds of far more beautiful women with your touch than me."

"I love you," he said simply.

He immersed her into his being, and into consummation with him.

22.

As the clock slipped into twilight, Henri placed a gold band inset with a sparkling bezel of black sapphires onto Angie's ring finger. "Vampyres are very casual about these things. 'Til death do us part' doesn't exactly work for us or the mortals we join with." He paused. "No other can take you as long as I claim you, Angie. But I can release or divorce you, whatever you want to call it, when the sun comes up if you do not want me."

"I do," she laughed lightly, kissing him.

He rose, and moving to the living room window that extended from the ceiling to the floor, used an automatic opener to open the blinds.

The mists were gone. A panoramic view of the city sparkling with lights below the mountain in the last trails of night filled the room. It was breathtaking.

Angie's eyes traveled over every centimeter of Henri De LaCroix, memorizing him as he stood in front of the window naked, looking out at the twinkling city.

Broad shoulders, strong legs, muscular chest, strong ... other attributes. "Breathtaking," she murmured.

He stood silently in front of the window for several minutes, then said slowly, choosing his words carefully, "She was beautiful. The most beautiful woman I had ever seen."

"The Lady Jane?"

"She would meet me every night at a stone bridge, and I would drown in her laughter, her fragrance, her smile. We would talk until just before sunrise. Then, laughing, she would flee from me into the woods. Everything inside me told me I should flee from her, but the danger in her smile was an enticement within itself. I burned with so much desire for her, I could not see the lightning in my own soul. So I became hers. And traveled with her for decades. Then Nicholas became her obsession. Fearing his holy companion's interference and influence, she killed the priest. Then the siren's song called to Nicholas relentlessly every night, and he weakened. She told him he would have to leave his cross on the stone ledge of the bridge beyond the abbey before he could have her, so he left it on the bridge. When he tried to put it back on the next morning, he thought it was going to burn a hole in his heart. But the only holes were in his neck. From the Lady of the Night. And—one other. Do you want me to go on, Angie?"

"He became an immortal with Jane," Angie said under her breath.

"We are not immortals. We—just—can't—die. Have you forgotten your nightmare so soon?"

He turned to her and the sapphires in his eyes were penetrating. "I shared the House of a Hundred Rooms with her."

"Why aren't you still with her?"

"She's a witch," he said simply, with a shrug.

She joined him at the window and he held her wrapped in his arms until dawn approached, two bodies clinging to the last threads of night, clinging to the only safety net they had—each other.

At dawn's breaking, Henri became restless. Night was waning, yet he was reluctant to yield to the dark sleep. The sleep that would take him from her. He was as desolate as death itself.

He glanced at the cross on the coffee table and looked away. "I release you. You are an innocent."

"Well, that was the shortest marriage I've ever been in," she said in dismay, then looked up at him unhappily. "And how do I dismiss the longings I will forever feel for you, Henri? What do I do with each empty night now?"

"It's the empty days that worry me, chéri," he said. Then he gave her a sudden, hopeful smile. "We could catch a red eye across the U.S. and be in Connecticut by tomorrow night. I have a—secret place."

"Works for me," she smiled. "What's in Connecticut?"

"Just a damned village," he said.

Her smile erased. "That doesn't exactly sound like the Sandals, if you're cussing it."

"No, no," he said, laughing. "It's really considered damned. Cursed. Haunted. It's the ruins of a town supposedly built by early settlers in trees so thick it's barely visible, and closed in by the hills around it, filled with their shadows, creating perpetual shade. Only a few building foundations here and there remain. It's off limits to the public now, and only a few trespassers ever venture in—if they can even find it. Mostly just occasional ghost hunters and such try to make their way through the trees. The dark entry road is dim and hazy, sunless, uninviting. We would be secluded, safe. Strange stories haunt the town's history, discouraging visitors. Stories of settlers who went missing, women who eventually became hysterical—insane—or killed themselves. People who saw strange creatures and red, glowing eyes peering through the thick trees, and were also declared insane. Dead animals, missing animals, mostly cows, hysterical women, men who burned down their homes—the stories do not report the reasons, but let's suffice it to say I had a few friends who fell victim to house fires. Historians say the ruins of certain large holes in the rocky ground are root cellars, some with sod grass tops that could be pulled over them—"

"You can stop there," she said. She was getting the picture. Clearly.

He closed the window and nodded toward his bedroom door. "I have to sleep now, Angie. Don't go in there, and don't take that cross in there. If it touches the room, I will suffer each time I have to return."

He went into the room, closed the door and locked it.

Angie stared wistfully at the door for some minutes. She was already lonely. Her gaze fell on his goblet, tranquilly shimmering on the breakfast bar counter.

Glimmering in the light from a pale dawn graying the horizon, the cup was beautiful. Heavy crystal in forest green, bejeweled and rimmed with gold. A goblet that she knew was for his use and his alone.

A few drops of residual wine left in the bottom sparkled in the day's first touch of pale light. Slowly, she circled the golden rim with her fingertip.

Strange pleasure pelted her.

"You know what it would do to you if you drank from that, don't you?" she heard a woman's voice say in soft surprise, directly behind her. "Where his lips have touched?"

Natalia moved slowly around to Angie's left side. "Drink from it," she enticed in a whisper with a twisty smile. "You'll remember what it's like—forever."

She laughed tauntingly, lightly, so lightly it was no more than a tinkle of a tiny chime on a night breeze. Light—and wicked, and delighted as she also remarked in deeper surprise, "You want to, don't you?"

"Isn't it a little past your bedtime?" Angie said, unafraid of the saucy vamp but terrified of the truth in her words.

The vampiress moved closer, her eyes on Angie's carotid artery.

Angie's eyes narrowed. "Touch my neck and I'll take you out, Natalia. And I won't need a stake to do it."

"I believe you could, couldn't you?" she responded, and backed away a little.

Then her voice became acrid, bitter as quinine as she swiftly left the subject of the goblet behind and revealed her purpose. "Do you know what you've done? They will kill him."

"What is it you know about all this, Natalia?" Angie demanded.

The dawn became tinged with pink. Natalia fled.

As she returned to the couch, Angie began to feel strange, odd, bombarded by perceptions within her that felt like hands reaching out from a mirror, and it frightened her.

Yanking on the jeans and blue top Christa had brought her, and her cross, Angie wrote Henri a quick note and hurried to the door to jump in her car and beat it back to the city. To get help for him from the Shadows.

Before her hand had even touched the doorknob, Henri was beside her.

"You can't go out there. Not alone. The Lammergeier has only one purpose here, Angie. To kill me. And take you prisoner. And Nicholas also, in the end, will have only one purpose. His own preservation."

"He was helping the school teacher, Kara Milstead ..."

"Ah, yes. Kara. Sweet little minion, I'll wager she became, after meeting the mighty Nicholas."

"Minion? But she wasn't a vampyre!"

"Minions can also be mortal. Slaves. To do the master's bidding."

"But Nicholas saved me from the phantoms," she stammered.

"Did he? Are you sure? Are you sure the holy water he just happened to be carrying in his cape pocket at that moment was so holy?" He paused. "We are masters of illusion, Angie."

Angie looked into his eyes reflecting things that needed to be said, but fear he would lose her love if those things found a voice.

"Nicholas is here at Jane's bidding, Angie," he began reluctantly. "And she is here at the Realm's bidding. She is here, with the help of her paramour, Nicholas, to abduct you and sell you to the Realm—if the Lammergeier doesn't beat her to it."

"Sell me?" Angie cried, horror-struck.

His eyes became piercingly sad. "The Realm wants you. But not to kill you, Angie. They want you because you are a Black Rose."

Angie felt sick.

The flower on her pillow …

"You have royal blood in your veins," he admitted slowly. "They want to join you to a descendent royal—who is destined to become a vampyre Royal. And the firstborn male child of your blade union, when he comes of age, will follow. And you, Angie, they consider a very special Rose. They plan to establish a lineage of mystical vampyres with you. Royal mystical vampyres. Powerful."

She shook her head as though trying to shake away a terrible, horrible dream. The vision of the caves deep in the earth with her as their singular dweller swam in her thoughts.

"No," she said, stepping back, numbed, refusing to accept what he was saying. "My birth mother's name was Wessin. There's no real proof yet."

"Your grandmother changed her name to protect you, and your mother," he returned. "You know in your heart of hearts it's true. And it appears a slayer may have killed Allison."

A slayer had killed her mother. "How do you know it wasn't Nicholas?" she tried.

"Do you seriously think Nicholas would use a nail instead of fangs?" he countered drily.

A sob rose up in her throat and spilled out through her eyes. "My grandmother said my parents were killed in a car crash."

"Or your grandmother invented that story to keep your true past in darkness, hidden from the Realm."

"How did Jane find me?" she sobbed openly, agonies of sorrow now ripping at her.

"Your cross," he answered. "There is only one like it in existence. Your mother had it made—to protect you specifically."

"We have to make a plan, fight them. Help me, Henri," she pleaded. "Empower me."

He pulled her brusquely onto the couch with him. "Sit down beside me and listen, Angie. I bit you, and not just a pinprick, remember? I carried you into my world. Jane is my—master. She could know your every move—through me."

"Then you have to fight her and the Lamm-whatever it's called—through me."

His brow furrowed, perplexed. "Are you sure?"

"Yes."

Sweeping her hair behind her shoulders, he pressed her against the back of the couch and bared his fangs. He bit her hard on the neck before she could even comprehend what was happening—

Until she felt something warm and wet flowing down her neck and seeping onto her blouse and her arm.

"You bastard. Did you play me?" she said weakly, collapsing under his spell as his being began to immerse deeply, powerfully, into hers. "I'd like to kick your sorry ash and dirt back to France."

"I am empowering you to fight her. Is that not what you wanted?" he said, drawing back quickly, confused. "She's an Old World vampyre, a powerful one."

He reeled and drew his hand across his chest. He had lost his heartbeat.

"Am I your minion now?" she asked weakly.

"Do you feel like a minion?" he smirked slightly, emanating mystical essence all over the room as the streams sparkled in his veins.

"I think I should slap you."

"Then you're definitely not my minion."

23.

The door to the mountain lair kicked open.

Carrying an elaborately carved stake of mahogany wood infused with silver and engraved with Latin symbols, Andre, with the Shadows behind him, rushed the room.

Henri was on the sofa, his arm draped around Angie's shoulders.

"That's a little excess avant-garde, don't you think, DuPre?" Henri smirked as he looked at the demolished door. "The door wasn't locked."

Andre glared as he caught sight of Angie's blouse, then his gaze burned toward the vampyre.

"Give her to me!" Andre demanded, his eyes blazing as he held out his hand.

Henri pulled her close, his arm tightening. He didn't want to give her up.

"Release her! Now!" Andre said, his hand curling around the stake in a tight grip.

James's crossbow became taut, ready to send a bolt. But he did not want to risk hitting Angie if she moved to protect the Royal.

Which she did.

Angie lunged, threw herself in front of the vampyre's chest. "Don't hurt him!"

"Go to them, Angie," Henri said, reluctantly releasing her.

"Don't kill him, Andre," Angie pleaded in torrents of tears. "He didn't understand. And God help us, Henri De LaCroix is in atonement."

James looked at her neck, and his eyes shone with a hard glint. "That doesn't look like much atonement."

"You would be killing an atoner," Angie cried in a sob. "You're sworn to safeguard them."

With his arm tight around Angie's waist, Andre began pulling her with him backward toward the door while his troupe kept an eye on the vampyre empowered with mystic strength.

His stake remained ready in his hand.

Henri moved toward the window. "I will not engage you, Andre," he said.

Andre studied him curiously. There was a strange tone in his voice. Sorrow? Sadness?

Henri became a visage of fog. The window slid open. The fog rolled away and down the outside wall just as a sliver of sun began casting a gold net across the thick canopy of old growth forest.

Andre began pulling Angie down the porch stairs and toward the drive—she resisted him, looking back desperately.

"That Lammer thing will kill him," she sobbed.

"Get us out of here," Andre said, tossing his keys to James.

Andre threw her onto the back seat, then slid in beside her while they sped away with her.

"We should have staked him," James said as he glanced back at Angie's blouse streaked with blood. "Look what he did to her, Andre! And you let him live?"

"No. She let him live. She swore he's in atonement."

"He thought it was what I wanted," Angie sighed, then leaned her head against her guardian's shoulder as her thoughts began to mingle with Henri's and the venom seeped.

At the next stop light, she undid her seat belt and tried to lunge out of the van.

"He's calling to her," Andre said, pulling her back against the seat. "Hurry, James."

"He isn't calling me. We have to help him, Andre. He's betrayed Jane. And the Realm."

"You can't help him if you're half-vamp," Andre said. "We have to burn the venom."

As soon as they reached the apartments, Andre flew up the stairs with her to his rooms. Tossing her onto the bed, he shouted for Mack, told James to hold her down, then turned her face to the side and smoothed her hair away from her neck to appraise the damage. The sight of the two punctures buried in purplish bruises made him swear hate for the vampyre with a vengeance, atonement or not. "I'm so sorry, Angie," he whispered sorrowfully.

The bedroom door flew open and Mack hurried in. Angie looked up to find the other slayers standing just outside the door, their gazes intense.

She closed her eyes, drifting somewhere between space and time and Henri.

The Shadows' voices became far away.

"I can't believe he once let her live. Then did—that—to her."

Then Andre's resolute words. "If either of those vampyres tries to call to her and she tries to go to either of them, tie her down."

A sigh. From James.

Andre's voice again. "Let's get it done."

Mack pressed her arms against the bed. Angie bolted up against the arms holding her down. "Where is Henri? He'll kill him. He'll kill you all!"

"Right now we have to keep from killing you," Andre said. He motioned urgently to James as he took a small wooden box from a locked drawer. "Hurry."

Taking a wooden-handled iron in the form of a cross from the box, Andre ran to the kitchenette.

When he returned, the tiny branding iron was glowing red-hot, and his instructions to Mack and James were simple. "Hold her down."

They each took an arm, and held them pressed against the mattress. But they did not have to use much pressure.

"I know the routine," Angie said.

Mack studied the deep punctures. "The bastard did a number on her."

"In a moment, she's going to be fighting us like a cornered wildcat," James said.

Andre took a vial of olive oil, centuries old, from the wooden box and placed it next to him on the night stand.

Then pressed the hot iron against the punctures.

Angie screamed and fought them, struggling to be free. Unable to break their grasp, she dug her fingers into the bed covers, clinching the folds into her hands.

The slayers held her down.

Finally, she sank against the pillows, paralyzed, paralyzed by liquid fire.

"Easy, Angie," Mack whispered. "Come back easy." He looked frantically, helplessly, at Andre. "Why is it taking so long?"

"It just feels long, Mack," Andre said quietly as Angie continued to cry out, her body tensing into hard spasms.

After what seemed an eternity, her breathing finally calmed, and the muscles in her arms relaxed.

She gazed at him, through sobs and tears. "It hurts, Andre. It hurts."

"I know, bébé. I know."

"I'm not afraid to go after him, Andre," James said, his tone angry, demanding justice for her.

"No!" Angie cried.

Mumbling, "The Lady Weston's niece. Her niece," through a foggy voice, she let the pillows carry her away again. When she opened her eyes, Andre was uncapping the vial of oil and putting several drops on his fingertips.

"If it burns, you are a vampyre and will have to die, Angie," Andre said quietly.

She closed her eyes, not wanting to see the silver dagger James was easing from its sheath at his belt.

For several moments, the tears rolled, unfettered, from under her lashes.

Then she felt James move close to her. He would be swift and merciful, but that didn't help the fear that made her begin to shake uncontrollably.

Andre rubbed the holy oil across the burned punctures.

Then faced his Shadow warriors. "Angie is deeply in love with this creature. If she has given herself to his darkness, we will have to—destroy her. Losing a Shadow is not something we want to contemplate, but the possibility does exist."

A silence as heavy as a lead apron fell across the room.

He turned back to Angie. The oil was cool against her skin.

Drawing back, he exhaled with relief. They had not been too late.

He poured the rest into the wound, the antidote for the venom.

"Welcome back, Anj," James said, putting away the dagger. "That was too close for comfort."

Angie forced herself up, bracing herself on her elbows. She had to make them listen, make them understand. "He's dangerous, Andre," she sobbed.

"You said Henri is in atonement."

"No. Not Henri. Nicholas."

"What are you saying?"

"Nicholas is Jane's lover. He wavers. He may kill you all. For her. To take—me. If she finds out I'm still alive." Her voice trailed off. "So will the assassin."

"She's in some kind of delirium," James said. "From the venom?"

"Are you the descendent of The Lady Jane Weston?" Andre asked in awe.

"That nasty spider is not a lady!" Angie cried. "She wants to sell me to the Realm! And Nicholas is her lover. If he doesn't sell me himself, to that Lammie thing."

Andre's eyes shot through with a sweep of emotions Angie couldn't identify, and his voice was like gravel. "He walked right into our midst, to mock us."

"Henri kept calling him a vanguard?" Angie queried.

"A vanguard is the warrior who goes in first, the front line," Andre said. "The vampyre vanguards of legend are cunning, evil. They go in with well-planned deceptions, to deviously cloud the senses, clearing a path for those who would follow."

"The evil thing offered us his wine, and we drank it," Taniesha said.

"You're the Royal mystic," Andre breathed, then addressed his warriors. "Anjanette Carter is the missing royal babe. And a Royal vampyre stumbled onto her in a park. Destiny had a hand in this."

Weakened from the loss of blood, Angie sank into her pillows and closed her eyes, to rest. Just a moment or two.

When she opened her eyes, it was nearly midnight.

The slayers were still in Andre's room, watching over her.

Then suddenly, moving like lightning, they slung open Andre's closet and began assembling their weapons of war.

"What's going on?" Angie asked, staring in open astonishment. These were not belt packs. They were spears of wood, javelins of silver welded with splinters of wood, crossbows, holy water in sprayer tanks, and one golden cross.

"The cross seems so small," she said.

"The mustard seed," Andre said. "The smallest can often be the strongest. This belongs to Stephen De LaCroix. "

The slayers were exchanging glances but saying nothing.

"Why are you …?" Angie began, then her senses sparked, into a pyrotechnic explosion. "Henri! He's here."

Taniesha glanced toward the door, beyond which was the stairs, beyond which was the vampyre. "Do you think she would go to him?"

"Oh, for crying out," Angie began and started to get up.

Andre blocked her. "Stay with her, Taniesha. If he's here for her, she may have a struggle resisting his call. She's still weak, and still reeling from her experience with him."

"The bastard has come right to our front door," James said, his jaw clinched tight.

Weapons at their sides, the slayers descended the stairs to confront the Royal.

Stepping from the shadows, Henri glided into the apartment lamp light.

"You have four slayers ready to kill you at my command, Henri. Why are you here?" Andre demanded in a tight, but controlled voice.

Henri moved into full view. "Is she—all right?"

"If you're here for her, you can't have her," James said, stepping forward with his crossbow.

As his eyes swept the slayers, and the weapons ready to take him, every muscle in the vampyre's body tightened.

"Your strength is coming from her," James said angrily, raising the bow.

Henri bristled and stepped forward in challenge.

With a wave of his hand, Andre warned James to back off. Then he asked again, "What do you want?"

Henri smoothed his hand across the front of the soft, white cotton shirt he was wearing. "I would ask only that when you come for me in daysleep, you do not—slash—my shirt. I wore it in—happier times—and would like it to remain untorn." He paused. "My deepest hour, and my weakest point of resistance, is when the sun beams its hottest. Place a cross and slay me then and you will have me. But that day is not today, Andre. For you know my strength. And I do not wish to kill your troupe."

Andre's grip on the stake relaxed. "I have a better idea. My mystic slayer tells me you are in atonement. Why don't you just—go see your cousin, repent and stop feeling sorry for yourself?"

"I might die if I enter Stephen's church and that sanctuary light hits me," Henri exclaimed as though the suggestion was ludicrous.

"You die if you don't," James said with a shrug. "What's the difference? The church, the Lammergeier, the Lady Jane, or us at high noon? Your pick."

"Go to Stephen, Henri," Andre said. "The Realm and the Lady cannot touch you once you're with Stephen. We will protect the mystic."

A small smile of irony curled around Henri's lips. "So Stephen finally gets his wish. He will probably have every nun in the convent singing victoriously all night just to torment me."

Briefly, Henri wondered if Stephen would welcome him with open arms, or throw holy water at him. And whether facing the Lady Jane could be worse than the serene little cathedral reeking of cedar and incense and purity.

His black trench coat flowing out from behind him, Henri stomped off in a huff down the sidewalk. For the moment, he had no choice but to go. The crossbow had moved into position, ready to burst his heart.

He did not go very far.

He had no intention of deserting Angie with the threat of the Lammergeier looming over her—

A beat in his heart again—and an unholy chill thickening the air.

Henri's eyes darted toward Angie's bedroom window.

A single lamp came on. James was entering the room.

Henri pulled his black trench coat closer. One of the only chills a vampyre could feel besides a ghost was—

Yes, phantoms were on the premises.

And Jane, if the perfume in the sludgy air was not deceiving him.

24.

As he flew back toward the apartments, Henri could see the Lady Jane Weston relaxed in the crook of a limb next to the window, her body stretched out across its width.

But as everyone knows, he thought, *the pose of idle rest is the position from which the feline predator leaps and pounces on its prey.*

Her violet eyes shone delightfully as though from a light of their own, a light that chilled Henri to the core yet excited him with strange heat.

As it always had.

Damn her. She was about to do what she did best.

Seduce.

And her victim was the crossbow slayer.

Jane scratched at the window. Lightly. With a crimson red fingernail.

With Angie sleeping deeply from a sedative Andre had given her, James had busied himself by stacking some empty boxes and was now ripping the packing tape from the flaps of the one box that remained unopened, the fax machine box.

At the sound of the scraping, he stopped.

Henri felt a wicked sensation begin to pelt the night like needles, an evil permeating the very walls of the room, almost making them weave. A phantom was in that box.

The slayer left the box and pulled apart two of the slats on the venetian blinds cautiously to peer outside.

A pair of violet eyes gazed in at him from out of the darkness.

Instinctively, he reached for a stake from his utility pack.

"You are the crossbow slayer," she smiled, then the violet orbs reflecting the moon moved to his ring. "And more, perhaps?"

He glanced at his ring, his brow furrowed in puzzlement.

What did she mean? Henri wondered, his own brow furrowing deeply.

The Lady smoothed her cape away from her shoulders, and let the folds blow seductively around the branch as she drew her knees up under a silken white evening gown. A side slit extended all the way up her thigh.

"You are a seasoned slayer," she said in a soft, come-hither voice. "So you know that our cloaks carry the essence, the power of what we are?" She kneaded a bit of satin white between her fingers.

"I didn't think you wore them to fend off the cold," he answered flatly.

Damn you, don't you dare try to take her down! Henri thought, flying faster. She was outside on the branch, he was inside. She could fly in the wink of an eye, or knock him off balance if he opened the window and pursued her out onto the branch.

And Angie would be left unprotected.

Henri tried to force his being to fly even faster, his starling wings beating the air with tenacity. But his power of flight and of flash were to his surprise diminished.

He was beginning his return to humanity.

At the moment, not a good thing.

"Any other time," he muttered.

He pummeled the wind, forced his body to respond to his commands. He lifted a talon, stared at it. A sensation of warmth above the bone.

Jane would have the upper hand if this return to Oz continued.

"I don't need a heart at the moment, thank you very much," he twirtled to the sky. "Or a brain. Just courage and power. To get us out of this mess. Then I'll be human again. Then I'll be a happy, middle-class, blue-collar, have-a-nice-day nine-to-fiver. We'll get married, settle down, get pregnant, have babies. I'll work in a tire store or something, the whole mortal enchilada."

Only, just not right now...

Jane was feigning a pout at the slayer's wisecrack. Moving a perfect, pale, silky leg so the slit would widen, she stroked the windowsill sensuously with her hand. "I have a name, James," she said softly. "I am Jane."

"I know. And I'm not inviting you in—Jane," he said firmly.

"Am I asking for entrance?" Her eyes gazed provocatively at him from under a black canopy of thick, luscious lashes.

She was keeping her eyes on his, Henri realized, to distract him from the evil growing in the room like a mushroom cloud—behind him.

Damn it. The Shadows had brought that phantom with them like a nasty camel spider hiding in the fax machine box.

The wad of tar crawled out onto the floor, then rose to tower silently, his glowing red eyes slanted malevolently as he awaited his mistress's command.

Jane moved slightly and eased her hand along the smooth skin of her thigh. "I want the mystic, James. Are you strong enough to resist me and keep me from her? I want to see how powerful you are."

"Give it your best shot," he said.

Don't challenge her, you fool! Henri cried inwardly. *She loves to play!*

Her fingertips followed the slit to its source along her silky skin, beckoning his eyes to follow. "How did you get that nasty little burn scar on the inside of your forearm, James?" she asked sweetly, sympathetically. "It must have hurt terribly. Was the fire your fault? No, of course not. Your stepfather found out what you were and tried to kill you. But of course, you thought the fire was your doing." She leaned in toward the window, and her eyes became excited, wild. "You were trapped—in the fire. Were you terrified, fearful you would not escape the flames? We don't like fire, either, James. Let me take you away from the fire. Come out the window and fly with me. I can give you an ecstasy no mortal can."

Her hand glided in under the slit. "You would be so strong, James," she whispered, her eyes moistening.

Henri used the wind to propel him. He was almost there ...

"I could have worn nothing. But I love this gown, don't you?" Jane was saying coyly.

She arched back, the slit opened to full breadth. "I decided instead to wear nothing under it."

James stepped back, wary of her seduction.

Her lips turned down and she glared, not having received the look of lust she had wanted—desire pelting him unmercifully. But just as quickly, her smile returned, her voice mellifluous. "It was a laboratory fire, wasn't it, James? From an explosion? He mixed the chemicals in the college laboratory so they would combust when you lit the Bunsen burner."

"What are you saying?" he said, his mental control momentarily wavering as he fought to control his emotions in the face of her words.

It was the moment the vampira and her phantom had waited for, a singular moment of weakness. His mind was theirs to shatter. She pricked him with visions of fire—and smoke. The air became so hot it could incinerate a man's lungs.

But there was no fear in the slayer's eyes. He stared at the illusion of fire, fascinated.

With a corrosive laugh, Jane spread her dark wings and danced delightedly on the branch. "James, you are wonderful. Invite me in, and I will let you look at me again. I am more beautiful than the human or that sullied vampira could ever be, am I not?"

"Except for the fangs," he said, his tone flat.

"Burn, slayer," she smiled sweetly. She drew her wings back in and sat back down on the limb.

Henri crashed through the bathroom window.

Since the damned thing wouldn't open for him.

The phantom was forming into a chimera, the lion head nodding toward Jane as though he had received a command.

The mistress of evil was about to play a horror game. Henri could literally smell burnt ashes as he stepped from the bathroom and into the illusion of fire.

A lit candle appeared in the phantom's cloven hands, and Henri cast a worried glance toward Angie. She was weak. The illusion could manhandle her if she awakened in the center of flames she would mystically be able to see.

The odious creature with the body of a goat dropped the candle. "Oops," he said.

Drops of hot wax splashed across the carpet, and tiny flames began to form on the drops, burning the carpet fibers with a thousand little fires.

The little fires rolled across the floor toward the drapes.

The drapes burst into open flame. Towers of red began to lick at the walls and the bed. Henri could smell the smoke, feel the hot haze. This mistress of the undead was powerful.

The phantom chimera, its razor-sharp wings outstretched, moved through the smoke.

Moving between Henri and the bed where Angie lay.

A burning bed …

"Get away from her," his deep voice commanded from within the smoke.

The phantom dissolved into the floor.

Jane's rain bell laugh filled the room. "Henri, you have joined us! You delight me."

A dark silhouette moving through the smoke, Henri moved toward Angie's bed. Sitting on the edge, he took the sleeping mystic's hands in his.

"What the hell are you doing back here?" James cried angrily, combating the smoke, trying to cross the room, trying to find his crossbow, keep the vampyre from stealing the mystic.

"Saving your butt, apparently," Henri smirked, tossing a glance at the slayer trapped in the center of a circle of flames, surges of brilliant yellow-orange tongues of fire rising up around him.

Jane began pirouetting on the limb like a wood nymph in senseless mirth. "Slay him, James!"

"This one is more venomous than an asp, in case you hadn't noticed," Henri said, his blue eyes cutting coldly to her heated, violet ones.

He raised his arm and flexed his hand toward the window, toward her madness. Glass cracked and crashed. Flying pieces of pane showered the branches and leaves around her.

She stomped her foot against the branch, and flapped her wings in anger. "I hope the Lammergeier kills you, Henri De LaCroix!"

"If he doesn't kill you first for trying to kill the mystic," Henri retorted.

Enraged, she turned the room into a volcano.

Scorching heat fell from the ceiling at her command, shot up from the floor, dripped off the melting metal rims of the Victorian bed posts.

The phantom slithered across the floor like a snake, then rose toward Henri with razor wings.

"Kill him, my sweet chimera. Kill him!" the vampira cried, clapping her hands in mirth.

The phantom flew at him.

Henri slapped the phantom into an ink blot on the floor. It puddled away into the burning drapes.

A floating piece of drape landed on James' shirt, burning through to his skin. He cried out in pain.

The chimera rose again out of the shreds of drapery and kicked the slayer in the midriff with a cloven hoof, a powerful, driving blow that sent him reeling against the wall and right into the fire. His scarred arm began to burn unmercifully.

Henri grasped the phantom, splintering it into ashes.

"You should have behaved," he said.

The burn on James' arm became a thin line, the skin became smooth.

Henri tossed him his crossbow and quiver. "I really think we should get the hell out of here before she gets pissed and really sets the room on fire."

Angie looked up through half-closed eyelids at the master vampyre lifting her from her bed. "Henri!" she smiled in surprise, lifting her arms and sliding them around his neck. "What are you doing here?"

"Angie, are you awake enough to join your power to mine?" he whispered urgently.

"Mmm. No prob," she smiled drowsily. "What's going on? Besides looking like it's a bonfire in here?"

Wrapping her into her blankets and quilt, Henri lifted the mystic into his arms, hurried to the bathroom window and climbed out onto the limbs of a cottonwood.

James clambered out after them.

The bedroom door kicked open and the Shadows rushed the room.

"Go back and get your goonies," Henri commanded James. "You're going to need them."

The Lady Jane Weston was flashing from the tree, screaming like a banshee, calling on her forces.

Within moments, the alley behind the apartments, black as pitch, became sparked with crimson eyes, crossbow bolts and stakes slicing the air with fire trails.

A full raiment of power from the crossbow slayer, a shower of bolts, sprayed the air like deadly splinters, and in the wake of the arrow tips, swords and stakes and knives and fangs flashed and clashed, punctuated with Andre's shouts, phantom screams—and the light, lilting laughter of the vampira. She clapped her hands in glee from a fifth story fire escape like she was at a riotous play.

But Henri and Angie weren't there for the encore.

They were in a cave miles from town.

Angie sat in front of a fire pit dug out of the cave flooring, watching a curtain of rain drape the cave entrance.

Henri took a small tin cup from a stone shelf, caught some of the drops and held it for Angie to drink. The flight had been difficult for her. She was still somewhat weak.

Hell, the flight had been difficult for him. He was still somewhat human.

And the insufferable rain had started pouring out of the sky on them like a reservoir turned upside down. He threw another log on the fire and checked to see if the blankets he had spread across the cave boulders were dry.

They were warm and toasty. He wrapped her in her blankets and draped his coat over her as well. "Better?"

"Better," she smiled. "Where are we?"

"Safe. For the moment."

Henri had spirited her away while Andre's troupe kept Jane and her entourage busy.

Angie had protested, of course, and Andre had to practically kick her in the butt to get her to go. She was fiercely loyal.

One of the reasons Henri was senselessly in love with her.

"What is all this?" Angie asked, glancing around the cave. Besides the fire pit, there were matches, oil lamps, flashlights, and a coffee pot.

"Teenagers like to come up here and play house," he said. "Sometimes after they leave, they even get to play mommy and daddy." He paused and studied her. "You were too weak to fight, Angie. And Andre had an obligation. He could not let you fall into Realm hands."

"I know."

He sat down beside her at the fire and tucked her blankets closer around her.

"I don't think I like caves very much," she said, staring into the blackness of several tunnels and remembering her vision. "Where do they go?"

"These caves lead under one of my castles," Henri answered simply.

"One of his castles," she murmured to herself.

"Feel like spelunking?" he smiled.

She wrapped her blanket around her and trudged along beside him through the rock-walled tunnels until they stepped through a camouflaged hole in the mountainside and out into fresh air.

The rain had stopped, and the black towers of a castle poked at the disbanding clouds from behind a tree-shrouded, massive wrought iron fence.

A metal plaque with a soul-shuddering inscription was above the gate, an epitaph.

As you are, so once was I,
And as I am now, so shall you be.

The gate was locked with heavy chains and an iron padlock.

Henri honed his gaze in on the chain and lock.

Nothing happened. Not even a quiver in a link.

"What's wrong?"Angie asked.

"Humanity," he answered, and not pleasantly.

Cupping the lock into his palm, Henri turned a steely blue gaze on the rust-coated iron. After several moments that seemed an eternity, a slight scraping sound emitted from the hollow of the lock.

The lock popped open.

He pulled the lock from the chain links, pushed in the shackle, rubbed away a little of the rust and slipped it in his pants pocket.

"Why didn't you just break the links and the lock with that whoop-ass strength of yours?" Angie asked.

"It's an antique," he said simply.

25.

Wide-eyed under her curtains of dark lashes, Angie gazed with wonderment at the creature returning from the dark. He was fearsome more than reassuring. Demanding more than requesting. And every request was a command. But she couldn't deny the fires shooting through her at this moment, warming every vein.

Henri De LaCroix had stolen her heart—lock, stock and barrel. Henri pushed the gate open.

A stone and mortar behemoth, the castle was grandiose with its stained glass windows, but not friendly. Fierce faces of gargoyles bared their fangs from the parapets. And the tower windows were jaded—and jailed. Grated with spiked iron.

The massive castle doors opened on their own as Henri stood before them.

Henri handed Angie a flashlight from the cave. "You have never been in a vampyre's castle before, sweetums, and this one belongs to the vampyre you are in union with."

"Is this a definite tourist must-see?" Her smile was shaky.

"A simple tourist would think he was only shuddering at the cobwebs in the halls and his own imagination," he said. "But you will sense much more from these living walls."

"Castle walls couldn't be ..."

"These are my walls," Henri said tightly. "And haunted as hell. Trust me."

He took her chin in his hand, lifted her face so she could not break his gaze. "When you enter, you will feel as though the breath is being sucked out of you. Take a moment to gather your wits about you."

She stepped across the threshold—

The dark palace enshrouded Angie so quickly she gasped and sank against the vestibule wall.

Besides sensing vampyres—everywhere—and strange occupants passing close but unseen, a blade of cold encompassed her. "I feel as if the ghost just did a hit and run on me again," she cried.

"It's possible he did," Henri said. "Our watcher is still with us, I have a feeling, sticking this out to the end."

"It's the gray ghost," Angie breathed with relief. "I thought perhaps Jane was calling the very dead from the grave to attack us."

"No one, alive or among the undead, has the power to touch the final grave," Henri said. "One and One Only retain that power."

A strand of fog momentarily passed over. They were dusted with pasty, pale light from the stained glass windows.

The intricate patterns fell in soft hues against the floor, but seemed to form the shadows of creatures from the imagination's darkest side.

A sound of slight rustling above them, high above them.

Angie looked up. And wished she hadn't.

Vampyres hung from the vaulted, Gothic ceiling as viscous as spiders that could drop and kill anything below them in an instant.

"They will not descend," Henri assured her as he gently squeezed her fingers between hers. "They are mine."

As a dark form zipped close, she knew he also had dark companions.

What else was living on the premises?

Best she not ask, she decided.

Henri led Angie up a wide staircase carpeted in red and antique gold, and down a tapestry laden hall to a room in the farthest wing, his bedroom.

The bedroom was as large as her whole apartment and richly furnished. But the forest green window drapes were heavy, blocking out whatever sliver of moon might be brave enough to hang over this dark kingdom.

The bed with a pale blue comforter in a fine brushed fabric, was a welcome contrast to the heaviness of the room. A lovely painting of a winsome, mossy stone bridge at evening hung above the headboard.

"Wow! Not bad," she said as she plopped onto the bed and dissolved into the soft, luxurious mattress.

The dim room was also Febreze fresh. "Shouldn't there be a warm chocolate cookie or mints, or something?" She smiled up at her rescuer.

He pulled open the night stand drawer, and popped a mint her way.

She laughed, caught it and unwrapped it.

In the hall, a shirring sound like many wings came. Then it stopped. Just outside the door of the room.

"They are here to protect you while you sleep," Henri said.

"Are they loyal?" she asked, nervous.

"They are," he said. "They have their reasons, not the least of which is their hatred of Jane."

"Where will you be while I—sleep?" She fought panic.

"With you," he smiled and nodded at the bed. "It's a Cal-King."

Moving to a far wall, he pulled aside a tapestry revealing a small, almost imperceptible panel in the wall.

"Any vampyres worth their salt have escape routes—in the event they need a quick escape from a slayer—or the Lady Jane."

Angie bent and dipped her head into the small enclosure, but pulled back quickly, sputtering at the cobwebs clinging to her face. "If anything goes awry, this will take us, or you if I am not able to go with you, to a tunnel, then upward to the highway. There is a car with a full tank of gas hidden in the brush and trees. V-8, black with smoked windows. Grab it and drive like hell to Tuscon or Phoenix. No clouds, no rain—desert sun. Do not go back to Stephen. There will be Realm loyals thick as wasps watching the grounds."

Smoothing the tapestry back in place, he opened the door beside it.

A large square sunken marble bath tub beneath a skylight glistened with warm, fragrant water. Angie could only imagine how beautiful this room was on full moon nights.

Flower petals floated invitingly in the water.

A sink in a marble vanity with gold faucets was in a separate alcove with an oval, gold-framed mirror.

Angie turned from the tub to him. "This is for me?"

"You could not use a few moments of relaxation?" he smiled.

"Oui. I could."

"Enjoy," he said, kissing her. "I am sorry there is not much moonlight."

"S'okay," she said, then looking back eagerly at the warmth waiting for her.

Practically ripping off her clothes, she dove in. "Oo, this is wonderful!"

"I'll see if there's any food in the house," Henri said, and left her to herself to luxuriate.

By the time she finally forced herself to leave the water behind, Angie found a floor-length black satin gown and robe waiting for her on the bed, and a tray of fresh fruit and vegetables.

She slipped the gown over her head and nibbled on a strawberry.

Then she spotted the little lacy black negligee tossed over the back of a tufted silk chair.

She kept the black robe, but exchanged the gown for the sheer shortie.

"Thought you might like that one," Henri said with a sly smile as he came through the door with a bowl of soup.

"I like," she said with a smile. "Do you?"

"I would like to take it off," he said.

And he did. Slowly, with deliberation.

As soon as the bit of black lace was on the floor, his shirt tumbled next to it. His pants also fell under her deft fingers. They tumbled onto the bed into a pile of soft pillows. She ran her hands across his chest. Touching him lit her with fires that burned all the way down. A moan escaped her lips.

She wrapped her legs around him and he groaned with pleasure, rocking in her liquid warmth as she arched and receded and kept him on the edge of the dream with kisses and caresses until he was driven deeper, longer and harder, and finally into release. Then he lingered, pressing her into more sweetness with him.

Nestling into Henri's arms, Angie released her body to him once more, then slept. A sense of security enveloped her, strange though it was. Her bodyguards were vampyres.

When she awoke, Angie smiled dreamily. She smoothed her arm across the pillows to find the master of her heart and let him excite her.

Empty pillows met her touch.

She sat up straight and slid off the bed.

Was he hanging from the ceiling in the closet? Mousing around on the rafters? Passed out cold under the bed in a box of dirt?

Whipping on the black satin robe, she rushed to the bedroom door and opened it a slit.

A pair of red eyes peered into hers from the darkened hallway. Her breath caught in gasp.

The vampyre stod, a sword in his hand, its blade resting across his shoulder. "Do you need something, my lady?" he asked politely.

"I—I—Where is Henri?" she stammered.

"He had a visitor. He will return shortly. Is there anything I can do for you, my lady?"

"No. No, that's okay. I'm fine." She closed the door. Quickly.

And realized she wasn't breathing. She exhaled.

Returning to the bed, she sat anxiously.

Like a prairie wind, barely visible to her, he was suddenly through the door and beside her.

"Sure," she said. "Use my body, then take off in the middle of the night." Her smile teased, but the somber lines in his face swept her elation into trepidation—again.

"The crossbow slayer is downstairs," he said, and not happily. "I suppose you should hear what he has to say."

26.

Angie yanked on her clothes and shoveled her feet into her shoes.

"You are still in great danger, chéri," Henri said gravely as he took her downstairs. "If what the slayer told me is the truth."

He walked her out to the road where an SUV idled in the shadows of the trees.

The only occupant was James.

"The Shadows were ambushed while I was getting coffee for everyone," he said, his tone burning the air. "Mack thought it was the pizza guy when the buzzer rang, and buzzed them in. They bit the hell out of the day maid, then left her tied up and instructed her to tell me they will be waiting for you. They know you will try to rescue the Shadows."

"Where did my aunt stash them?" Angie cried, anger turning her violet eyes to black ire.

"She couldn't help playing one more night game," James said. "She left that one for you to figure out."

"Jane is obviously using them in pretense of an exchange, you understand that?" Henri said.

"The maid said Jane's vampyres descended on Kathryn with a vengeance," James said, his tone a frozen Arctic wind. "They stoned and flailed her with silver clubs to punish the defector, the protector of atoners. When she tried to extend her wings to fight and help the Shadows escape, Nicholas broke them. They plan to kill her first."

Angie's eyes flew to Henri's, filled with fury. "Henri! We have to stop them."

"That's not all they have planned," James said. "They're going to throw Henri in a sun well, and you in with him so you have to watch him burn before the Realm hauls you off to break your will and find the secrets to your power."

"And we are alone against the vampyre woman," Henri added. "Where are the envoys?"

"Sweeping the city," James responded. "I left messages, but I doubt they'll be able to join us in time."

Angie grasped Henri's sleeve. "Nosy Natalia will know where they are! She's Nicholas' minion."

"So I suppose this means we are not going to Connecticut to-night?" Henri sighed with a small sad smile, his blue eyes tracing hers.

"Not tonight," she said softly.

She jumped in the car. He slid in beside her. "Mystics," he said, kissing her lingeringly as though it might be their last. "We are in a pickle, aren't we?" He stroked her hair as torrents of tears spilled down her cheeks.

"Cry later," James said roughly, tossing his cell phone to the back seat as he scattered gravel with the utility truck tires and sped away from the castle. "Right now we need reinforcements."

"Come on. Pick up, pick up," Angie said, punching in the number James gave her.

Angie clutched the phone, hoping an envoy would call back, and call back soon. They needed the cavalry.

At the edge of the city, James whirled the SUV into a trashy, rundown cul-de-sac.

The old Victorian three-story Natalia inhabited was behind scraggy trees and wild brush.

James screeched to a halt at the curb. They leaped onto the rick-ety porch, and as Angie summoned the strength within her and took the doorknob in her hand, Henri stepped back. This night was hers.

The smell of the dead in the dim vestibule with soiled carpet almost knocked her over. But the mystic slayer emerging into her power was undeterred.

"Natalia!" she called out forcefully.

Angie did not relish climbing the fiendishly cobwebby stairs, but she knew she would rip the house apart to find the flippant vamp.

The vampira appeared, easing out of the shadows in a black lace tank top and skinny jeans, and towered over her in five-inch wedge heels. "It would seem you walk through locked doors with the greatest of ease, my dear. Do you also walk through walls? What are you?"

"Where would they go, Natalia?" Angie demanded.

"Who?" she asked with a twisty smile.

"Don't play games," James said, moving toward her.

Her smile disappeared.

The carpet on the stairs beyond them seemed to move.

They had walked into a nest.

"What makes you think I would know? Or tell you if I did?" Natalie said testily. Nastily.

Angie slammed her hand against the wall next to the vampyre's head.

"I don't have time for this," Angie said, her patience lost. "Now where would they go?"

Piles of rags rose from the dingy stairs, mottled the stair rails.

Henri bristled, ready to fight them. "Call them off, Natalia."

As James's hand moved to pull a bolt from his pack, Natalia's eyes fell on his ring. She raised her hand and motioned toward the stairs. The vampyres retreated.

James frowned down at the jewel shining as though from an inner fire, and his brow deeply furrowed. "What is it about this ring?"

The vampyre reared back somewhat, in surprise. "You really do not know, do you?" The splashy smile returned to her lips. "This should prove interesting." She moved closer to Angie, as close as she dared. "Are you ovulating, I hope?"

"Natalia, we don't have all night," Henri said warningly.

Her red lips pushed into a pout. "She's taking them to that hovel on the hill called Stony." Then her eyes glittered toward Angie and she laughed oddly, as if at a joke only she knew the punch line to.

Henri stepped in front of the Russian vampyre and instructed James firmly, "Take Angie to the car."

"I'm not going to ..." Angie began in protest.

James grabbed her by the arm. "Yes, you are. This is not something you want to see."

Ten minutes later, Henri was back in the car, in the back seat with Angie, his face somber, his muscles taut. "Let me see that ring," he said over the seat to James, his voice coffin-cold.

James did not argue. He slid it off and handed it to him.

Henri studied the symbols engraved on the inside of the band, then handed it back. "You are both children of the Realm. And they want you. I have a castle in the Black Forest where I can hide you."

"Look, ass," James said, glancing back over the seat. "I don't know what this is about, but I'm not abandoning the troupe. You can go with me or you can run hide in your hole, but I'm going after the Lady Nasty and her pretty boy, and get them back."

"Let's just barrel into hell and rescue the world," Henri retorted, no love lost in his voice for the slayer.

"Are you with us?" Angie pleaded.

Henri looked into the violet eyes needing his power, his strength. "I can refuse you nothing." He cupped her chin in his hand. "I can also promise you nothing. I cannot promise I can protect you, Angie. But I can promise I will fight by your side to the death."

"I'll take it," she cried elatedly, throwing her arms around his neck in an ardent embrace.

James tore away from the curb, but was brought up short by an eighteenth-century coach and horse thundering from the alley, blood dripping from the wheel spikes.

He threw on the brakes. The car spun sideways.

Angie and Henri leaped from the car, weapons drawn, but stumbled to a stop. The monster emerging from behind the velvet window coverings was an evil neither of them had counted on.

He was human—with an Uzi. They had expected to fight the forces of darkness, not the living. The shooter never pulled the trigger. He leaped back into the coach. The horseman slapped the reins, the horse neighed, and the ghost coach raced away into the night.

His goal had not been to kill, but to taunt.

To detain.

Their battle tonight was to be spiritual as well as physical. Battles of mind and will as well as flesh and blood. Jane wanted to break them, so they could be taken easily when they reached the House.

"Well, at least you know what you're in for," Henri cast toward James as they raced the SUV toward the nearest airport.

With Henri's arm around her shoulders like an anchor, Angie gazed out the car window, her heart on a rollercoaster. She had discovered she had a psycho vampyre in the family album. One of Drac's nephews, or both, were poised to impregnate her then hit the vampyre circuit. And she was in love with a master vampyre who might die trying to defend her.

And she had no idea what had happened to her mother's diary after it went flying out of her grasp. She leaned her head against Henri's shoulder and wished she was in Connecticut.

27.

Blue-black clouds sagged above the trees in dark bracelets along the road leading to the House of a Hundred Rooms. Not even a surreptitious moonbeam slipped through to create brief semi-light.

Angie could see her aunt's demon smile, and her blood rushed in hard pulses. "She's about to strike again."

A white cloud encased the car. And within the pale core, the forms of winged things—ravens or bats, she wasn't sure.

The cloud mass seeped in around the window weather stripping up through the floorboard, in through the vents. Vapors with a sweet scent.

"Damn her, she's drugging us," Henri said.

The road soon seemed to weave and twist at odd angles, lost in a cloud punctuated with eyes.

Vampyres, far away then suddenly in their view, latched on to the windshield like tree frogs, then let go and floated away into nothingness.

A vampyre slapped against the vapor-drenched window beside Angie, licked his tongue against the glass. Lick. Lick. Lick. Bared his fangs. Clawed at the glass.

"I'm getting really tired of this," she said. Surprising both Henri and James, she rolled down the window—and grabbed the assaulting creature by his hair. Pulling him partially inside, she said through clinched teeth, "You want my blood, do you, punk? Well, do ya?"

She staked him—he screamed and died. She shoved the dissipating skeleton out the window and rolled it back up.

"Pedal to the metal, James."

The car shot through the white cloud like a black ribbon.

A black sky studded with a myriad of crystal stars emerged. The road was tranquil, clear.

"You probably need to know," Henri said to James, "that I'm under sanction."

James shot him a hard look. "Thanks. Yeah. I might need to know that. Now we have to fight a Lammergeier."

Angie turned Henri's face toward her, looking into the blue waters full on. "About that statement, children of the Realm—"

The ghost appeared behind him floating top hat and all outside the rear window. "So what is Henri De LaCroix looking for tonight? Comfort for a guilty conscience? Peace for his wretched soul? Security in heaven because he has found that he has none in hell?"

"I guess he wants an answer, or he'll keep hanging around," Henri said, turning to him. "Hope for forgiveness," he replied simply.

"Ah, then it is hope he seeks." Silence. Then, "Is it a false hope?" Then he leaned in through the glass, his face to Angie's. "You seem to have a dilemma."

"Help us," she implored.

"You are near your destination. Trust the atoner."

"Think he means you?" James tossed back at Henri with a smirk.

The dead gray eyes penetrated James and the ghost's voice changed, becoming feral. "The castle is close, just three miles into the foothills. But the road will be long for you tonight."

The face retreated back through the glass. He floated away.

"I think he must be condemned to wander the netherworld until he pays his dues or something," Angie remarked. Then she studied the crossbow slayer. "He seems to think James is special. Everyone and every *thing* seem to think James is special."

A heavily forested road jutted off to the right. The road to the House.

So why was James slowing down again? "Allez tout droit! Speed up!" she cried.

"The road's blocked," he said, coming to a full stop.

Dead ahead, a nine-foot, half-human, half-demonic figure with the head of a gargoyle sidled back and forth. His skin, slick as oil, was reddish-orange. A cat, contemplating its prey.

"What the hell else is running around out here for Jane?" Henri muttered, climbing from the car. "Let us pass," he ordered.

The beast pulled his tail into his hand, then whipped the sharp edge against Henri's leg. "Don't think so," he said.

Henri's knee buckled and he winced in pain as blood spurted.

"Henri!" Angie cried, running to him.

"Stay back," Henri demanded.

But of course, she didn't. She loved him.

He smiled in spite of his irritation with her.

The tail swished toward Angie in a red streak of nasty temper, but she leaped over it.

"How does it feel to have been the one who caused him to break the vow he made so recently, broken for you?" he threw at Angie. "The vow that was lifting him from hell's grasp? He has lost his heartbeat. Because of you."

A great sob rose up in her throat at his words.

He moved closer to her. "The memory of what he wanted with you is still strong within him. It tears at him, and he burns. As you burn. I will be watching his soul tonight, mystic."

Desperate, hard breaths filled Angie's lungs. Henri was now on the devil's hit list, as well as everybody else's.

The gargoyle body transformed into the semblance of a man, perfect, unblemished, with raven wings that shimmered like black oil in sunlight.

He brushed her softly with his wing tip and held a crystal goblet in front of her. The ruby red liquid glimmered. The glass sparkled in every crystal facet.

"Taste the pleasure and the power as you share my cup," the voice said, horrifying seductive. "I would take care of you, Anjanette. I would be your protector."

Henri knocked the goblet from his hand.

James moved forward with a stake.

"Roland! He wears the ring," a woman's voice shouted from the trees. "Fly!"

Angie leaped to stop his retreat. The cross on her neck swung against him and he lost his wings, becoming no more than a vampyre in a black-collared cape writhing in Henri's grasp. He screamed, an unearthly cry of terror.

James knelt over him. "Goodnight, hot shot." He drove the stake in like a dagger. "Your imitation of the devil was poor, by the way.

You forgot the horns."

Terrified, the vampira swirled away through the trees to the ruins of an abandoned abbey.

"Do we pursue her?" Angie asked as James beheaded the master vampyre then rose to his feet.

"Playing cape and dagger in monks' cells with vampyres is not my idea of a fun night and it would delay us even more," James said. He picked up the vampyre's cloak with the point of the stake. Turning it skyward, he flicked the stake out from under the folds, and the remnant of evil power hurtled upward. Spreading across the moonlit sky like an abandoned sail from a lost ship, it blackened the moon briefly, then vaporized.

"That was the Marquis we just took out," Henri said.

"Well, he's a dead marquis now," James responded. "He seemed a little drunk on his own power. Best he go to hell and learn some humility."

The three warriors hurried back to the car and rocketed toward Jane's vacation home. In dead center, a tower took the house to almost six stories in height. Chimneys dotted the jagged roof, dipping and weaving and rising across the hill to connect the wings.

As they parked at the edge of the woods and climbed out of the car, the trees were thick with wings and eyes.

Henri bristled, ready for war. James raised his crossbow.

And Angie stood stupidly next to them—wondering what to do. Henri had used her holy water. She had used her last stake on the vamp who had clawed the car window. All she had was—

An F-5 power that amazed her, rising in a vortex within her. Pure strength. Her own.

"Hold, Henri De LaCroix," a voice said from the thick foliage.

A master vampyre stepped partially into view. "We will not engage you. We are leaving—by another's command." He paused. "But be forewarned. She has her entourage."

His eyes fell briefly on Angie, glowed with dark desire, then his eyes rested on James and glowed oddly. The red orbs with fire like rubies traveled to his ring. He lowered his head in a brief nod as though acknowledging a prince.

In the next instant, the vampyre was in the air and a black cloud, like a cloud of locusts, rose from the trees to follow him, winging their way to the far mountains.

"What was that all about?" Angie asked, turning to James and staring at his ring.

"Beats me," James shrugged, twisting the band. "Perhaps we fought somewhere in the past."

"What did he mean by another's command?" she asked.

A heavy silence followed her question. Neither Henri nor James apparently wanted to answer her.

28.

"I'm not taking another step until you answer me, Henri De LaCroix," Angie said, planting her shoes solidly in the dirt. "I want to know what Natalia told you."

"So do I," James said. "We have to the right to know what we're getting into here if Dracula is involved."

"Dracula?" Angie blurted. "But he's dead—isn't he?"

"He's died more times than I can count, pardon the pun," Henri answered.

"It was known the Count had two descendent nephews," Henri began resignedly. "Apparently, there is a third. You. After you—procreate with Angie, the Realm is giving you to Jane and taking Angie. The Realm offered Jane protection for her lands in exchange for arranging a joining of the Black Rose with the Count's bloodline. And right now you're the bloodline conveniently located."

Both Angie and James fell silent.

"Sure you don't want to go hide in my hole with me?" Henri smirked toward James.

"Why did she agree to their offer?" Angie asked. "She struck me as being an independent selfish vamp, not the needing kind."

"No one refuses an offer by the Realm," Henri said simply.

His night bird sailed noiselessly onto his shoulder.

Angie stepped back a little, watching it warily. The bird had a thing for eyes.

"Is the crowish princess coming with us?" she asked.

"She may prove—useful," Henri said.

As they slipped into the house through the servants' entrance, the bird flew ahead, disappearing into the recesses of an endless, crooked hallway that wound through the wings crawling all over the hill.

"I don't know which I'm hating the most—the Lady Jane, or this interminable house!" Angie exclaimed, her breathing become rapid in the close, uncertain corridors.

Henri glanced at her worriedly. The collar of her shirt was becoming moist with perspiration. "Do not yield to the fingers of evil playing on your heart's strings right now."

"I'm terrified."

"So am I. I lived with her."

The bird returned and made several soft clacking sounds.

Henri turned to Angie. "Eleanor has found the slayers wandering without direction in the tunnels. They broke free of their captors." He pointed to the far end of the hall. "Through that set of doors. Hurry."

They ran.

But the unseen breath of cold that hit James as he shoved two massive oak doors ajar made him halt abruptly and wince. "God! I hate that ghost!"

They edged into a dingy dining hall. Tarnished silver candelabras huddled on a long table, remnants of the grandeur of a lost past.

"Angie! Above you!" Henri warned, pulling his rapier from its sheath.

The vampyre dropped from a dusty chandelier, fangs bared. Angie stifled her screams and her fear, and moved like lightning. Pulling him from her like a monkey spider, she threw him to the floor, breaking every bone in his body.

Henri's eyebrow arched appreciatively.

"Did you forget something before checking out?" James said, kneeling beside him with a stake.

"Just a taste," the vampyre said, groping with a broken hand toward Angie as he died.

"Stay here, you two," Henri said, meaning every word of it. "I am going to fly with Eleanor and configure a way in, so we don't run into any more guests. Do not leave this room."

It was not a request.

After he had flashed though the door and the room was silent, Angie turned to James. "No offense, but I'm not going to have sex with you."

"None taken," he said with a grin, and placed his hands on her shoulders reassuringly. "Look, Angie, I don't know how this is going to play out, but I promise, I would never hurt you."

"I know," she said in a small, shaky voice.

"Care for a bit of libation, m'lady?" he said in a light tease, picking up an ancient, cobwebby flask as he plopped into a carved, high back chair and rested his foot on the table. "While we wait for the Court's Royal to return?"

"The Court's Royal?" she asked quizzically.

"He hasn't told you?" James said, sitting forward in surprise. "Damn, girl! You might want to know who you're sleeping with."

Henri was returning. Angie ran to him and clasped his hand hard. "Did you find them?"

"There are grated gates in the tunnels, sealed with Jane's power. I will need our combined strength to release the bars." He opened a window with shredded drapes and released his bird. "Fly my winged pet. You are free now."

Henri closed the window quickly and ushered James and Angie into the hall toward a narrow flight of cellar stairs. Once in the stairwell at Henri's silent signal, their flashlights began to glow.

Angie clung to him, her flashlight quaking in her hand. She didn't want to die here. The stone-vaulted recesses of the descending well were chilly and damp with water seeping through the mortar in the walls.

And she didn't want to conceive a child here in this God-forsaken cobweb cave—then be given to the Count afterward. To become a forever-after sex toy.

The mystic glow, he called it, the power that would pleasure him, every part of him.

Henri had left that part out. But she knew. She knew what they had in store for her. She had caught it within Henri's knowledge, as he told them Natalia's dirty little secrets. She had seen the Count's plans for the mythical, mystical Black Rose.

Ain't gonna happen, she swore silently. *I'm not glowing for anybody.*

At the bottom of the narrow steps, James opened a door, slipped through and was swallowed by the dark.

"Don't let go of my hand," Henri told Angie firmly.

She let go. Her hand fell away from his when she dropped her flashlight.

The door behind her slammed shut. Slamming Henri on the other side.

"James? Henri?" she ventured in a small voice into the dark.

No answer.

As she groped in the darkness for the flashlight, she heard a pair of boots running through the shelves, followed by a sound like a bag of cement being dragged across the floor.

Then nothing. Only deafening silence.

Angie felt around on the floor, found the flashlight, shook it, and a tiny amber glow wavered in the globe, briefly, then darkness again. She shook it again, tapped on the glass cover. A bit of yellow light glowed dimly, then out, then on.

When in doubt—hide, she heard smack her thoughts.

Henri. Sending threads.

She crawled into a dank corner and pulled her knees up to her chin and hid, shaking with cold and fear. She did not feel very powerful. She felt—

Alone.

An unexpected vision of herself in the black depths of the earth, sitting like this in rags, her knees drawn up to her chin, waiting for the next "procreation," ripped Angie with terror.

She clenched her fists. She would die before she would yield, she swore silently.

She could hear the plop, plop of water onto the stone flooring and a scratching, scurrying sound within the wall beside her.

Then a hand, electric hot, jerked her flat to the cement while another hand moved swiftly over her mouth to stifle her cry of surprise.

"Shh!" Henri whispered. "Jane's minions have taken James and now they search for you. I couldn't reach you because Nicholas sealed the door. I had to crawl through a crack in the mortar as a mouse!"

She scooted on her belly with him backward into a grated vent in the cellar wall. "Hurry," he said, pulling her in.

Beyond the grating, he retrieved his rapier from a crack where he'd stashed it. Then pulled out a bag of arsenal for her. "Found these on the floor," he said.

The pouch was Brandi's.

Sinewy strength rippled through his shirt in warm slashes against her as he enfolded her tightly. They clung to the tunnel walls, inching along in the dark. "Just in case we don't die," she said, "I'm—"

"In love with me. Yes, I know," he said, kissing her quick, hard, wanting her to live, fiercely wanting her to live. He helped her up a set of ladder-like steps. "These lead upward into an acreage of weeds and thicket Jane affectionately likes to call her estate garden."

"Insane Jane," Angie smirked.

"We have to get to your friends without placing you in peril. We can go through the gardens."

They climbed from the lightless manhole—

Into a circle of shapes of twisted smiles, glowing eyes and rakes of bone with wing.

And all were in those rich, wondrous capes the color of night ...

And none of them were happy with Henri De LaCroix.

"You betrayed us, De LaCroix."

Angie and Henri drew their weapons.

"We need to stop this insidious murdering of innocents," Henri said.

"Mortals have been torturing and murdering and warring with each other for centuries. Without concern for those they kill. The percentage we take is no more than a thimbleful compared to their own bloodletting."

"Except to those who love them."

"Love," a voice within the ranks scoffed.

The familiar voice shocked both Angie and Henri.

The circle of wings parted, and the librarian from the English library stepped forward out of a swirling mist of fog.

"You have brought a mystic into our midst, a mortal mystic. Do you love her, Henri? We are going to take her as our prisoner. For eternity. But you—we're going to kill you. You've committed high treason. Through you she knows our secret places, and you refused to send her into death." She paused. "Of course, that did work out to our advantage."

Angie felt her blood turn to ice in her veins.

The woman pushed a stray strand of gray hair back behind her ear and returned to the mists.

The vampyres advanced.

"You are the darkest beings of this world," Henri said, drawing his sword from its scabbard.

The vampyres converged to subdue him. And take the mystic.

Henri hacked at them, killing as many as he could while Angie fought beside him, agile as she whirled with blades and stakes blazing.

Screams, unearthly wails, pelted the countryside. Followed by yells to take Henri alive, shouts to burn him alive in a sun well. He whirled and turned and leaped and flew—his sword blade flashed with blackened blood that flowed down his arms and onto the ground in rivers of burnished red liquid.

But there were too many ...

Standing back to back, Angie and Henri let their weapons drop. Turning her toward him, Henri held her tightly and sent a single thought spiraling through space and time before the circle of angry capes closed in.

Angie, I—love you.

29.

Chloroform.

Angie recognized the sickly sweet scent.

As her head cleared, she realized she was on the floor, flopped against the edge of a dilapidated bed. A candle in a broken pewter plate clung to life on a wobbly-legged, grime-encrusted table next to it.

The only window in the whole place was a tiny rectangle far above her.

She was in the tower.

She was also laced with bite marks. They had delighted in her while she was unconscious.

"Angie," a voice whispered.

She looked up toward the high window. "Henri?" Her heart spilled with a cascade of happy heartbeats. He was alive!

"Shh."

"How did you escape?" she whispered excitedly.

"A vampyre named Pighead likes me. He arranged my escape. I gave him one of my castles."

"You gave him one of your castles."

One of his castles. Of course.

"I'm going to help you escape," he said. "But not just right now. Her roadies are thick as thieves, and wary. And her power has this room sealed. We will have to wait. Can you play the game?"

"I will try."

He looked through the bars around the room. "I used to live in this room."

He had explored that room towering into the sky in countless forlorn attempts to find escape. Night after night, he would pace back and forth in the room in the impenetrable darkness, and in the echo of his footsteps, he could hear the steps of the shadow that kept pace with him. She had sent a phantom to warn her of any attempts at freedom. Night would deepen into a black abyss, and the phantom would be joined by a chorus of shadows—every morbid creature at her command—to torture and torment him. If a stranger passing by the House of a Hundred Rooms came to investigate the torturous cries that could be heard across the court-yard, he soon ran away in terror.

The black tower became Henri's universe. She sealed him in, waiting for his hunger to become unbearable. Then and only then would she bring the release his condemned soul was driven to seek—a tavern wench or liquor-drenched beggar,or runaway ... He fell farther into her hands, into her dark world, letting her have him while he grew stronger in the strange, unassailable power that accompanied his crimes in the tower and claimed his soul.

Not even Jane had realized how quickly, how massively his power was growing, fueled by the fire she herself had created—hatred.

Henri had discovered he could simply become a vapor that could slip under the tower door, or that he could push the door from its hinges if he chose—or become as tiny as a starling and leave the iron bars of the window behind.

He chose to fly ...

"She's coming," he warned, and his face disappeared from the window.

A floor-length, blood-red hooded cape lined in black satin floated in through the door and to the bed.

"A mystic slayer in love with a Royal. Intriguing," the cape said, without expression.

The hood fell away from the face.

In spite of her attempts to remain hardened, Angie was awe-struck by the oval, angelic, ivory face framed in waves and waves of raven tresses that showered down her back. Her ancestral aunt's violet eyes seemed to shine from a light of their own and her lips, parted in a slight pout, were a perfect rosebud—sensuous—the color deep as though her blood or whatever blood she happened to be using at the moment ran perpetually hot.

The reckless, flawless beauty of a Gothic heroine.

Only she was not the heroine.

She was the villain.

"Auntie Jane, I presume?" Angie said thinly. "Did you kill my mother?"

The violet eyes rested on her neck, on Henri's bruising punctures. "No wonder the Realm and the Master Slayer are up in arms! A joining no one wants." She laughed, lightly. "You are giving them rabid fits, my dear!"

"Where are the Shadows?" Angie demanded tearfully.

The words that followed rolled from the vampira's rosebud lips like honey. "Do you not wish to know where Henri is? He did not fly very far after he left your window, Rapunzel."

Angie felt her heart smash into her throat. "What have you done with him?" she cried.

The heavy tower door groaned on its iron hinges and opened, and James was tossed into the room by four vampyres, tall, with sunken eyes as though emaciated, bluish-gray in their pallor.

James' hair was matted, his clothes torn, his body tatted with lacerations and bruises—but no punctures. Apparently Jane had commanded he be left pure.

As he spotted Angie, fairly littered with puncture holes, James' eyes flickered, but only briefly.

Jane's smile became a tight purple line at being denied the pleasure of seeing human distress even crease his cheeks.

He pulled himself from the floor.

"If you take one step toward me, to kill me, James," she warned, taking an instinctive step back, "Nicholas will kiss her, then kill her. Behave yourself and she will live."

Nicholas slipped into the room and took hold of his arm.

"If she kills the Count's mystic, there will be nowhere on God's green earth she can hide. Does she realize that?" James said in a lowered voice.

"I'm sure she knows that," he said.

"Will she keep her word?"

"You have no choice at the moment, but to believe she will."

"I want your bloodline, James. But you must first take—her," Jane said, her voice filled with disgust for the mystic. "Afterward, I want a master slayer of slayers. Andre and his troupe are running around in the tunnels like lost rabbits. It should be easy for you."

"You're so damned crazy."

She flew at him angrily and slapped him full on the face. Then bared her fangs.

A thrust of heart stopping terror rose up in Angie's throat. "No!" she screamed, grabbing the bed post to help her get up.

"Hold her!" Jane ordered her minions sharply. "Or I will have you for breakfast!"

The vampyres moved like lightning and squeezed Angie's arms into their bone-thin, icy hands.

Angie cried out in pain. *Henri, where are you? Where is your strength?*

Jane's eyes blackened. "Sedate her! She's trying to call up his power."

They slapped a rag soaked with chloroform across her face. Just enough.

Jane drew her fingertips coyly across the slayer's shirt front. "And would you not want me to share your bloodline at least a little with me before you bed with her? You're so strong, James, so virile."

Angie shook with sobs while the creature with flaming, hungry eyes let her fangs drop.

Jane scraped her lips and fangs against the nape of James' neck, closing her eyes as she felt the pulse, strong and even, but fast.

"You're afraid," she whispered.

"Terror's a better word," he said unflinchingly.

"But you are intrigued by your terror, studying it," she said gaily, bringing her face to his. "You are enjoying the way your heart is racing."

"Do it," he said, pulling her into his arms roughly.

She laughed. "When I first lighted in this city, it was to find and sell that horrid niece. But this, this is an added gift."

She drew his eyes into hers.

He surrendered. She weaved back and forth softly in front of him, watching as his eyes followed the violet command to yield his will. "You're enjoying this!" She pushed him away. "We will join when you're finished with the mystic."

Within moments, the foul group was gone and a heavy lock could be heard sliding into place.

Angie stood in the middle of the room, angry tears of betrayal streaming from her eyes. "What happens now, James? Sex and the new race? Then fun and blood games with Jane?"

He sighed. "I played the game to buy us time, Angie. I'm a Shadow, a stealth fighter, remember?" He began feeling the walls, the door, the handle, looking for a way out. "Any ideas on De LaCroix's whereabouts? We need him. Can you thread?"

The streams to Henri were vacant. "Nothing," she said in agony, hope against hope. "Why would there be nothing?"

"It doesn't mean he's dead," James assured her. "It just means Nicholas and Jane and the lamb hawk have sealed the house." He placed his hands on her shoulders. "This isn't easy for either of us. We're both trying to recover from the shock of our pasts without any time to absorb the shock, and now we've ended up here and we don't even know if either of the beings we love are still alive. But we have to assume they are."

He looked into her eyes, and his gaze was one of resignation. "We don't have a choice in this, Angie."

"James, I can't," she began.

He placed her fingertips over her lips. "It's the only way to get us the hell out of this room. We can't fight the enemy from in here."

She could feel him hard and ready. She felt her legs go weak, her heart's promise of forever love to Henri being torn from her, sacrificed.

"I'm gentle, Angie. I promise," James murmured.

"It's not that. It's giving them the child they want," she said, putting her hand against his chest. "Would you want your child raised for breeding if she's a girl, or become a vampyre if it's a boy? They want to create a race. A race of powerful beings. To dominate us. To make humans their serviles. And I would be their Eve, to begin the creation of their weapon of mass destruction."

"Then our friends will die, and so will we," he sighed.

"The lives of the few to save the future lives of many."

"I have two brothers or cousins or whatever they are still out there, Angie. And what's to stop the Realm from finding another mystic royal? It has to end here, now. Alive, we have a chance to end it. Dead, no one will even know their plot and we will have died senselessly. We will have saved no one."

His arguments held substance she could not deny.

They waited. An hour later, the lock on the outside of the door released.

The Lady Jane floated into the room. James uttered a cry of pain as she sank her fangs into the nape of his neck—and drank deeply.

She jerked back, retching, spitting out his tainted blood all over her impeccable white satin gown.

Andre had sworn the vampyre who fought him and won would regret it. He ingested the concoction religiously that he said would taste like poison to the vampyre stupid enough to bite him. And James drank with him every night.

Enraged, the scorned, hungry creature turned on her victm in fury, lifting her hands in a fierce gesture as if to rip him to shreds.

Then her hands dropped. "I will take you when you're cleansed," she said.

Angie felt talons of sorrow grip her heart.

James Lauren. The quiet, strong, mystery slayer who had an undercurrent that ran silent, yet oh so deep—the Count's bloodline.

If he became a vampyre ...

Where is Henri? Angie thought helplessly.

Nicholas, in a cape of royal blue, glided back into the room, toward her, his hand outstretched.

Angie sank against the bed post, shrinking from him. A single tear rolled down her cheek. "You played me."

"Don't be too hard on yourself, Angie," he said with his vain, beautiful smile. "I'm just very good at what I do."

"You're a common criminal," she breathed.

He frowned, disliking the human reference.

"You're evil. You're murderous!" Angie cried. "You're a murderous fiend!"

The smile returned. "Now that's a compliment I will accept."

Why the hell didn't you take off with Henri while you had the chance? he threaded toward her.

Roughly, he pulled Angie away from the post, and holding her wrist hard, pulled her to the door

"Let go of me, you dirty, damn dirty—" Angie cried, writhing against the iron grip.

Help us, Nicholas!

I—can't.

Nicholas began pulling Angie out the door and down the tower steps.

"You can still make a decision for good, Nicholas. There is good in you. Don't do this," Angie cried, as she grasped futilely at the wall with her free hand.

Her hand slid along the stones, her fingernails biting painfully into grainy ridges as he drug her behind him.

"Do you not see how beautiful your aunt is?" he said. "A man in his wildest dreams could not hope for so much. That she would be obsessed—with me."

"She uses you. As a tool for her own brand of perdition," Angie refuted, but she could find no further words for her grief and fury, or the strength to fight the creature holding her in a vice grip. The drug continued to dilute her mystic strength. She hung limply, like a rag doll.

30.

Night was a small, round hole. At the top of a circular well that widened in circumference toward the bottom.

Angie slid to the iron floor.

The young woman staring back at her from the polished black stones of the cylindrical wall across from her was wearing a mocha colored satin camisole and short black skirt—in shreds. Gingerly, she pulled a bit of ragged strap back onto her shoulder, and pressed a stray golden tendril back into place.

A slight rustling in the dark.

"Henri!"

She flew to his arms.

He drew her close, kissing her face, her hair, her cheeks, her lips, kissing her and kissing her. "I am sorry, chéri. It seems I was detained in my efforts to rescue you. It would seem I am also not very good at saving you, I suppose."

She smiled. "Well, it seems at least you tried, or you wouldn't be in here."

They sat together on the floor, leaning back against the well wall, and gazing up at the tiny, circular universe of stars above them.

"Your beauty surpasses your aunt's, you know," he said.

"And you are a handsome devil who flatters." She laughed lightly. Then she leaned into him, resting her head on his chest. "You really do love me, Henri?"

"Yes. But I am also not very good at atoning, it would seem."

"You're a master. It would take some time. I would have to be patient."

A deep laugh escaped his lips. "Patient? Liora Anjanette, patient?"

The stars began to fade. The circle above them became silvery gray.

But not with moonlight.

Angie tensed. Dawn was breaking.

An arc of pale light began to appear on the floor. Layers of salt became dimly visible. Other unfortunates who had passed this way.

Morning began to light the black glass of the wall, mirrors to reflect the sun. The semi-circle of pale light on the floor began to widen infinitesimally toward them.

As the crescent grew, Henri moved in front of her, and spread his cape.

"Why are you wearing a cape?" she asked, having never seen him in one before.

"The Realm did not give me a choice. It was to be my death cape," he answered. Then he smiled. "But today, it will protect me."

"How?"

There was no protection in this hole!

The back of Henri's cape began to smoke.

"No!" Angie cried, closing her eyes tightly, clinging to him. She refused to look into the mirrors, refused to watch the fire.

"We will be fine, Angie," he whispered.

Oddly, she felt no heat. She opened her eyes.

The well was becoming darker again. The sunlight on the floor was returning to a thin crescent.

"The eclipse!" she breathed. "Henri! How long does an eclipse last?"

"Long enough to fly," he whispered. "You did not really think I was going to let them burn me, did you?"

"You are so arrogant," Angie cried, slinging a kiss onto his lips.

"They do not know I am a shape-shifter," he said. "But I had to wait until they brought you from the tower. I couldn't enter and rescue you because Jane's strength holds the house. So I simply let them capture me."

She watched, fascinated, as he shadowed and his form began to change. "I can't open the door from within the well. I will need you to join your power to mine to release it from her power on the other side. We must be quick. The sunrise returns in seven minutes."

The tiny starling that emerged from his shadowing flew to the round hole. And out into the false night.

Angie pressed her ear to the door, but quickly became frantic. "I cannot sense his presence now. Something is blocking me." What was blocking the threads?

"Nicholas." Hatred smothered her voice. "He is within the halls, and not yet in daysleep because of the eclipse."

She closed her eyes. *Build the wall, brick by brick by brick. Brick on brick, build it tall, build it strong.*

Henri, I love you! Hold on! she cried as she struggled to break the vanguard's hold.

"Thirty-nine seconds, Henri, and it returns to full sun," she murmured, looking worriedly at her watch.

Use the power, Angie. Henri's words spiraled through her. *Use the strength I gave you and break the seal. Together, we are the more powerful.*

"Use it, Angie!" she heard through the door. "Use it now!"

She pressed her hands against the door. And pulled the iron handle, strength pouring from her in rivulets.

The door heaved.

She leaped from the room to stairwell windows throwing shafts of sunrays, and a cape pouring with smoke.

Uttering a multitude of French words of disgust, Henri tore the cloak from his shoulders and threw it to the floor.

He handed her a flashlight and they raced into the snaking cellar tunnels in hopes the Shadows were still alive.

In the flashlight beams, their silhouettes on the walls seemed to form a phantom vampyre and his lover rushing, flying, to battle their destiny.

Oppression, thick and heavy, soon weighted the stale air. They were intruders in a chamber where mortals never went.

Except to die.

Lost mortals could wander in these dark depths for days and never find a way out, finally succumbing to the natural terror that accompanies endless dark and fatigue.

Something crackled under Angie's foot, like a dry twig breaking. She flashed her light across the floor. As the light illumined the dark beside her feet, a simultaneous exclamation of shock and horror escaped her lips. The surface of the floor was strewn, littered, with bones and bits of bone. Some were brittle-brown and ancient, others were white and small. And all of them were human.

They moved on, Angie wincing as they crunched their way forward into uncertain darkness. The low arched tunnel ceiling created a ghostly echo as the wind whistled through the cellar passageways.

"Use your mystic senses, Angie," Henri said. "Can you sense them?"

A short distance farther on, she stopped at a door cut into the tunnel wall.

Henri pushed the door open.

The room was empty except for a few rats. She sighed forlornly, tears glistening her eyes.

"I am sorry, chéri," Henri said. "I should not have brought you into this world. Your life was simple, innocent."

"I would be simple, innocent and dead if you hadn't been there," she reminded him. "We'll find them. I just have to focus."

A bit of pebbly dirt fell from somewhere above them.

"A vampyre has not yet retreated to the secret places within the castle and is still awake," Henri said. He sniffed the air. "Natalia, get your butt down here!"

A pair of high heels sailed downward, touched the ground noiselessly.

"I thought I saw you here at the House of Horrors, hanging around on the tower ceiling," Angie said. "Did you enjoy all the fun?"

"I was actually hoping you would kill her," she said curtly.

"We could have used some help," Angie returned irritably. The peppery little Russian vamp was the last creature she wanted to see right now.

"She would have killed me. You don't know her."

"I don't want to know her."

The bloodsucker in spandex moved closer. "I know where the slayers are and where Jane has taken off with your crossbow slayer."

Angie leaped like lightning and grabbed the vampyre by the throat. "Where?"

"That's not the best way to get on my good side," Natalia choked. Natalia's eyes flew to Henri, but he stood back and did not interfere with the mystic slayer.

Angie released her but watched her carefully. "What do you want, Natalia?"

"I know the envoys will sweep the entire countryside now."

"And?"

"I want your word I will be passed by."

Angie stared at her incredulously. Allow a vampyre who enjoyed her bloodlust the way this one did to live? Incredulous that she could even consider the bargain.

But consider it she did. "You can hide in the recesses of that wooden tower. They will not return there. And when you come out, don't touch anyone, ever, who treasures life—or I will hunt you down and kill you. Do you understand?"

"You're adding strings ..." she pouted.

"That's her deal," Henri said with a tone of finality. "Take it or leave it. And don't lie to her."

"All right, I agree," she said sulkily. "The Lady Jane once lived under this thing she calls a house. In case there was an atomic war. You know. The sixties Cold War thing. And that's where they will hide—until they can come back and try again to abduct you." She glanced at Henri. "And kill Henri." Natalia moved close to Angie and in a conspiratorial whisper said, "You want to live, to drink from his cup, don't you?"

"Where are the Shadows?" Angie demanded, ignoring her remark.

Natalia's mouth turned down. She didn't want to save the life of a slayer any more than Angie wanted to save a useless half-life.

"The wall is an illusion. Study the panels with your mystic vision."

"Why are you so willing to tell us this?" Angie asked, still suspicious of the cagey vampira.

"We don't like her either," Natalia said, moistening her lips.

Angie blocked the fire in her brain from the vampyre about to attempt to mesmerize her as two white fangs appeared.

Henri took hold of the vampyre's hair and jerked her head backward. "Put them back in your head, Natalia."

She gasped in pain as she felt the Royal's touch burn into her.

"You aren't much fun anymore, De LaCroix."

Natalia promised to hold her hunger in check if Henri would

let go.

He released her.

Briefly, as she sealed the bargain, an odd little thought crossed Angie's mind. How many vampy friends was Natalia probably going to try to cram into that little tower room? Had she just struck a bargain that might be protecting not one, but a whole bevy?

"If he takes you, your veins will bleed for him," Natalia said. "And he will have you every twilight to use as he likes. He will toy with your mortality, your desires and needs, to win you. Then if you do not join him, he will break and crush you. He will deepen your sense of hopelessness and despondency and crush your spirit."

"James is not a vampyre yet," Angie said.

"I was not referring to James, dumb cluck. Dracula wants you."

"We've made our bargain. Get out of my sight," Angie said, trembling.

The vamp flashed out of the room and was gone.

The deceptive wall revealed the obscured tunnel, and Henri and Angie soon found the Shadows.

The walls bore the scars of battle. Kathryn, with only the one wing still hanging, causing her to walk somewhat like Quasi Moto, was nevertheless healing, the multitude of lacerations had become thin lines on her skin.

Andre leaned on Mack's shoulder, weak but walking.

"We need to get you to a doctor," Angie said.

"No, we need to hurry," Andre said quickly. "If we are to save James."

"Jane is not known to be patient. He may be dead to this life already," Henri said. "And deadly."

31.

"If I'm right, we are not far from the Great Room where she sleeps," Henri said, as the group ascended a ramp back into the house. "There may be a secret passageway from that room to the underground city."

"If you're right?" Angie blurted.

"I have not been in this house in a few centuries," Henri explained, glancing around. "It seems she's been refurbishing."

"You call this refurbishing?" Angie said, staring as they traveled a labyrinth of crooked hallways, leaning staircases and lopsided doors that opened not into rooms but sheer falls to the Lady's gardens. "This house is a trash pile."

"Looks like she's added some new piles," Henri said. "I'm not familiar with these wings, but—"

"I think this is the room," Henri said, halting at a door.

"And behind door number one is a stonework room with candles and columns, and a stone slab ornate with reliefs of Roman gods and goddesses. A mausoleum," Angie said as they entered. "What's behind door two and three, or should I ask?"

While Andre studied the room, Henri sat on the elaborate coffin slab, and Angie slipped next to him. "I was afraid I was never going to see you again."

"We are together in this moment," he said, brushing his fingertips against her cheek softly. Then he kissed her, a warm, slow moving, I'm-damned-glad-you're-alive kiss that set her heart on fire.

"I'd tell you to get a room. But it looks like you're already in one," Mack addressed Henri, interrupting them. "Think you could take a break, Cuddles, and help us look for vamp holes?"

One corner of the room receded into an alcove with a seat of stone tiles that had the semblance of being a window seat—without the window.

Angie's eyes circled the seat. "One of the stone slabs moves in my vision, Henri, outward toward me." This was a new facet of mysticism she had not experienced. Fascinated, she rose and touched the tile in panoramic 3-D vision. "This is filled with the Lady Jane's touch, her essence. And it's loose."

Henri heaved the stone to the side. The seat was hollow. An escape well. "The steps are steep but not treacherous. And they seem to lead downward, perhaps to the secret city."

"Hurry," he instructed the Shadows. "Time is not on your side. A storm is in the making, and the clouds will hide the sun. They will feel no need to sleep."

The tunnel at the bottom of the narrow well of steps continued for only a short distance before unfortunately slanting upward.

It ended in the outer gardens in a labyrinth of high hedges.

"Well. That didn't work," Angie clipped.

"We need to pyramid," Andre said. "To look over the grounds from the top of the maze so we're not detected, to see if there is anything that looks like an opening that would lead underground. Angie is the smallest and lightest. We will hoist her to the top on our shoulders."

"I have a simpler idea. I can take a look from ..." Henri began, but he could see edges of distrust still sharp in the master slayer's eyes.

"All right, the mystic then," Henri said. Easing behind Angie, he put his arms around her waist, pulled her against him, and rose straight up through the air with her.

"Whoa!" she exclaimed as she watched her feet suddenly dangling.

"I don't suppose we could just hang a right at the second star, and on 'til morning?" he said into her cheek, wrapping her securely in his arms.

When they reached the top of the hedges, away from Andre's watchful eyes, Henri hovered and pulled Angie closer.

"Did the crossbow slayer—have you, Angie?" he asked into her ear.

"Never," she said in a small voice.

Lightning began to flicker through the seams in the thick, angry clouds that had gathered, lighting up one hundred, fifty rooms and a hillside.

"Oh God, Henri!" Angie gasped suddenly, folding her arms over his tightly as a garden walkway stone lifted and flipped to the side.

Two vampyres rose out of the ground.

One of them held a small bucket.

And one of them was very angry.

•

"You have brought a slayer into this house! Our house!" Nicholas accused angrily. "A new prize to add to your collection." His eyes were pits of fire. "His blood has the stench of rotting road kill."

"He's royalty. In a few weeks, he will be pure again," Jane countered, hugging her bucket.

"You need to take off that dress. It smells like hog slop."

The seed pearls forming leaves on the bodice were laced with red.

Setting down the bucket, she smoothed the folds of her bloodspattered white dress.

And yanked James by the hair of his head from the hole and onto the ground.

He was covered in leeches.

Dropping to her knees, she let her blood scented hair fall across his face while she drew her mouth softly along his jawline. "Can you not see, Nicholas? Can you not see the resemblance? Do you not see his bloodline? Did you not see his ring on his finger? James is—magnificent!"

Though weak, James kissed her, hard, to incite the vanguard, then pushed her brusquely away.

"So that's why you want him. To replace me—with him," Nicholas said. "Because of who he is."

She returned to the vanguard, caressing his face. "Not to replace you, Nicholas. I would never replace you."

He jerked her hand away, holding her wrist in a hard grip. "I have been with you for hundreds of years. Do you think I do not know when you are lying? I should kill you where you stand."

"Why don't you, then?" James challenged, raspy.

Jane smiled at him. "The venom is seeping, in spite of that nasty potion."

Nicholas ripped the bodice of her dress to her waist and threw her against him. "Now you can both stink."

Reaching up, she grasped the vanguard's legs, cast her violet eyes into his, then ripped his pants with her long fingernails, leaving deep scratches on his thighs through the cloth.

"Prove you are mine," he said, sliding against her. "Right here, right now."

Easing from his grasp, she picked up the small bucket. "I have to purify him. We can bed later."

She pulled a leech out of the bucket and slapped it on his neck, barely able to contain her want as she watched the leech grow bulbous with blood. She was bleeding him to pull out the poison blood, bleeding him out slowly until fresh blood poured through his veins.

She licked her lips.

Then whirled and bit Nicholas. He pulled away. "I will not slash my wrists for him. So don't ask."

"Jealousy does not become you, Nicholas."

"As far as I'm concerned, Dracula's bloodline is sputum."

"Bring him into my chambers. I want to be with him. I command you!"

"You have never commanded me. I did your bidding because it was my choice. You do not have my will. You never did."

The wind began to shake the trees, sending leaves and sticks somersaulting across the courtyard.

"I won't tolerate having to live in the same house with another one of your pets," Nicholas yelled across the wind.

"He's not a pet. He is nobility!" she screamed at him through the gusts.

Their capes began to blow around them like sails in a phantom storm.

"You envy him," she accused. "You envy what he is, what you can never be, and you covet the ring he wears!"

"Don't you think I know your game plan? You, the great Lady Jane Weston, would be the royal aunt of the royal niece who would breed the new hierarchy, and as founder of this fine bloodline, would sit beside the Count himself and rule the Realm with his nephew as your lover."

Henri crushed Angie to him protectively as he felt her tremble at their words.

Lightning danced in the courtyard, joining the wild wind.

"I want him, Nicholas! I want his youth. His noble blood," Jane screeched.

Angie's brow wrinkled in puzzlement as the powerful vampyre vanguard's aura paled oddly.

Then she understood.

Jane wanted power, position, to rule the Realm and later the world. Nicholas just wanted to retain his position and have a golden house or two—with Jane. The Realm be damned.

Nicholas suddenly became the most fearsome being Angie had ever seen, even in Henri's thoughts within her. His cape swelled in the gusts of stormy wind, vile wrinkles contorted his face, and his eyes were volcanoes. Even the Lady Jane seemed startled by the power surfacing against her.

"And you believe he will swear himself to you, the Realm's bastard," Nicholas chided through the wild wind.

Jane's hand swept out from beneath her own cape, and her fingers stretched taut and rigid as she glared at him. "I am your master ..."

"You are Henri's. Not mine."

She softened her gaze. "You desire me, Nicholas. We traveled the highways of the old world together, you and I, and Henri. Do you still not—want me, Nicholas?"

"I want to throw you to the dogs. My Lady," he mocked.

She stepped back, furious at the mockery in his voice.

"You would like to claw my face," he said as she bared her fangs and began to hiss at him. "And scratch out my eyes perhaps? Torture will not endear me to you, Janey. It never did."

His hand caught hers by the wrist as she swept it toward his cheek. Bending her wrist backward, he forced her to bend with it. "Save your claws for your new playmate. I no longer want to play."

Lightning struck the tree beside them, splitting the trunk in half. She retrieved her arm and hurled him against the split tree, then against a fountain where Pan poured blood into a pool filled with wind-driven waves.

Angie lost her breath and almost collapsed in Henri's grasp.

Jane fled from the vanguard across the courtyard and toward the house.

He tore after her, sweeping into the foyer entrance like a black raven as she screamed she would kill him with every phantom at her command.

A jagged flash of lightning lit up the night, and Angie could see them through the windows, running up the stairs, through the corridors and rooms. Jane's hair flew wildly, and she kept looking back at him as though in terror. He caught up to her in one of the rooms and for a moment it appeared they were locked in embrace ...

A pulse-stopping, jarring scream pierced the night and curdled through the labyrinth.

32.

"I don't think we're going to have to worry about staking the Lady Jane Weston," Angie said with a forced breath as Henri descended to the ground with her. "I think Nicholas just did."

Stakes drawn, the slayers and Henri made their way through the hedge walls into the courtyard, yet James was nowhere in sight. They hurried into the house and up the stairs.

As the troupe neared the top of the staircase that should have led to a landing and the bedroom Angie had seen from the hedges, they realized the house itself was a maze. The last step ended—at the ceiling.

"The contractor's blueprints erred on the side of stupidity," Angie quipped.

Before Henri could stop her, Angie ascended the stairs to get closer to the ceiling. "Perhaps there's a secret opening."

Something stirred in the darkness in the small space between the last step and the ceiling planks. A rat?

The bat flew at her, hitting her head and knocking her backward.

But her blade was quick, backed by Henri's power, taking its head before it could bite her. The bat became gray dust.

"I am so tired of all this," she cried.

"Remind me to be careful around you when you're tired," Henri said, arching his eyebrow.

"We must hurry," Andre said. "In his weakened state, James is fair game for Nicholas."

But the maniac mansion became filled with twists and turns and doors that went nowhere, and steps that went everywhere, and halls that ended—just ended.

They chose another staircase.

"There is a sheer drop between the stairwell and the wall," Henri said, "of about twelve inches in width, enough to trap a man bodily if he were to slip between them—or enough to allow a vampyre to diminish and slide. So be careful."

"I'll never keep up with all of you," Angie said, aware her small legs needed several more inches on them to keep up with the taller, fast-paced Shadows and Henri.

"Well, I'm not going to carry you," Kathryn said. "And neither is Henri. You're a mystic slayer. You can probably outrun all of us. Look within you. And stop pretending you don't know your own strength. It is not all Henri's."

The witch is back, Angie thought happily. Kathryn was almost completely recovered from the attack against her.

Angie ran with them through the Fun House halls barely five feet high and two feet across, and halls with walls so high they seemed to rise into a wooden sky. Crooked doors, slanted walls and a ceiling that shrank inward had them at their wits' end.

Then one hallway became rigidly sane, ending in one door, one room.

The lady's budoir.

"This is the room," Angie said, opening the door.

A bed almost eight feet long filled one entire wall. The head extended to the ceiling with carved columns at the front corners that supported a tester. Carved, it was inlaid with gold.

A writing table with ivory stationery and a quill sat under a window draped in heavy scarlet.

"Why would she sleep on a slab when she had this?" Angie asked.

"A vampira's bed is not for sleeping," Henri answered quietly.

A sharp piece of splintered bed post covered with blood lay on the carpet by the window—and a pile of dust under a blood-red cape.

"Nicholas is here, somewhere, DuPre. We just can't see him," Henri said warningly. Slipping into an obscure corner, he shape-shifted into a starling to check the rafters.

Picking up the cape with the tip of his stake, Andre opened the window and flipped the cape into the air, sending it sailing, a red-black shimmer dissipating against a slip of moon rising above breaking clouds. "The cape is hers." He looked back at the floor, frowning at the pale pile of ashy dust. "That is not."

Glancing through the window out over the courtyard at the red and pale blue strips tingeing the dawn, he shook his head. "He is the king of deception. And she his queen. He would do anything for her. But he would not kill her."

"He would die for her," Angie said, her eyes glazing over. She started walking toward a closet door as though in a trance.

Angie threw open the closet door, then leaped away. Nicholas was in the closet hanging from the ceiling in the dark. He dropped, and stepped out, bristled, ready for war.

He glared at the Shadow slayers, then looked at the tall, high windows.

The drapes fell away. The panes began shaking, the glass breaking, shattering, flying, falling toward them in a cascade of death.

In an instant, Angie whirled and a halo of energy shimmering with light as though the very sun itself had taken refuge in the arc around her, surrounded her. She spun, the jagged pieces caught in the iridescence were crushed, floating to the floor in a harmless waterfall of bits of light and crystal.

"A mystic royal," the vanguard murmured, not exceptionally startled. "A mystic royal slayer with the power of a Royal vampyre. I thought I had seen it all."

His eyes darted toward the door and windows as if seeking an avenue of escape. But the only door was beyond her arc, and only one small window, high, almost to the ceiling seemed to offer a way out.

A small starling had lighted on the ledge and was peering down at him.

The slayers advanced, spurred to avenge their fallen comrade. Nicholas flew to flash beyond them, to reach the tiny window.

Henri materialized on the ledge. "I think not, Nicholas." Nicholas returned to the floor. Henri floated down to confront the vanguard. "Should I use theatrics, Nicholai?"

Nicholas reared up to slash him with his raven wings.

The Shadows stepped back, Kathryn grabbing Angie as she tried to rush forward and join them. "He would be distracted trying to protect you," she said sharply.

The two powerful vampyres circled each other slowly, hissing.

Henri flashed and threw the Russian vampyre against the wall.

Nicholas spread his wings to fly at the atoning French vampyre. Then he fell, a bolt protruding from his back through his chest, through his heart. Blood poured out from under the wood bolt and across the floor in rivers.

James was in the doorway leaning on the frame, his crossbow in his hand.

Henri nodded acknowledgement toward James. "Well-planned. He was deceived in his own devices."

"Wasn't my bolt," James said. "I just got here. I've been roaming these crazy halls for hours. Jane drugged me with those damned leeches. Thinking she would come back for me later, I guess."

The Shadows began seeking every possible point of attack, puzzled.

Weakly, with his last drops of existence, Nicholas reached up toward Angie. "But is she not beautiful, Anjanette, your ancestral aunt?"

"Where is she, Nicholas?" Angie demanded.

With waning strength, he slid his hand into an inner pocket of his cape. "You may want this," he said, handing her a small dirt-smudged book.

Allison Weston's diary.

"Read it, Anjanette. You will find it rather interesting."

A strange gasp escaped the vanguard's lips. His eyes widened and he didn't move again.

Angie tucked her mother's diary in her pouch and left the lifeless vampyre on the floor.

Henri pulled Angie gently out into the hallway. "In life, I was a distant cousin of the royal family, and therefore part of the court. A Royal. In the Realm, I retained my royalty by birth and power, a Realm elite." He paused. "And now, a Realm outlaw. The Lammergeier is after us. Jane is after us. We do not know who threw that bolt. We do not know who will come looking for a Realm reward for us." He looked into her eyes. "Do you want to go, or do you want to stay?"

"We would always be looking back over our shoulders if we go," she said.

Angie walked to the hallway window. Below her, from the courtyard, the gray ghost tipped his hat and smiled his ghostly smile at her.

A crossbow's prod appeared between two branches of a deodar cedar. Angie's hand moved to her pouch like lightning. Henri was behind her speaking with Andre and James, vulnerable, his back to the window.

Imperceptibly, the room was suddenly enveloped in a strange, black shadow. An almost indecipherable whizzing sound followed. A horrible hush crawled across the walls, then the room cleared. The Shadows' gazes flew from one to the other frantically to see who had been hit.

The ghost stood, leaning against a wall, legs crossed casually, his hand on the bolt jutting from his heart.

"But for you tonight is not yet forever, Henri De LaCroix. You are in atonement."

He dissipated. The bolt dropped to the floor.

Angie turned back to the window, rods of fire in her soul.

With her mystic senses she caught a glimpse, a blur of brown, through the deodar branches. The thin birdlike thing was about eight feet tall, bone and wing and not much else. Except evil and a pair of blood red eyes.

"Henri! What is that horrid thing?"

He jerked her away from the window. "The Lammergeier. The lamb hawk. And you are the lamb. There is only one way to end this. We must take him down, my love."

He nodded toward James who slipped out of the room. The rest of the Shadows hurried to the gardens to search for the assassin or assassins.

Henri led Angie into a clearing in the courtyard. *Pretend you are looking through the nearby trees*, he threaded.

The English librarian in camouflage and hunting boots stepped out from the cedars, crossbow string drawn taut as though not believing her good fortune that they were open targets.

"Meddlesome ghost," she muttered in disgust, glinting through her glasses. In the next instant a bolt flew toward Henri.

Catching the librarian's bolt through a flash, he tucked it into the dirt behind his back and fell as though dead.

The human librarian's smile twisted around her dentures. "Well! I thought I missed!"

She started to laugh and send a second bolt into Henri's heart, just to be sure, but her eyes glazed oddly and she looked down at the shaft tip protruding from her own chest.

She turned to look behind her.

James lowered his crossbow.

She fell face first into the dirt.

I don't like him, but I'm damned glad he's a marksman, Henri threaded to Angie.

A slight rustle. In the cedars. The blur of brown darting back and forth between the low-hanging branches. Coming closer.

It's hauling ass through the trees toward us! Angie threaded.

It entered the courtyard to begin the kill, the red eyes pinpointing every slayer. Then it would take her. She could sense his purpose.

The hawk glanced at Angie in curiosity, wonderingly, then the red orbs moved to Brandi as she emerged from the brush. "The Nebraska slayer child," he murmured, licking his thin blue lips.

He dodged the holy water Angie slung from the window in his direction as she popped the top of a new vial.

But a few stray drops found his arm.

The bony appendage shriveled to the elbow and he fled. But not before he sent a bone-cold thread, *I will return for you,* hurtling toward Angie.

Henri swept past James after the hawk, and commanded fervently, "If I do not return, you must protect her with your life or the world as you know it dies."

A pair of long, thin-boned legs leaped the courtyard wall into a python pit, one of the Lady Jane's refurbishments.

Henri leaped in after it.

Silence followed. A stillness without even a puff of dust.

The Shadows searched the pit. There was no sign of the Lammergeier.

But the pythons seemed happy.

Unfortunately, there was also no sign of Henri.

Andre declared him dead.

Epilogue

For almost an hour Henri stood before the window in the forest hilltop cabin gazing down through the trees at the distant city. A light mist glistened on the treetops and rooftops, and car lamps sparkled in the dark on the faraway streets.

He was shirtless and barefoot, wearing only his Italian pants.

Angie sat on the sofa wearing only a sweater with the emerald necklace he had given her for her birthday, her only other adornment.

She tied her birthday cards together with a red ribbon.

Opening a little wooden chest with a lock and key, she placed them inside and put the chest on the coffee table.

"It was a great party."

"I liked the after party," he said, his eyes traveling to the luscious thighs below the sweater's hem.

"I read my mother's diary," she said unexpectedly, looking up at him. "When the train derailed, the slayer lunged at Nicholas and missed, hitting the school teacher. Nicholas exchanged the teacher's handbag and belongings for my mother's, then told her to get the hell off the train and make a run for it. She hightailed it out of the train car. He made up the story about the spike, and the world thought Allison Weston was dead. The entries after that are of days in the park with me, how she had so much fun with me on picnics, swinging me in the swings, things like that. And dinner dates and things with a man she absolutely adored. A man she married. The entries stop on January 6, 1991, the day my grandmother told me she and my father died in a car wreck. So in a way, both my grandmother and Nicholas told the truth." She paused thoughtfully. "Why did he help my mother, do you think?"

"He was a vanguard, highly regarded, with wealth and power, and Jane. The advent of a new order would have changed all that. Relegated him to the pig troughs, a foot soldier—obsolete, archived and forgotten."

She slipped the diary in the box and locked it.

"And what else is in that diary worth locking it away?" Henri asked, arching an eyebrow.

She flashed him a conspiratorial smile. "I've got a crazy grandmother who's just been transferred to an undisclosed location. I don't even know where she is, but gee, she's just crazy enough to blab all of Allison's secrets. Crazy enough to blog, twitter and blackberry every envoy on three continents. And one of those secrets is the Count's—various locations." She patted the box. "Right here in Allison's little old diary. He's probably going to be kept busy relocating for quite a few centuries—if he lives that long."

She joined Henri at the window. "You were pensive at times tonight. Was it the crowd I run with?"

He smiled. "I think I fit right in. We're all a bunch of misfits. Ex-vampyres, vampyres, relatives of vampyres, an old slayer from somewhere on a mountain top, a couple of smart ass kids who play with stakes and run with knives."

"Then a penny for your thoughts?" she coaxed.

"How was your visit to the doctor?"

"Interesting."

"Interesting as in you're pregnant, or interesting as in you're not pregnant?"

"Interesting as in I can't get pregnant. I'd say they'll lose interest in me pretty quickly now."

"Nonetheless, you are powerful and it will be dangerous if we stay and join the Shadows to fight the Realm and Jane. They will not believe I'm dead for long."

He lifted her into his arms and kissed her, soft and long, moving his mouth caressingly over hers.

"You realize," he said, "You have become a mystic slayer and the Realm masters will never know as they haunt the night that you move in the shadows behind them, until you touch their thoughts with your threads?"

"Speaking of touching," she said. She pulled her sweater over her head, shook her hair free and used her real power, the power of a woman, to decimate him, wrapping her legs around him in just the right place.

"Don't need to read your threads," he moaned, aching pleasurably as her soft hands moved downward.

I love these pants, she threaded.

• • •

ELIZABETH BROCKIE

A native of Oklahoma, Elizabeth Brockie graduated from the University of Oklahoma with a bachelor's degree in English Literature. After graduation, she relocated to Southern California, became a college instructor, and began a career in writing.

When she isn't at her laptop, she works for a grant program at the local high school district, enjoys cooking and trying new foods with her husband, and spending time with their golden retriever, Summer, and cat, Taffy. Her two children, presently residing in California, are her best critics and loyal supporters of her writing.

OTHER VAMPIRE ROMANCES
YOU MIGHT ALSO ENJOY:

CPSIA information can be obtained at www.ICGtesting.com
Printed in the USA
BVOW081002220113

311274BV00001B/10/P